DR SAD

For David,

love + best

wishes.

David B. xoxo ♡

UNIVERSITY OF CALGARY
Press

DR SAD

a month and a day

David Bateman

Brave & Brilliant Series
ISSN 2371-7238 (Print) ISSN 2371-7246 (Online)

University of Calgary Press
2500 University Drive NW
Calgary, Alberta
Canada T2N 1N4
press.ucalgary.ca

This book is available as an ebook. The publisher should be contacted for any use which falls outside the terms of that license.

LIBRARY AND ARCHIVES CANADA CATALOGUING IN PUBLICATION

Title: Dr Sad : a month and a day / David Bateman.
Other titles: Doctor Sad
Names: Bateman, David, 1956- author.
Series: Brave & brilliant series ; no. 18.
Description: Series statement: Brave & brilliant series ; 18 Identifiers: Canadiana (print) 20200234021 | Canadiana (ebook) 20200234048 | ISBN 9781773851037 (softcover) | ISBN 9781773851044 (PDF) | ISBN 9781773851051 (EPUB) | ISBN 9781773851068 (Kindle)
Subjects: LCGFT: Novels.
Classification: LCC PS8553.A8254 D7 2020 | DDC C813/.54—dc23

The University of Calgary Press acknowledges the support of the Government of Alberta through the Alberta Media Fund for our publications. We acknowledge the financial support of the Government of Canada. We acknowledge the financial support of the Canada Council for the Arts for our publishing program.

We acknowledge funding support from the Ontario Arts Council, an agency of the Government of Ontario, which supported David Bateman in writing DR SAD through a Chalmers Foundation Arts Fellowship.

Printed and bound in Canada by Marquis
♻ This book is printed on Enviro Book Antique paper

Editing by Aritha van Herk
Copyediting by Naomi K. Lewis
Cover image by David Bateman
Cover design, page design, and typesetting by Melina Cusano

hand splint for limp wrist

saw himself limp wristed
in months becoming days
young men waning into autumn afternoons
languishing from midnight
through some intermittent May
into dooms of disaffection
unrelenting dispositions
a mincing manic chaos
wrung from some December'd knotted fray
contriving splints for all his panics
populating words blithely ordered
by day in evening when light fell
Bacchic chants began
throwing grapes of euphuistic—
sashayed syntax out the window
grading verses for a month of Sundays
scanning lounging gaily
on some bargain store divan
draped in scenes from othered frays

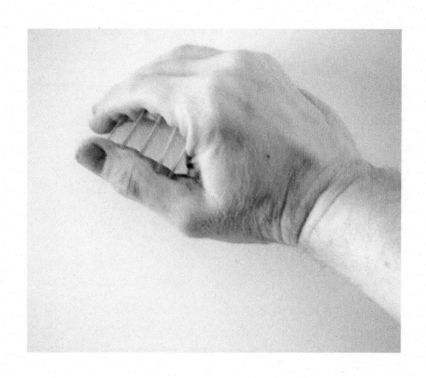

PROLOGUE—EAST TO WEST

Tkaronto—December 25

the world is made of plastic the heavens are made of dust
hell's on the earth we've laden
particles that fail to rust

"Are you going to die soon?"
  "No."
  Stephen could have knelt beside the boy, the soft glow of the coloured lights illuminating the left side of his tiny brown face, and gently said to him, "Well, sweetheart, I hope not. I am old now, but I think I still have lots of time left to do fun things with you and your dads. And today, well, what a fun day today is, the most fun-filled day of the year."
  But he had just said no, gently, and that was the end of it. Children could be easily placated with a simple one-word answer, sometimes. Other times they would bounce into that interminable question period. *Why not? Are you going to die before my dads? Are you scared of dying? Are you going to heaven or hell?*
  Stephen was grateful that today, just a soft simple reply to a single six-word question sufficed—because any more questions about death would undoubtedly send him into some sad new hell that he would have to smile through, and this wasn't the time for that. Today, his smiles would be genuine and filled with seasonal love. So instead of embarking on a complicated little death chat with a five-year-old, he set his mimosa on the floor, and just said, gently, "No."
  But, of course, he had no idea. One of his favourite sayings had always been, *If I had money, I'd be dead in a year.* But he

never did have money, not for any prolonged period. And now he was on social services, waiting for an upgrade to disability.

And on this particular day of the year it was even simpler for the boy to ask the dreaded question, and then quickly return to his pile of freshly unwrapped plastic joy. There was the shiny package of plastic race cars, the little plastic train pieces with a red caboose and golden boxcars inhabited by squat square little plastic people with vacant expressions on their painted plastic faces. But the little boy's favourite was the volcanic island with attachable molded plastic pieces, replete with tiny plastic chips to fill the volcano's pristine erupting plastic hole. Plastic. Plastic. Plastic. Plastic. Plastic. Like a gently rolling island of erupting emotion—a planetary bracelet of love surrounding the earth with nothing more than fabricated, complicated feelings.

But the volcanic chips didn't really look like lava. They looked more like little chocolate particles fleeing from an abandoned cookie. And this special day of the year would not be complete without hundreds of tiny plastic bits scattered all over the carpet, between ribbons and bows and scraps of torn gift wrap, and sad little bits of scotch tape just past their usefulness, to be vacuumed up before ten guests arrived for a festive dinner late in the afternoon. Stephen preferred dinner at eight, but children were hungry long before he was, the contented guest, happy to comply with a queer brand of postmodern familial tradition.

Plastics. It had been his favourite one-word utterance in American twentieth-century cinema. It set the tone for the rest of his life and for what was left of the planet. When the businessman uttered that foreboding solitary word to Dustin Hoffman, in *The Graduate*, in 1967, Stephen had been eleven and unable to see the film for several years because of its R rating. During a cocktail party scene, highballs in hand, as Dustin is about to embark upon a life of supposed upper middle-class wealth after graduating from college, a family friend walks up to him and says plastics. That ominous one-word unintentionally foreboding advice, like tiny bits of faux lava in a child's toy—a tropical volcanic pirate island made of PLASTIC! The one word—*plastics*—like the one-liner *are you going to die soon?* sets the tone for a lifetime, or at least one part of one lifetime, when the whole damn thing, life and all its ramifications, is called into question, the past the present and the future, with just one to seven little words—*1/ Plastics. 2/ Are 3/ you 4/ going 5/ to 6/ die 7/ soon?*

Dad Number One: "Where's your mimosa? Let me top it up for you."

Stephen picked up the long slender-stemmed glass, drank the last bit of bubbly late morning breakfast libation, and handed it to his host. The little boy continued to play by the decorated tree, and then his second white dad came back into the living room from the kitchen with a heaping tray of cinnamon buns and a pitcher of orange juice lightly inflected with fizzy transparent booze. They all gathered around a round table by the tree and toasted the holiday season and their time together. In the centre of the table a small plastic angel glistened in the starry glaze of the LED lights and tinkled the notes to Silent Night. But it was morning. And much too early to be awake. But that's what so many children are trained to do during this most wonderful time of the year. Wake everyone up only seven hours into the twenty-fifth day of the twelfth month. Luckily, he was a quiet, well-mannered little boy, and his early rising was not rambunctious, just gently annoying.

After breakfast, they opened the last few presents. It had become a tradition, the four of them gathering the night before and opening a single gift each, then rising early and opening most of the remaining gifts before eight, then a light breakfast, and then the rest of the presents. The mimosas were a fabulous addition to the Christmasy atmosphere. There was a child present, and they were mature adults with a strong sense of decorum.

Stephen had unintentionally saved his gift for the little boy until last. Pirate Island and all the other worlds the boy inhabited through these delightful objects dominated his young consciousness as he lost himself in the swift ravaging of giftwrap and the gleeful uncovering of yet another microcosmic fantastical site. Cars, trains, islands, planes, racetracks, pirates, inflatable superheroes, synthetic beach towels, bath products, edible oils, and indelible drawing utensils dominated the festive scene, and they were, for the most part, all made of plastic.

The boy's tiny fingers eagerly ripped the carefully wrapped package open, and three flat objects separated and fell to the floor. A package of felt-tipped coloured markers, a large pad of drawing paper, and a children's storybook.

"Say thanks to Uncle Stephen."

"Thank you."

And then he hugged his real pretend uncle and went back to his tree-side play with his new conquests. He seemed to like the markers and the pad, and began to draw for a few minutes before returning to his volcanic island. But he didn't really notice the storybook. One of his dads picked it up and briefly scanned the back-cover description.

"Wow. Interesting. Where did you get this? I don't know a lot about the Shuswap. This is great!"

It was a children's storybook, with illustrations, about the Shuswap people. Stephen had bought it when the boy was three, but kept it for two years before giving it to him now that he had moved back to Toronto from B.C. He bought it in an art-gallery gift shop in Tk'emlups—translated by English colonizers to Kamloops. Stephen's own blanched heritage had never acquainted him with the Shuswap. There were no storybooks about Indigenous history and colonization when he was a child, at least not in his childhood home in southern

Ontario, or in the decidedly British influenced classrooms dominated by very particular views of the past. But in his twenties, during his undergraduate studies, Stephen became familiar with the frequently flattened, simplistic sound of an English translation. Kamloops sounded like a colourful breakfast cereal made of little hoops of tiny toxic-looking oat'ish particles—like residue from the faux volcanic lava all over the carpet. Tk'emlups sounded more complex, broken, and yet somehow connected by a lone apostrophe in an unlikely spot, giving it a linguistic elegance, consonants aligning themselves without the aid of softening, frequently intervening vowels that reduce varied sounds to fluid oversights. Tk'emlups—where the rivers meet.

He bought the book there, in Kamloops—no, Tk'emlups—when he was teaching. Poetry—where the rivers meet.

After breakfast, opening the final gifts, and a quick cleanup, the child and his dads went for a short nap. Stephen sat in the large overstuffed easy chair by the tree, sipping a more robust mimosa—a pale orange rather than the brighter version mid-morning—and scribbled a few notes into the blank book, with Wonder Woman on the cover, that he'd found in his Christmas stocking. Excavating memories from his bittersweet time in Tk'emlups, he began to make rough notes for a poem.

on Main Street he sits on an upholstered plastic stool in Oriental Gardens / ginger drowned in sweetness / wasabi's sharp intrusive blend / as foreplay to sake's inebriating glow / overlooking soft pink treeless mountains / skirted by two strands of water meeting for one final toast to shores and land / mall-like casinos white sushi rolling snowboarding bartending moonlight'ing white cowboys serving fey fledglings / only miles away from ravaged full green forests dwindling into nights of bewildered half happy tumbleweed / thrown back across a valley on a busy street at dusk / soft brown becoming rose slaked

*by skies of blue-eyed blond-white muscled peaks / sun grazed
becoming well-groomed slopes of plastic snow / caucasian'ed
wilds wrought through to stalwart stance of stately buildings /
once the home of residential schools for stolen children / there
is a bargain store some village'ed Mart nestled somewhere in
this maze / the landed detritus of this and that / the rows and
racks of kitsch coloured rugs depicting vistas / deer and doe
grand antlered beauty named as beast / husky driven sleds race
through foregrounds fear and froth woven from pasts / wearied
carpeted by theft restless young and multi-coloured ghosts of
aging dreams of bric-a-brac / the second hand of cultured lies /
we tell the children we have stored among the numbered days /
the silent din the deaths of dreams the hope we lie in graves*

He sipped his mimosa, closed the notebook, smiled, and
thought to himself—*Merry Fucking Christmas . . . and a happy
new year.*

DR SAD

Vancouver—October 1

A gorgeous spray of flowers, funereal yet gay, the size of a small tree, a burly sapling perhaps, sat in the darkened foyer. Pot lights were strategically placed to wrap the Calla lilies in varied shadows, mingling with large white and yellow chrysanthemums, tulips, baby's breath, shards of random greenery, and variegated roses—all collected in a cut glass vase placed below a languid light. It set the tone for a couple of hours of elegant debauchery on Davie Street, behind a subtly identified doorway and up the stairs to some kind of purchased bliss. Putting the promise back into promiscuity was a short walk from here to there.

Stephen paid his entry fee, took his key and towel, and headed for his little room. As he walked down the dimly lit corridors, he could hear the familiar sounds of other patrons already engaged in what some might term nocturnal encounters, emissions, what have you. But it was late afternoon, and Stephen's bus to Kamloops was mid-evening. Just enough time for a quick plunge.

Just as his key went into the hole, he saw the shadowy silhouette of a man, a young man, early twenties, standing in the corridor, looking at him, or so he thought. He viewed youth now, from his middle-aged perspective—verging upon elderly—as a blurred existence. Youth seemed such a dead-end street. Age, on the other hand, was a comforting cul-de-sac. Being elderly'ish was easier to bear, or so he thought. He looked the other way and saw another young man, and knew of course that they—the two young men—were engaged in a corridor-long flirtation that would inevitably become an intimate clutch.

Stephen tried to think of these bathhouse visits as a kind of lone romantic sojourn, sex something he had relegated to duty long ago, in his late twenties. Get the job done. Enjoy it, and retreat back into the daily drudgery and excitement of trying to have a life. So he went into his room, disrobed, turned the dimmer switch to three quarters to give himself the benefit of flattering unadulterated tones, and reclined on the pristine white sheets of his single bed, with his door wide open, waiting for his first engagement. It didn't take long, ten to fifteen minutes, until a suitable candidate appeared. A man who seemed very close to his own age. They had safe sex. Kissing followed by carnal means of this and that. It was all just tugging, pumping, lightly biting, and a bit of luscious licking around the edges, the rims, of desire. They were located on the Pacific Rim, so it all made a kind of socio-sexual-geographic sense. It did the trick. Besides, what on earth was considered safe sex in an unsafe world? And he had lucked out. The man was beautiful, rugged, collaborative in his initial approach and subsequent landing—and muscled, covered in a masculine coat of fine dark hair, from light beard down through round soft chest, and then that final lightly feathered flush of landscape from just below those buxom man breasts past the navel to a lush garden of dark follicles surrounding that pulsing branch of in and out with the rhythm of low-pitched moaning. All in a day's work. Nice. If you can get it.

Fuck. It was all poetry culled from popular songs and Stephen's florid, euphuistic tendency toward the decorative in language. He couldn't escape. Words. Twenty-six musically inclined letters he was lyrically bound by, even when he was flat on his back enjoying what was supposed to be the opposite of verbal communication. SEX. He rarely spoke during sex. Even though there were times when, in his reeling desire-ridden head, he counted his partner's moans in haiku syllables.

4

uhh uhh aw awwww uhh
ooohhhgh uhh uhh aw awwww uhh aaaaaaahhh
uhh uhh aw awwww uhh

For the most part, Stephen silently sang along with the rhythm of what some called his nature, poetry implanted in his crotch—like some pubic bard awaiting the encapsulating froth of that final verse that rarely, but sometimes, never came.

He had been with men who chatted all through sex. He always tried to quiet them—shut them politely the fuck up—with a few well-chosen vowels and consonants becoming sentences of implied silence. He didn't come here for conversation. Some did. He came to take care of something that had become a carefully guarded activity and nothing to do with the intimacy of his real life. It was just pleasure—corporeal cacophony, as he liked to call it, a pleasurable sin of the flesh. If this was sin, then bring it on. He liked his fleshly sin to be surrounded in silence, in sprays of flowers, in corridors flashed by white towels and bodies in shadow, with old, middle-aged, and young men whispering through some interstice, caught by their own youth—or lack thereof—between each other and the bars of crafted light and the expanse of bodies some gods and goddesses had randomly given them.

The man's straight dark hair, his light brown skin, and his big wide smile reminded Stephen of his favourite song by Buffy Sainte Marie. Like Buffy's lyrics, the encounter was fun, *gay*, lyrical, with a subtle sense of play beneath the identities of the men involved in this very human interaction. It was perfect. They barely said a word. Perfect strangers. Kind to each other without sharing much verbiage at all. Gently navigating with robust thrusts and groans. This was when sex worked best for Stephen. The posed, euphuistic poetry of promiscuity—of casual sex, of florid physical expression bathed in little light. When the unspoken rules of his preferred form of carnal engagement were followed without having to be set out in spoken words, that was when Stephen felt completed by the world his craving body inhabited.

As he left the premises, grinning and humming Buffy's tune, Stephen caught a final glimpse of the spray of flowers, and noticed the young man again, early twenties, standing just a few feet away from the vase, his face mostly obscured by a great big pinkish mum. And once he had left, he missed the mutterings of this young stranger eagerly chatting to a potential late-afternoon paramour—hidden from Stephen's view by a swath of tulips mixed with a clump of baby's breath the size of a large gourd—a man who had just taken off his big white hat and reconsidered leaving the sex-tablishment when he spied the young man eyeing him.

Jeffrey, the young man, muttered, as the stranger drew closer, hat in hand—"Fuck, I know him. That guy that just left. He's teaching poetry this term. Shit. I hope he doesn't remember seeing me here. Lily would totally fucking freak if she ever found out."

Jeffrey's new acquaintance replied, "Naw, I just had him. He's a nice guy, and it's pretty dark in here, probably won't even remember you. Wanna fool around?"

And then they fondled each other's public parts, kissed, and walked down the corridor to Jeffrey's little room.

Day One—Tk'emlups—Tuesday, October 2

the boy on the flute is a fright / his face is a horrible sight / when he walks his knees knock / it creates such a shock / his braces light up in the night

Stephen's doctor's appointment was scheduled for 1:15, and his poetry workshop started at two. The bus ride from Vancouver had taken an extra hour due to bad weather on the Coquihalla. Satisfied yet flustered by his late-afternoon bathhouse escapade, he had missed the bus the night before, had to stay in a hotel and catch one early morning. When he arrived, he would still have time for a bagel and some herbal tea before his appointment at the campus clinic just before class. There were six remaining manuscript proposals to go over, and an exercise on limericks and villanelles to prepare. He could have graded the last half-dozen proposals on the bus, but listened to a mixed CD of all-female vocalists instead—a homemade collection made by a deceased friend who had hand labelled the tape *Mostly Ladies*. Falling asleep halfway between Hope and Merritt, he woke up in time to see the sign advertising the country-music capital of B.C. On his antiquated portable CD player, Alison Krauss was just finishing up "My New Favourite," and Norah Jones followed her with "Come Away with Me."

As Stephen opened his eyes, he found himself sweaty. He had been drooling on his own shoulder, muttering the lines to a limerick he had written in high school English class as he woke. The limerick exercise had involved giving Grade 9 students the first line; then they were expected to complete the poem according to the form they had just been taught, and they were not allowed any notes. They had to listen. The point of no notetaking was to ensure that the structure of the limerick was imprinted on their brains long enough to write one of their own. It was an old-fashioned teaching strategy, before laptops littered the classroom and memory sticks were a dime a dozen.

Stephen's high school limerick, from more than four decades ago, had something to do with an unattractive yet musical young man whose face was not a pretty sight.

the boy on the flute is a fright

He was required to rhyme the word fright with another word, and then make up three more lines comprised of one original couplet, and one more rhyming word in the final line that corresponded to the last word of the opening line.

his face is a horrible sight

Stephen didn't have a scientific, structured brain. He was a Virgo Monkey, extremely organized with a foundation of chaos underlying everything he fastidiously attended to. He found himself struggling with strict poetic forms. The seemingly rigid quality of patterned poetry, ranging from the villanelle to the sestina, always confused him. The limerick was his favourite. He considered it a simple perfect rhythm for the comic edge that invariably seeped into his poetic voice.

when he walks his knees knock

A precocious wordsmith from an early age—an idiot savant of sorts—Stephen's talent for writing short poems, poems that the teacher often thought he had stolen, was quite sophisticated by the time he entered high school. He once wrote a poem about snow for another student and the teacher refused to accept it, claiming it must have been plagiarized from a poetry book.

it creates such a shock

Stephen didn't think it was a great poem himself, and had tried to keep it simple for the student he was writing it for, but as it turned out, the student was a strange-looking creature with grimy braces and no mental capacity whatsoever when it came to poetry, so it was a wasted effort and created no small amount of conflict in the schoolyard immediately after English class.

his braces light up in the night

"Ya fuckin' homo! I told ya to write somethin' easy for me to understand. Like about a snowman or hockey, for fucksake."

And then the brazen bully kicked Stephen in the shin, followed by a swift punch to the stomach. Stephen suspected that his crotch had been the intended focus for the first kick, but knew from experience that the witless bully's aim was never very good. It hurt, but could not really be considered much of a physical injury. He was more concerned about the unsightly rip in his trousers, and whether his mother would be able to mend it in a way that would conceal the offending flaw.

Later in life, Stephen wished he had kept a copy of the snow poem he had written for that taunting halfwit. But alas, it had been lost to the great humming canister of unsung literature, sucked into the not-so-literary stratosphere like so much vacuum cleaner detritus. He especially liked creating metaphors for vacuum cleaners. When they worked properly, vacuum cleaners could solve the most mundane of daily problems, erasing the crass material excess that surrounded them. Had he owned a giant vacuum cleaner as an adolescent, he could have taken it into the schoolyard and vacuumed up all his shrieking detractors, those who shouted names like sissy, pansy, and girlyboy. There was one name he never quite understood. It was always shouted at him by the little blonde boy Caleb, who went to Jamaica every winter for Christmas. He was taken out of school for almost a week, then came back to class midwinter with a tan that the little girls, and some of the little boys, loved to admire.

Caleb had relatives in Jamaica, and his parents visited every year. When he shouted names in the schoolyard, the one Caleb seemed to have saved especially for Stephen was *batty boy*. Stephen thought it was because he was so bad at baseball that everyone moved in toward the pitcher whenever he was up to bat. When Stephen was in the field he went as far out as possible, because all the other kids would shout whenever he tried to throw the ball, "Ya throw like a girl." But Caleb always shouted, "You throw like a batty boy, batty boy!" Caleb was tiny, with blonde hair, and just as effeminate as Stephen. The taunt never worked, because Caleb's boyish bravado was outwitted by his own effeminacy. They cancelled each other out. The other kids would just laugh at Caleb when he shouted *batty boy*, and Stephen would feel sorry for him. But they never became friends. They feared the reflective surface that their childhood bodies mirrored when they looked each other's way. It was too painful to see someone else, someone they felt powerless to help. Caleb passed more than Stephen did. It was all limp wrists and lazy tongues for Stephen as a boy—a batty boy.

As the bus rolled into Tk'emlups, about an hour after he woke, Stephen put the finishing touches on a poem of historic and culturally astute proportions about a certain vacuum cleaner that revealed his penchant for finding the erotic within humorous semiautobiographical modes. This carnally charged form was a style he had cultivated during his late teens and early twenties, something he had become known for as a middle-aged poet whose presence at readings was sure to arouse no small amount of laughter—and some shock—from an amused audience. The poem was semiautobiographical, with a light academic subtext that would allow people to laugh and feel slightly intelligent at the same time. It was loosely based on an experience he remembered fondly. But whenever he did remember it, he always felt a little alarmed and very lucky that he had never injured himself in the process of his adventurous and creative adolescent carnal experiments.

McLuhan's Bride

Once, at a graduate student soiree
the professor's wife told him that
McLuhan's Bride was afraid of her first vacuum cleaner
he was clearly shaken, and hesitated to add that he
on the contrary, felt little techno-based fear
when it came to small appliances
and all the strained emotional ties
they liberate their lovers from, and had, in fact,
experienced a prolonged affair, late sixties
with his mother's first vacuum cleaner
an avocado green Westinghouse
amply accommodating his great pubescent shaft
in a most delightful way
stored in the basement, this Mechanical Bride
this compact galaxy of carnal pleasure
pre-dating certain ground-breaking
post-structuralist thought

stood proud alongside boxes of old clothes
hunting rifles, bewildered WWII army uniforms
broken rear view mirrors, pocket westerns
and his father's liquor bottles stored in heating ducts
among the detritus of lives infused with sex and booze
standing squat and satisfied, his thoroughly modern
fully equipped paramour, astute and wild-eyed
in 'her' stolid ambient purring
giving him uncomplicated joy
strengthening his love for his mother
her taut brisk arms pulsing strong
around her fervent breasts, pressing that small appliance
into layers of 1950's synthetic pile
the charged erotic ways of her domestic engineering—
reminding him of the ways in which
she kept her house in order
providing sons and lovers with the necessary tools
to survive in global villages where
as McLuhan once implied
we live centuries in a decade
and telephones remove us from our bodies
inspiring one to think
when you are screwing a vacuum cleaner
you have no conscience, no need of one
save the sudden onset of a short circuit
as you engage in one final perfect act

of consummate industrial self-indulgence

and the grand sweep of oral history

that will one day go the way of items

stored in a musty basement

works of art, mechanical reproductions

boxes of old clothing, hunting rifles

bewildered WWII army uniforms

thoroughly modern, fully equipped paramours

canisters, astute and wild

having borne silent witness to

the grand eternally pubescent shaft of time

Stephen didn't think it would be a good idea to share his new household appliance poem with his students. Generally speaking, bringing one's own work into a creative writing class that one was teaching was frowned upon. He did it the odd time, but because of this one's sexual nature, he felt it might be best to show a little restraint this week. Little did he know, as he scribbled the final words of his poem into a notebook, that written sexuality would be the least of his worries by the time he arrived in the classroom at 2:15. He apologized for being a quarter of an hour late and began to improvise limerick exercises from his rough notes. To hell with villanelles. Fuck sestinas. They could wait until next week. Under the circumstances, the limerick was all he could withstand for now.

Despite being visibly shaken by the news he had received at the clinic, Stephen managed a bit of pseudo-prudish humour by telling his students that he would prefer that they did not use the word Nantucket in their limericks, because it had become such a cliché within this particular form. And then, as quickly as he had cautioned them, he retracted and said, wryly—"Use whatever words you like."

Faintly vulgar innuendoes often managed to work their way into his teaching style. It was something he couldn't seem to resist, and on this particular afternoon, it lightened the load of his astounding diagnosis. Although he had told the doctor not to call him regarding test results over the weekend, she still managed to leave a message. Stephen ignored it, and decided to see her at the previously scheduled appointment when he got back to campus. He had said to her, clearly and emphatically, that he would be out of town on both Saturday and Sunday, so there would be no point in contacting him until he returned on Monday. He had expected the news to be something about another round of antibiotics for a bacterial infection he had in early September, just before classes started. But she was clearly misguided. He felt perfectly fine. But the blood test was routine. There was no need to worry.

Worry. From the paraphrased words of a country-music-singing Rhodes Scholar with a name like a fairy-tale writer, *worry* was just an alternate word for nothing left to lose. As for freedom, Stephen had given that up for an academic career. But he would have the summers off.

The first thing the doctor said to him after revealing the results annoyed Stephen instantly.

"A lot of people are prone to suicidal thoughts when they first get the news. Perhaps you might consider counselling?"

He had one gay nerve left, and she was all over it.

She had ruined his weekend. So he retorted, as gently as possible, without resorting to an excess manifestation of his signature sarcasm—yet managing to fill each word with a subtle, underlying rage over her forgetfulness about his wishes regarding the results.

"I appreciate your concern, but, no, I won't be experiencing any suicidal feelings. I am well acquainted with the immediate emotional effects of this news, and on several occasions have helped others deal with their initial response. But thank you for your time. I have to run, or I'll be late for my limerick workshop. I'm really looking forward to it, especially after you've managed to inject such a strained poetic rhythm into my weekend. I'll contact you later in the week if I have any more questions or concerns."

As he walked toward the classroom, Stephen thought of how he often liked to alter the final rhyme of a limerick in order to punctuate the narrative with a jarring tone, bringing faint chaos, and a kind of contradictory open-ended closure to an otherwise ordered poetic microcosm—*the man with the lisp is afraid / he hides his rage in a cage / as calm as can be, he makes merrily, concerning his status / regarding* HIV

11 a.m.—Tkaronto—HAPPYBACK

The S.A.D. lights had been on all day. They really did work. They lifted Stephen's mood from melancholy to lightly cheerful. Any degree of false happiness was an improvement at this point, but was it false happiness if it was the result of light bulbs he bought at Canadian Tire? Perhaps not. But he would try not to spend too much time thinking about that, and he would burn out the bulb trying to get his happy back.

That's what Irene said whenever she visited. As soon as he opened the front door, she would burst out, in a cheerful nauseating tone, like it was a one-word question but not a full sentence.

"Happyback?!"

At least that was better than the typical phrase when a concerned friend inquired about his frame of mind.

"How are you feeling?"

"Fine. I am feeling just fine."

F.I.N.E.

Just like the word *sad* had become an acronym for seasonal affective disorder, fine had become one for Frustrated, Insecure, Nervous, and Excited.

If it was on the phone that Irene asked about his disposition, he would cheerfully say yes. Stephen was careful to answer the telephone in a happy voice, so callers wouldn't bug him about his mood—especially Irene. But if she was at the front door, and he was unsure of how sad he actually looked, he would sneak a peek into the mirror beside the door, and if he wore a grimace or a light frown, he would put on a big fake smile, open the door, and say, "Yes, Irene. I'm filled with joy. Please come in." And she would enter, sit down, ask for a cocktail, and spend the rest of the evening complaining about her latest boyfriend. And they would laugh and laugh and laugh, and sip and sip and sip.

They loved to laugh together, and drink, and shop. Especially when they were unhappy. She was much less happy than he was. On that particular dispositional point, they would agree to disagree. "What's your misery compared to mine," she would say to him, laughing. And he would chuckle, and she would cry, and call him an unfeeling asshole. And they would both laugh again. Finding themselves, on any given evening, in superficial conversation, mixed with feelings about everything from furniture to fucking, followed by a brief shopping sojourn across the square and into the mini metropolis of the Eaton's Centre and its many appendages, feeling a little tipsy, eager to guiltily purchase some unnecessary, eco-un-friendly items. Only a week before they had succumbed, late afternoon, to retail therapy. Stephen had thrown his last gulp of Pinot Grigio into his gullet and howled menacingly.

"I really have to cut down on the drinking. You want to walk over to Canadian Tire and buy some new molded plastic Adirondack chairs? Mine are cracked. There's a fall sale on. September sell-off."

"Sure. We can stop at the wine boutique on our way home."

"I thought you had a date tonight."

"Fuck, yes. I almost forgot about him."

And then they wandered into Canadian Tire, happy as larks, melancholy as nightingales.

Transnational Bliss

sometimes I like to wander through Canadian Tire

look at all the lovely things

the bikes the lawn furniture the shelves the faux ferns

the uncomfortable pull-out couches
the Barcelona chairs with matching ottomans
and imagine myself sitting in one of those fancy
five-hundred-dollar classic designer chairs
wearing an incredibly large diamond ring
a ring so large it forces my forearm to the floor
scratching the laminate to shreds and lifting the sheen
a ring so large it befits the world's oldest living whore
I mean whore in the most loving sense of the word
a whore one feels no pity for
because pity is not a whore's best friend
but a whore who knows bad art and worse literature
when he sees it and loves it
a whore who knows the Barcelona chair
may look contemporary to some folk as they wander through
their nationally named store
when in fact it is over ninety years old
was designed in 1929
for the German and the Barcelona pavilions
at the Ibero-American Exposition in Spain
Imagine that, eh? We've come a long way as a country
now we have ninety-year-old designer chairs
for sale at Canadian Tire
for a fraction of the price they went for
before they could be reproduced
in cheap knockoff form

sporting poorly made faux leather cushions
Yes, sometimes I just like to wander through Canadian Tire
look at all the lovely things
imagining myself the oldest living whore
sitting in a white faux leather Barcelona chair
(for some reason the leather always looks dirty)
wearing a diamond ring so large
it forces my limp wrist and forearm to the floor
and I would sit there all day
scratching laminate and lifting sheen
and telling people pithy historic details regarding home décor
they have little to no interest in ever knowing
about themselves, the world of fine furnishings
and my disambiguated patriotism
as it manifests itself within my love for wandering mindlessly
through Canadian Tire

Stephen and Irene bought orange plastic chairs the colour of pumpkins. And then they said goodnight.

A month later, post Canadian Tire, it was uncommonly warm, but damp and cloudy. Pleasant weather for the perfect eerie autumn event. Stephen felt sad, but cheerful, and had eagerly pulled one of the brightly coloured, recently purchased Adirondack chairs into the front hall and assembled plastic faux-clinical instruments beside it on a small table draped in white satin. Orange and white. A perfect colour scheme under the circumstances, with a little black around the edges of the mise-en-scene. The candy, purchased at Shoppers Drug Mart, was wrapped in colourful translucent cellophane. He placed them in orange plastic bowls from Dollarama, set them inside a large painted wicker trunk, and then closed the trunk so visitors wouldn't see them right away.

It was only eleven a.m., and everything was in place. The oversized bottle of rubbing alcohol (aka Isopropyl) he had made from a Javex bottle, with a skull and crossbones drawn onto the plastic, and big black letters below identifying the contents.

ISOPROPYL—AKA—CHEAP BOOZE

And there were rolls of white bandages hanging from the small crystal chandelier above the Adirondack chair. Sparkling synthetic cobwebs everywhere. But no blood. That, he thought, would be tasteless. It might frighten the children. And there wouldn't be many of them. Only the ones who lived in the building. Twenty-five to thirty at the most.

Through the glazed translucent panels on each side of the apartment door, he would be able to see their shadows as they approached his unit. They would knock. And there he would be. In a white satin uniform with a thin black tie, a hot pink stethoscope around his neck, and topped off with an Elvis wig. Stephen had a big smile on his face as an old Moody Blues CD played one of his favourite songs. Nights, white satin, unsent letters, ideas, and images floating through a haunting melody. Later in the evening, it would be Patti Smith, *Horses*.

All the songs that haunted him as a teenager when he lived alone in the condo overlooking the Don Valley Parkway, in the mid-seventies. It had been a two-bedroom unit, no balcony, covered in a sea of white shag carpet. After a day of classes in a graphic design program, he would take a streetcar, then a bus, all the way from King Street East to Don Mills, and then sit in front of the television for most of the evening. Ending up on the couch and in front of a TV table and a glass of Lonesome Charlie wine—his Nana's favourite cheap rosé—a plate of fish sticks, lemon wedges, and broccoli, watching whatever was on. It didn't matter. *Lawrence Welk*, *The Mike Douglas Show, Laverne and Shirley*—anything. It was the sound of other voices that he craved then, when he was young. Not what they were saying or doing, just knowing they were there, in a little box, keeping him company but never requiring interaction or conversation—filled with false smiles, sympathetic tears, and sincere, comical emotion.

But now, in middle age, on the lapel of Stephen's white camped-up clinical satin uniform, as he laid it out on his king-sized bed in his one bedroom apartment near Yonge and Dundas, where he had lived for almost a quarter of a century—with time out for graduate studies in the foothills of Alberta—he fastened a tiny nametag with black letters, identifying the institution and the individual poet/physician whose work he had always admired.

HAPPY TRAILS HOSPITAL—DR W.C. WILLIAMS

"Could I have your attention please?"

Stephen felt compelled to say that at the beginning of a seminar. Students were loud and rowdy given half a chance, and he had to raise his voice as firmly and as politely as possible in order to gain any control in the classroom. He wondered if a more manly physical presence would have made a difference, but it seemed like a lot of trouble to go to for the sake of custodial order, himself a glorified janitor, a babysitter, a well-paid part-time prison matron. But those were the more extreme definitional modes he relied upon when he began to lament his role as teacher. Pedagogy had its good points. If all went well, yes, he would have the summers off.

He had considered buying a whistle to shut them up, but that would only add to his reputation as an eccentric professor of literature, composition, and creative writing. After he repeated his question three times, they finally fell silent, and he fell seamlessly into rhapsodic mode.

"Thank you, so much, for your eagerly anticipated attention. Now, today's exercise, the limerick, like any poetic form, is open to moderate alteration, so long as the intricate immune system, so to speak, of the particular lyric mode, comprising the general structure and thrust of the poem, is not compromised. If you wish to alter the rhyme scheme in your second attempt to write a limerick, please feel free to do so. The use of slant rhyme is also acceptable in this exercise. It can only add to your basic understanding of the many tools available to you as young writers of poetry. But be cautious at first. Structure can be very useful as a means toward complete agility and freedom when you tackle longer poetic forms as part of your completed manuscript project. Some people consider limericks to be a minor poetic novelty, a kind of slight, whimsical doggerel that conservative poetic minds feel lapses into vulgarity, thereby making the form of no real use to the serious poetic imagination. I, on the contrary, feel that the limerick has the ability to both amuse and enlighten, if it is carefully handled by a skilled practitioner. So, please, as you approach your first go at the limerick, consider the narrative first and foremost, and do not allow yourself to lapse into simple vulgarity. Vulgarity can be delightful and profound, but let's see if we can come up with some other narrative possibilities for the time being. And then later, perhaps, depending upon the outcome, we might decide to entertain more ribald narratives for our poems."

After he left his second poetry class of the week—on the use of limericks as alternative comic structural strategy—Stephen started to feel a bit better about the recent diagnosis. He still hadn't told anyone, so it was his secret, his and that goddamn overeager doctor with the bedside manner of a dead skunk. One of his favourite songs in his teens had been "Dead Skunk in the Middle of the Road," and he often hummed it to himself to lighten his mood.

After class, instead of embarking on what would cause light-headed boozy depression—a pitcher of beer, chicken wings, and some deep-fried pickles at the campus pub—he chose a walk in the urban wilds of a city he was beginning to love for its landscape alone. In between burgeoning housing developments clinging to the side of low-lying mountainous regions, there were still plenty of rough, elaborate walking paths along steep dusty edges of barren, desert-like environs. With his earphones planted firmly, and his hiking boots clutching the earth, he braved the blinding sunshine and the treacherous hillside, listening to Robin Gibb sing "I Started A Joke" over and over and over again.

It had been one of his favourite songs, for most of his adult life. He first heard it in 1968 when he was twelve years old, and it represented to him, even then, a perfect union of poetry and music. The haunting quality of the melody, combined with Gibb's pseudo-boyish voice, and lyrics hinting at pain both hilarious and heartbreaking, a commingling of styles he was drawn to immediately. Ridiculous. Sublime.

When he found a copy of the Bee Gees' greatest hits on vinyl at the Kamloops Value Village, he snatched it up, along with a small plastic record player, and then, after listening to the whole album twice, he went online and downloaded his favourite track onto his iPod.

If that doctor had only seen him, singing away to himself as he wandered those treacherous paths, with a slight lilt to his gait, she would have thought he was about to go over the edge, prompting her to call the police regarding a potential suicide among tumbleweeds and thistles. What a solemn joke she was. So serious and concerned. She didn't even have her facts straight, and gave him ten years of relatively good health, with medication, and all downhill from there, death the most likely career option, around sixty-four, if he was lucky, and careful. In ten years, he would be sixty. Of course, he knew that everything she had said to him was quite possible, but was also well aware of the fact that people were living happily and in relatively good health with HIV now. It was a very different world from when the pandemic first began. Stephen's greatest concern, if he ever did reach his mid-sixties, was—as the Beatles had so poignantly unsettled him with, in 1967—would he still be loved at sixty-four.

What he craved from that doctor at the campus clinic was neither shrill nor sugar coated, but a delicate mix of truth and possibility, tinged with light wit and jovial discursive foreplay. All she offered was dour, faintly factual data, sadly out of date and totally lacking in hope and possibility. She seemed to have no sense of humour whatsoever. Whenever he saw her in the corridors of the university in the days that followed that fated day at the clinic, she looked at him with a crooked smile overwhelmed by the worst kind of compassion, laced with sadness and regret.

Stephen prided himself on regretting nothing. He found himself saying—to himself—in the early days following the diagnosis, that he had never thought of himself as someone who had experienced a good sex life. Thrilling was a more fitting adjective. Bad sex was something he had been fortunate enough to avoid over a long and satisfying career as a thoroughly sexual creature. Having practised safe sex for years, he had become quite good at its requirements, but apparently not good enough. Although he was faintly aware that a sense of regret surrounded him, trying to make its way into the treeless contours of his somewhat arid emotional landscape, his strong sense of commitment to the memory of an utterly thrilling sexual past would keep him going with no regrets.

He could easily survive on his abundant memories of sharp, poetic, sexually astounding acts. He liked to refer to his exploits as a metatheatrical form with gymnastic overtones. Circle Jerque de Soleil was a term he tossed around whenever he remembered some of the more acrobatic group sex he had experienced. It had been thrilling, and taking a break from carnal practice for a potentially indefinite breather—on the brink of fifty—did not seem like too much of a challenge. Despite a slight sense of misgiving, he knew he was ready. Hadn't he been primed for a disaster of this kind for most of his life? Was it too much of a cliché for him, a primarily gay man, to have contracted HIV relatively late in his career as a very pro-miscuous person? His motto had always been to put the promise back into promiscuity.

So, there he was, in the midst of stunningly beautiful terrain, listening to an attractive, slightly odd-looking Australian sing in a strained, heady falsetto. Humming along, he wandered, lonely, as a cloud, or a clown, or something witty and faintly poetic?

25

12 p.m.—Tkaronto—CEMETERY

In the lobby were more than a dozen Styrofoam headstones painted grey, humourous inscriptions emblazoned across them. Stephen did have a favourite one:

DR. IZZY GONE — I TOLD YOU I WAS SICK!

The events committee had been using the same Halloween décor for over twenty years, ever since the building opened, in the early nineties, just before a conservative government came in and cut subsidized housing plans from the budget. Stephen had put his name in a lottery to get into a co-op on the island, but it was cancelled, so he took his first offer and ended up in the downtown core.

It was no isolated island paradise—neither was the island—but it had a wonderful view of Lake Ontario from the roof garden above the seventeenth floor. There was a second roof garden on the twelfth floor, more secluded and with a less spectacular view. He planned to one day suggest that a stone angel be set in one of the gardens.

Stephen felt lucky, happy to get in on the last gasp of socialized funding in a comfortable, affordable building in the downtown core, just at the southern tip of the gay village. A few blocks further north and he would be living on what his closest friends called *the buckle on the fruit belt*.

The term *fruit belt* made him think of a comical term used to describe large men with small penises—a button on a fur coat. It was something he thought about every time he went to the YMCA and spotted a large man with a small dick wander by the hot tub. And he would hum, under his breath, "all things bright and beautiful, all creatures great and small." He was no size queen, and was happy to embrace a member of the phallic chorus in any shape or size.

As far as Stephen was concerned, given the clothing accessory metaphor, he was living at the bottom of the zipper, a few blocks south of the fruit belt. When he first moved in, his zipper was always open. By the time he had lived there for a quarter of a century, his zipper had been permanently closed, with momentary openings for quick encounters of the distant kind. Otherwise it had been welded shut, emotionally and physically—for close to a decade.

As he pushed his powder-blue laundry cart through the lobby, past all the tombstones, he chuckled under his breath. He kind of hated them, and he kind of loved them. Why not a change every few years? Why not some bright coloured leaves and spooky ghosts and glamorous witches and finely carved pumpkins, with a few contrasting gourds thrown in here and there? The decorations could be put up at Thanksgiving and added to until the big night arrived, giving a lovely fall scene a decidedly ghoulish tinge by the end of the month, just in time for haunting. They could even add some tinsel and a tree in early December, cover all occasions in one fell swoop and call it Hollow Christmas. But no. It was all about death. Bad graveyard jokes in the lobby of a co-op that provided affordable housing and subsidies for people living with HIV and AIDS. It seemed tasteless, a kind of event-based looming death design. But a sense of humour was important, under the circumstances.

Stephen sometimes wondered if jokes boosted his immune system. Well-conceived jokes yes, but tasteless ones made him cringe, laugh a little. So he chuckled on his way to the laundry room, passing this makeshift cemetery, but not too loud. He wouldn't want anyone to notice. This time, unlike all the other years, DR. IZZY GONE, or BARRY D. HATCHET—REST IN PIECES, or I WAS FRED NOW I'M DEAD, or GIL A. TEEN—A TISKET A TASKET HIS HEAD IS IN A BASKET—they didn't seem quite

as funny. Just over a year after leaving Kamloops—the site
of his initial diagnosis—it was still a bit too fresh. So, when
he passed the tombstone that sported I.B. CRISP—FIXED THE
TOASTER WITH A KNIFE GOT THE SHOCK OF HIS SHORT LIFE,
and made his silent chuckle, he felt a little shocked by his own
sense of humour. To make matters worse, there was someone
standing by the mailboxes. He hadn't noticed him when he
got off the elevator. The stranger laughed out loud when he
noticed Stephen concealing his own amused state.

"Funny, aren't they? Corny and kind of stupid, but funny.
Ya think so?"

Stephen looked at him and replied, "Yeah, maybe a little
tasteless, but sure, yeah, for sure, kind of funny."

The man was tall, but Stephen didn't recognize him, had
never seen him before. His eyes were covered with a shiny
black half-mask.

Stephen looked him up and down and said, "You're in
costume very early today."

The stranger replied, "Party for my kids, at the community
centre. Just waiting for their mom to bring them down."

"Well, have a lovely day, and evening. Enjoy the party."

"Thanks. I will. And nice to meet you."

Stephen smiled and nodded, then wheeled his cart toward
the laundry. On the top of his laundry cart was a photocopy
of the poem "Spring and All." Stephen had been studying
it—making notes in the margins—for a poem he was working
on. He could see some of the words surrounded by the folds of
dirty laundry—purple sheets, bright red underwear, floral tea
towels, jeans, the faded, once vibrant mauves and pinks and
lime greens of an old beach towel with Tinkerbell's smiling
face emblazoned across it, half crumpled, but still discernible
just beside the last four sections of the poem, interfered with
here and there by a lone sock or some underwear. The poetry
of William Carlos Williams comforted Stephen with haunting
images of spring. Images and ideas of awakening, roots, and

the appearance of seasonal sluggishness drifted thought his mind as poetry and dirty clothes mingled in his laundry cart.

"Why don't people know how to talk about death?"

"Because it's frightening. It's an unknown."

And then he laughed.

"This is no laughing matter. If you want to talk about this, then I think we should be serious."

"Precisely my point. If I can't talk about death, my own death no less, and laugh, then I won't talk about it at all."

"Suit yourself. But I find it all a bit unnerving."

"And when I get tired of laughing about it, I'll cry a little. And when I'm finished crying, I'll get on with the gross tedium of being alive."

Stephen was having one of those irritating conversations that neither voice—both his own—could possibly win. Lying in bed, arguing with himself, he felt neither happy nor sad. He had expected the first few nights after his diagnosis to be restless, sleepless. But he slept like a log and woke feeling rested and empty of any easily recognizable emotion. The best he could come up with, when he considered carefully, was, *I feel numb, and a little giddy.* The first three mornings, after the diagnosis, he would stare at the ceiling, and then at the kitsch throws with the scenes of deer on them, that he had bought at the local Value Village and sewn together into a bedspread. And then he would say hello to all of the representations of woodland creatures assembled on his bed. This helped energy move through his body, motivating him to get up and start a brand-new fucking day.

"Oh, Hello, Bambi. Hello, Thumper. Hello, Floppsy. Hello, Grizzly, hey, Booboo, Yogi, Lassie, Gentle Ben. Come Dasher. Come Dancer. Come Donner. Come Blitzen. Hey, Rudolph, what's up? What's it like having that huge hunk of antler sticking out of the top of your head twenty-four seven? Rudolph! For fuck's sake. Do you even have antlers, or is it just that boozy nose that got you all that fame?!!!"

Stephen could never remember what kinds of reindeer had antlers.

More often than not, after Bambi, he would start to free associate and call them whatever popped into his head. He lapsed into rabbit names quickly, followed by bears, dogs, and assorted Disney characters, finishing up with the customary list of iconic reindeer he had known from childhood. But it was important to him that Bambi play a starring, introductory role to his run-on list of beloved creatures. Woodland creatures always made him think of a poem a friend had written years ago, when he was an undergraduate.

I am a slut of ill repute

With no redeeming features

A fact that no one will dispute

I suck off woodland creatures

During a dress rehearsal for a university production of *A Midsummer Night's Dream*, in which Stephen had played Puck, he scampered onto the stage for the prologue and recited his friend's verse instead of Shakespeare's metatheatrical lines about shadows, making amends, and serpent's tongues. His genuine affinity for vulgar verse, learned from his father's foul and relentlessly funny mouth, lived on in his own. The inheritance never failed to lift Stephen's spirits.

The third morning after the diagnosis, he woke to a day filled with sunshine, and the rustle of fall leaves outside his bedroom window. Birds fluttered about, making trouble in the eavestroughs. But that was the conflicted joy of living in a small town. Nature was everywhere. It couldn't be avoided. During his campiest, most bitter moments, he felt that if nature was in fact a mother, then she needed to be sent to a home for wayward women.

Feminism had taught him, however, that maternal metaphors could be dangerous, objectifying and essentialist. So he preferred to think of nature as a gender non-specific lover. That way it could be anything the individual experiencing it wanted it to be. Nature was lovely, whatever gender it chose to inhabit.

Yes, he felt that nature was lovely—small-town proximity to mountains, blighted evergreens, and terrifying animals. But Stephen missed the reassuring sound of helicopters landing on the roof of St. Michael's Hospital, a couple of blocks from his co-op apartment in Toronto, the helipad in full view from his balcony. Still, in the quiet, naturally haunting environs of residential Kamloops, during the first few days after his initial diagnosis, nature became an absent lover. Memories swirled around, in the breeze, in the leaves and the trees, even birdsong became heady sexual innuendo possessed by a strong sense of nostalgia for fuckfests long gone. His past loves were flying through the air in the form of dying blossoms, russet leaves, and long forgotten seedlings, a kind of carnal/pastoral melancholia—faintly overwhelming and filled with heady bouts of masturbation. The physical object of affection was nowhere to be found, airborne, windswept. In short, it was happy, and it was sad. It was sexually fulfilling, and it was empty. It was noisy and it was silent—sacred and profane, ridiculous and sublime, filled with love, loss, and laughter.

Before he moved from downtown Toronto to Kamloops, he had begun to worry that he would never be able to go to sleep without the chaotic sounds of helicopters and ambulances reminding him that at least someone was trying to save someone else from harm. But despite the din—or dearth thereof—silence in this leafy town was comforting, eerily so. The news about his health, even though it had come to him in a less than ideal manner, did arrive at a good time. He was alone in a quiet house with a spectacular view. This would give him time to consider his situation without the distraction of conversation, explanation, and inevitable expressions of sympathy. Thank the goddesses Irene was in Toronto. She would be beside herself with something thinly disguised as concern and sympathy.

Stephen found sympathy superfluous and condescending, difficult to accept without stupidly saying, *Thank you for your concern. I really appreciate it.* And then a hug, or worse, a few tears, or even more abominable—a prolonged crying jag. And he wouldn't be the one who was crying. There was nothing he hated more than comforting someone who was trying to comfort him.

Being alone in the house for a few weeks would give him time to think carefully about everything under the sun. It would give him time to avoid the emotional outbursts that constant contact with people inevitably involved. He would only have to relate to students and colleagues. They were all nice, but he had known them only a few weeks. It wasn't like they were going to be bothering him with personal questions that might motivate real human contact. No, it would all be very casual and friendly and meaningless, and filled with shallow verbal import and gratuitous innuendo of the heartfelt kind.

The first thing to consider would be who to tell first, and how to tell them, and how long to wait before telling anyone. He was in no hurry. And what was the proper etiquette? Would it be appropriate to let close friends know via email, or would a telephone call be better? He had little contact with family, and was living so far from his community of friends, that it seemed awfully time consuming to have to let everyone know. He could go all kitsch and darkly hilarious on everyone, and send embossed announcements in decorative envelopes with limited edition stamps of Anne Murray, his favourite butch-femme singer. No, that would be over the top, not to mention costly. In more practical moments, he felt that there should be a voluntary health registry, a way for people to fill in data about themselves that only a select group of friends and relatives could check on every now and then for crucial developments in a person's life. Of course, social media tried to do that, but he needed a more formal, less personal, strictly information-based medium through which he could channel this pathology-ridden news. If he was going to get on with whatever amount of living was left to him, then he wanted to skip the awkward part where he had to tell his friends back home about his new *condition*, so time consuming, tedious, and prone to evoke emotional outbursts. For the first few weeks, he went about his business, preparing for classes, going to movies, eating, sleeping, the usual routine, and trying to forget the unforgettable.

The seroconversion period seemed to have ended a week before he arrived in Kamloops, when his month-long bout with a flu-like illness in Toronto had finally ended. So he was feeling great, doing everything he could to ignore the onslaught of unwelcome information that had burst forth from that moronic doctor with the timing of a broken alarm clock. He arrived on campus in early September, and had his first check-up about the lingering after-effects of what he had thought was an end-of-summer flu, with a follow-up checkup scheduled for a few weeks later.

So on that third October morning, he got out of bed, straightened the bedspread, as he always did, even before leaving the bedroom, waved goodbye to the plush depictions of his furry forest friends, and went into the bathroom, where, like clockwork, he would go straight to the toilet for his first bowel movement of the day. But today he stopped and put his hands on the sides of the little pedestal sink and stared into the mirror. He looked tired, grey circles under his eyes. So he placed his palms on the skin between his eyes and ears and pulled gently, removing the creases and making himself look younger, madcap, wild-eyed. A temporary, makeshift facelift of sorts. He forced a little smile, widened the smile, and then, like a true drama Queen, bugged out his eyes, widened his smile even further, as far as he could, and said wryly, to his own reflection in the mirror, "oops!" repeating it over and over and over again.

oops oops oops oops oops oops oops oops oops oops oops oops oops oops oops oops oops oops oops oops oops oops oops oops oops oops oops oops oops oops oops oops oops

By the time he had finished repeating the four letter word, he was shouting, but not in an angry or frightened way, more akin to a joyful, head-splitting catharsis inspired by some of his theatre training, and based on the theories of people like Artaud, Grotowski, Peter Brook, Augusto Boal, Lily Tomlin, Joan Rivers, and Miss Piggy.

There, in front of the bathroom mirror, maintaining the widened grin, hands placed firmly on the sides of his face, at eye level, he was a sight to behold. A clown version of that skeletal fellow in *The Scream*. It was a good thing no one else was in the house. But if there had been, this never would have happened. He was a quiet, respectful housemate, especially in the morning. Being an early riser made it necessary for him to tiptoe, to place plates and cutlery gently on countertops as he prepared to leave for the campus. So this particular morning, being alone in a great big beautiful dwelling afforded him opportunity to indulge in the perfect, post-diagnosis outburst—or better put, a mini-semi-*hysterical* meltdown.

Oops was such a gentle word. It had a powerful cuteness, the movement from the double vowels to the simple hard consonant, into the final false pluralization. Could there be a single *oop* out there somewhere, he thought, looking for its partner in linguistic madcap'ery in order to make it a couple of *oopses*? He didn't know, but he did know for sure that his momentary obsession with the word *oops* that morning, as he shouted it into the mirror, and considered its absurd linguistic variants, *oopsie* and *whoops*, was too silly for words. So he stopped shouting, and he stopped thinking about it.

Although it would come back to haunt him.

After a light breakfast of cottage cheese, a bagel, some smoked salmon and arugula, with a hardboiled egg on the side and a tall glass of pure unsweetened cranberry juice, Stephen realized that the light morning snack he had planned was nothing of the kind. Subsequently, halfway to Value Village he needed another bowel movement. Should he walk briskly back to the house, or should he continue to the bargain store and use the public latrine there? But what if he had an accident before he arrived? Or worse, the Value Village washroom might be occupied, and he would miss his intended mark waiting outside the door between men's shoes and small appliances? That would be embarrassing, not to mention malodorous. He decided to take a chance and kept walking. And lo and behold, there was Jeffrey, one of his poetry students, coming toward him with a big post-adolescent grin racing across his face, back and forth, from cheek to shining cheek, shouting "Dr. Davis. Dr. Davis. I have a question about the next poetry workshop."

"Oh, fuck," he muttered to himself. "How am I going to get myself out of this situation without shitting my pants?"

"Hello, Jeffrey. You can call me Stephen. Nice to see you, but you know, I've just realized I've forgotten something I need at home, and I have to go back. Email me this afternoon."

"I could walk with you, and ask about the . . ."

"I am kind of in a hurry."

"We can walk fast."

"Okay, fine."

"I don't get the Villanelle, sir, sorry, Stephen. It feels weird calling your professor by his first name."

"Get used to it, Jeffrey. What exactly is it about the Villanelle that you don't get?"

Stephen felt the need to clench his buttocks as he talked, walking briskly, trying to focus on Jeffrey's questions and the state of his own lower regions at the same time. Luckily, by this time they were at the foot of the steps to the house.

"Wait here, Jeffrey. I'll be right back."

After a very close call with mother nature, Stephen came out of the house and found Jeffrey sitting in the middle of a pile of leaves, throwing a few gently into the air. He looked like he had been crying. Jeffrey was a nice young man, somewhere between nineteen and twenty-seven, who seemed quite mature, and very young, at the same time.

"Are you okay, Jeffrey?"

"Oh, yeah. I'm fine."

Jeffrey's cheeks were red and his eyes watery. A few tears sat motionless on the crest of his smile.

"I'm on my way downtown to Value Village. I like to browse there. Do you want to come, and chat on the way?"

"I love that place, Dr. Davis, sorry. Stephen. It's got great stuff. I got a pair of ski boots there last week. Me and my girlfriend, Lily, are going helicopter skiing in Washington soon. Her dad's taking us. He's fuckin' loaded. I hope I don't break every bone in my body. I'm a good skier, but I've never been in a fuckin' helicopter. It'll be wild."

"Yes, of course. Value Village. I like it a lot too. And skiing, but I don't do it much anymore, getting old. The Value Village here is just full of treasures. I've started collecting those old kitsch throws, with deer on them."

"I don't think I know what they are. What's kitsch?"

Stephen quickly thought of a faintly ridiculous analogy.

"Well, kitsch, it's an art form that comes from something that might be traditionally considered tacky, but there's something iconic, and as far as I'm concerned, graphically sublime about kitsch that gives it a special air, makes it appealing. Kitsch throws are to the world of wall hangings what limericks are to the world of poetry. I have four of them. I use them as a bedspread. I've always liked them. I think they're beautiful."

"You'll have to show them to me."

"If they have any. They only seem to get a few in every four to six weeks."

"You could always show me the ones on your bed."

Any other time, before the diagnosis, this would have seemed like a gesture on a student's part that would both excite Stephen and cause him concern. It hadn't happened a lot, but the odd time, when it did, he would instantly suppress any desire to engage, and change the subject. But with his recent health news, he felt a greater urgency to not only change the subject, but make sure it never came up again.

"Jeffrey, that wouldn't be appropriate."

"I really like you."

"Didn't you say you had some questions about Villanelles, that you might like to share with your girlfriend, Lily? She seems to be struggling with them herself, from the look of her first paper. I'm sorry. That was uncalled for. Lily's a good student, so far, and so are you."

"Thanks, sir, Stephen. Yeah, I do have some questions. But you know, I have other things on my mind, too. Sorry. I really am nervous, uh, about poetry. I've never studied poetry before."

"I think we should postpone this conversation, about poetry, until I'm on campus again. Email me and we'll make an appointment."

"Are you on campus at all today?"

"Tonight. But no office hours. Email me tomorrow."

Stephen made an abrupt left turn, and jaywalked across a four-lane street towards the avenue that led to his favourite bargain store.

Jeffrey didn't try to stop him or engage him further. He just stood there, with that same sweet smile, starting as a grin. It raced across his face with a slight tremor that made his lower lip undulate and fold, almost like a smirky, quivering pout. But what Stephen didn't see as he turned away were the tears welling up in the corner of Jeffrey's eyes.

He was taken aback by the young man's comment about the bedspread, and found himself feeling jittery and anxious. He had seen that smile too many times before, in the classroom, and it had been such a short time since classes had started. He was startled by what appeared to be Jeffrey's candid come-on. Perhaps he was reading too much into it.

As he browsed through the fabric section where the kitsch throws were usually found he came across a scene of a magnificent peacock in a forest setting with a velvety powder-blue sky as background. A peacock, of all things. It made him consider how inappropriate the interaction with Jeffrey had been, especially in light of his recent diagnosis. Nothing would ever feel quite the same again.

And besides, for such a cocky young man, why had Jeffrey been crying on the lawn? His red face and the faint tracks of his tears had moved quickly into that goofy, iridescent smile so seamlessly, without missing a beat. He was certainly a pleasure to look at. No denying that, despite the fact that pleasure itself was going to be more of a challenge for Stephen now than it had ever been before in his life.

After spending three quarters of an hour at Value Village, he bought the peacock throw and two new shirts, walked to Oriental Gardens for Sushi, crossed the street to the casino after dinner for half an hour of empty-headed bliss on the slot machines, then caught a nine-thirty movie, *Away From Her*, based on a depressive short story about Alzheimer's by

Alice Munro. When he returned home, he realized he had completely forgotten an evening meeting about taking on another course for a faculty member who had to take a sudden leave. So he sent a fabricated, apologetic email to the dean, and just before going to bed, began to formulate ideas for a new poem.

1 p.m.—Tkaronto—LAUNDRY

In that uncommonly warm October, a variety of insects—
ladybugs, spiders, house flies, tiny unidentified winged
monsters—dropped dead in mid-flight and fell into Stephen's
teacup. Lazy afternoons with varied bugs running riot in the
last few extra hours, days, weeks they had been granted, to live
live live till they died.

After apologizing to the fly swatter for killing the fly that
he could not seem to get away from, Stephen hung the swatter
up beside the rags hanging over the utility sink in the laundry
room, and took the photocopy of "Spring and All" out of
the laundry cart, setting it on the folding table. He poured
detergent into four separate washing machines and threw
colours, whites, towels, and sheets into their respective drums.
He loved doing laundry alone.

As he was filling the last drum, he heard knocking on the
laundry room door. Damn! Interrupted solitude at his own
private laundrette. How annoying. And knocking on the door
was unusual. Perhaps someone had forgotten their fob. So
he walked over, and there he was, the masked man from the
lobby, smiling and pointing to the door handle. Once the door
was open, they exchanged smiles, nothing said. A few seconds
passed with them just staring at each other and grinning, and
then the washing machine began to buzz.

"Oh, sorry, come on in. I have to close the lid." He walked
back into the laundry area.

The masked man followed him, and spoke. "Um, this may
seem odd. But I'm bringing my kids back around five or six,
and then I'll spend a bit of time with them at their mom's
place and be done around eight. Could I drop by?"

How do you say no to a masked man with a beautiful smile? He was tall, and filled out his costume very nicely. Stephen smiled and said, very quietly, "Yes, that would be lovely. There's a basket on the door. You can't miss it. I'm on the . . ." and then he whispered the floor number. Why whisper? He didn't know. Just a clumsy moment of awkward casual bliss.

"Great. That's great, can I bring some wine?"

"Yes, please do."

"I'm, uh, Graham, by the way."

"Nice to meet you, Graham. I'm Stephen."

Once Graham, the masked man, had left the laundry room, Stephen suddenly realized he had forgotten to put fabric softener in the machines. There was still time. So he opened each lid, poured in a capful, and fantasized about how the day might end.

And then he thought of the masked man again and felt the need to put a bit of fabric softener on his crotch. But that would be silly.

Day Four—Tk'emlups—Friday, October 5

In the second week of the poetry class, Stephen had given his students an unwelcome bit of advice. Most of them just ignored it, or rolled their eyes, but Jeffrey took it upon himself to resist the idea as soon as the words had come out of his professor's mouth.

Without raising his hand in the traditional, old-fashioned way, he just blurted out, "That never works, sir. Using a thesaurus? No. That makes poetry sound like a bad list. It's boring. Not very original to just go to an online thesaurus to find words."

Stephen curtly replied, "Well, Jeffrey, you're certainly entitled to your opinion. I was just suggesting ways of finding alternate word choices, in case, heaven forbid, any of you should lapse into some banal language. You, in fact, were the one who asked about repetitive words that mean the same thing. And yes, indeed, if you follow it too closely, a thesaurus can lend a predictable and tedious tone to your poetry. But as a basic tool, I do think it can be useful once you find other word choices, and edit the poem accordingly, and create something of your own from the limited words available to you."

Jeffrey insisted, "Using a thesaurus is too easy. I still don't think a thesaurus is a very original option."

Exasperated by the argumentative, resistant pose that Jeffrey seemed to take on in every class, Stephen found himself faced with a student who seemed to believe in the unique quality of his own verbiage.

"Well, Jeffrey, there are only twenty-six letters in the alphabet, after all. Good luck to you as you try to make every syllable come up sounding as unique as a special snowflake or a rock formation or some godforsaken wildflower. I'm just trying to guide you through language, and poetic form, in a way that might facilitate an interesting poem that strays as far as possible from the pointlessly sentimental and the brutally benign."

In the days that followed his diagnosis, Stephen's signature sarcasm had taken on a life of its own, and Jeffrey's vigorous discursive strategies seemed to bear the brunt of his queer professor's growing anxiety and impatience. So when he read the first stanza of Jeffrey's submission not long after the thesaurus confrontation, Stephen was startled, but not terribly surprised, to find a wry and surprisingly mature response— verging on adulthood, with a youthful tenderness—to his sarcastic retort to Jeffrey's anti-thesaurus sentiments. It reminded him of his own poetry.

the elemental danger of these rocks / the rudimentary beauty of this stream / the essential roughness of this bush / the basic panorama of this dream / lists of words describing nature make it seem / like blueprints for a topographic plan / planted in the rigid minds of men / who miss the call of nature in extreme / some prefer the wilder wordless way / of threatening dusty paths remote and tough / the driven trails that narrow, widen, wind, and then recede / the originary language of a bluff / the dry quixotic nature of a dreamy tumbleweed / the incessant adolescence of some diamond in the rough

Stephen felt that Jeffrey was a creature of curious proportions, an oddly anthropomorphized tumbleweed of the cocky kind, and not a bad poet for such a young—as Blanche DuBois would repeat—*young young young young* man. And he was starting to look familiar to Stephen. But he couldn't place that flowery, teary-eyed, allergic sniffing, smiling, resistant face, not for the life of him. Those moments in a Vancouver bathhouse when Jeffrey had recognized his new professor were remote, inaccessible, and the furthest thing from Stephen's mind now that he had a whole new life to live.

2 p.m.—Tkaronto—VASE

As Stephen folded the laundry, he read and reread the William Carlos Williams poem. Near the last of the bed sheets, he took the photocopy from the pile and sat down at the end of the folding table. He began to jot some notes for a new poem of his own.

When he was still teaching in Kamloops, he had told his students that looking at forms and images from other poems by established poets was a good exercise. Trying to imagine their own poems rising out of those images and notions, in a way different from the original, could inspire a person to write when they felt a creative block. His students resisted, because they felt that engagement was copying. Stephen disagreed with them. But maybe he was wrong. The construction of beauty in art and literature could be subjective, and young writers were so often hung up on the outmoded notion of the original—a notion that Stephen hated. Only twenty-six letters to work with in the English language, knock yourselves out! He loved beautiful objects made manifest in words or paint or penises or vases or vulvas or decoratively glazed clay, and he knew there were only so many ways to construct, repeat, revel in, and enjoy life and art.

Stephen kept a beautiful 1920s vase tucked away in his bedroom, in a little hexagonal commode beside his bed. It had belonged to his father as a boy. Some people thought it was ugly. Stephen loved it. Kitsch. It was, perhaps unintentionally, kitsch.

The story behind the vase was that Stephen's father had taken his teacher a beautiful bouquet of wildflowers, and she had placed them on her desk in an unusually shaped, brightly coloured porcelain vessel until they died. When the flowers did die, she gave Stephen's father—then only six—the vase. It was the one family heirloom he had left, and it wasn't worth a lot. The bottom of the vase identified it as hand-decorated Trico-China, made in Nagaya Japan. He did some online research and found that it might get a hundred dollars, possibly less. He loved it, but was afraid of breaking it. Every time he picked it up, he felt a mixture of extreme fondness, nostalgia, and terror. So he photographed it and set the vase below the photo for a long time, several months, always afraid it would get knocked over in his crowded co-op apartment. For a while he had it in the living room window and from a certain distance the top of the CN tower, dominating the Toronto skyline with an elegant vulgarity, appeared to be jutting out of the top of the vase. Stephen had stopped putting flowers in it. It was too pretty for flowers, and too unusual a shape. He often wondered how his father's teacher, so many decades ago, had managed to put the bouquet his dad had given her into a pleasing arrangement. Maybe it was ugly. Maybe it was sublime. The vase couldn't hold long stems, had a flat narrow opening for blooms to sit in. Stephen had tried short-cropped orange tulips and small yellow roses and lilacs, and, one Halloween, a cut branch of bladder cherries, thinking they were the perfect blossom for the vase and for the occasion—little lantern-like pumpkins hanging over the edge of the porcelain rim. But they didn't work either. He loved the vase, but he wanted to get rid of it. It was too precious. He wanted just the memory of it, and the photograph. That was all he needed.

As he read and reread the poem by William Carlos Williams, he realized that he also wanted to write a poem about spring and flowers and all that shit in a profound and moving way. Williams had been a pediatrician. Now Stephen had his own newborn medical pathology to add poetry and flowers and seasonal affective disorder to—s.a.d.

So there Stephen, an abbreviated DR, a doctor of a very different kind, a doctor of philosophy, sat. He sat for an hour, in the laundry room, getting up every now and then to finish folding, then going back to the photocopy to scribble more lines into the margins. By the time he left, he had a first draft, and in the entire poem, around the same length as the one by Williams—*Spring and All*—there was no mention of the story or his father and the bouquet of flowers.

Vase

winter rose

but now the effusive dignity of your form

odd curvature and sweep across your lower vessel

squat on pedestal orange as blood blossoms rest

atop an upper edge painstakingly glazed with yellowed hue

cloisonné-like sigh of leaves that stand

pert and crisp outside your dark flat hollow heart

spring tulip

but now the grace of petals

upright in their mood and haughty swing the pale green shank

narrow in its simple sway

garish sturdy leafage groans but stays

there is nothing all that grand in spring

save eternal blossoming of what immortalizes death

summer lilac

but now that lush quiet haze overwhelming grace

with riot disassembling seeded crowds

among grave gardens browning into sad sad fragrant tears

of going into earth of dying into soil and worm
of breathing august life through nostrils
freaked with blinding purpled jet

fall physalis alkekengi
but now the balls of bladder cherries making bulbs
in lantern likeness glowing crisp and even
dangled into nature's tease as one chaotic puzzled plant
named for robust nations misnamed for floral treatments
industrializing distributing fauna flower leaf and petal
the cutthroat destiny of blossom cell and stem . . .

Day Five—Tk'emlups—Saturday, October 6

Finally. The weekend. Those six remaining manuscript proposals Stephen should have finished on the bus were still lying on the carpeted floor of his bedroom, beside the chair he had placed by the large three-panel window so he would have a view of the river and the valley as he read, or graded papers, or slept. He put a little rolling table to the left side of the chair for his laptop, and a short, squat, sturdy pillar of large art history coffee table books to the right side, for a bottle of water or a glass of wine or a tumbler of scotch when his work took him into the wee hours of the morning.

The bright afternoon sun never distracted him. He could pull the window shade and focus on the work at hand. Evening was the best time for grading. Just before dusk, when the sides of the dusty mountains turned a pinkish shade, then suddenly grey'ish, with only faint traces of their signature pale pink, almost coral, before disappearing into barely discernible shadows. This was the time of day when Stephen's attention began to wander—nighttime—and he would lose himself in the growing darkness, only vaguely attentive when deciding the academic fate of his young wards. He was gentler, less harsh, in evening light.

That confusing time of day, light's disappearing act—not to be mistaken for sunset—when darkness appears, civil dusk, once the earth has rotated enough that the sun's centre is six degrees below the local horizon, marking the end of the evening—civil twilight. Not sunset, never sunset, but the point when the planet has spun just enough so the sun can no longer be seen as part of the horizon. This was when Stephen turned to alcohol-induced jet fuel in order to keep going for a few more hours. But rarely in excess. Those times when excess did take hold were easily identified by the papers he would find the next day with red lines and burgundy squiggles here and there, but not a single written word to remind him of what the squiggles or the lines actually meant. Some of them looked like checkmarks, others like little blood coils in the middle of a broken sentence. When this happened, he would have to reread the assignment and come up with an appropriate comment to match the squiggle. The squiggle became a joke among students, but the comments he made were, for the most part, articulate, sensitive, and helpful.

"Quixotic seems an odd word choice here—did you find it in a thesaurus!" He couldn't resist writing this comment on the poem Jeffrey had submitted, regretting it too late. He forgot to grade in pencil, changing to ink after a second reading. He wondered if this was an unconscious passive aggressive strategy on his part, in order to set his initial response in stone, no way of turning back. But in this instance, Stephen's scribbled sarcasm served Jeffrey right for being so familiar about the bedspread, and then the thesaurus.

Hard as he tried, Stephen couldn't get that silly encounter out of his mind. What was Jeffrey thinking, being so obvious with someone twice his age, and when he had a girlfriend—Lily.

Stephen couldn't help but notice how affectionate Lily was with her quirky classmate. They had seemed to hit it off from the start, and sat together every week afterwards, while the others scattered randomly, until groups had to be chosen for biweekly workshops near the end of the term. Lily and Jeffrey were a romantic portrait of postmodern heteronormative youth—but with a twist Stephen had not fully recognized.

So he graded and sipped, and the sky grew dark, the tightly bound spines of Chagall, Picasso, Monet, Manet, Matisse, and Modigliani acting as side table, big manly books catching bits of moon and lamplight that commingled on the carpet surrounding them. They needed some Morisot and Cassatt to strengthen the gender equation.

Without looking away from the manuscript proposal he was reading, Stephen lifted a large glass of wine from his makeshift cocktail table, raised it to his middle-aged lips, and sighed. Is this it, then? For the rest of my life, while my health still hangs on? Will I be reading undergraduate creative work every weekend, catching up on grading, and worrying that my own creative output will be blighted by exposure to the efforts of fledgling poets? Is my own poetry caught in some euphuistic glade of banal lyric intensity—overwrought and bludgeoned by too much wine and sentiment?

Setting his florid thoughts aside, he dove further into dull grading. He wanted to get this last sestet of early outlines out of the way so he could enjoy at least half of his two days off, and maybe even write some new poems of his own. But consistent Bacchic excess claimed his concentration. "Fuck it. I'm going out on the town. I'll finish these tomorrow morning."

He swilled the rest of the wine, switched off his laptop, put on his hat and coat, slipped into his loafers, and stepped into early darkness, his internal compass directing him due south, toward Value Village. The wine gave him unrealistic visions of a kitsch mecca of newly acquired throws that would shift the scene of his bedspread from a stylized forest of frolicking deer and antelope to a wintry landscape littered with dog sleds, brightly coloured fur-trimmed parkas, and predatory wolves drooling on the dusky horizon. He had noticed one a few weeks ago and now felt it was time to redecorate the surface of his bed. He was tired of Bambi, and wanted to experience the savage grace of Adolwolf, Adolphe, Lyall, and, best of all, Loba.

What would Jeffrey think if he ever had the chance to inspect his queer professor's bedspread? All these wild animals littering the classrooms and bargain stores of a small mountain city—it was becoming increasingly difficult to tell them apart—the wolves and the wolverines, the peacocks and the huskies, the beasts and the bambis. The ducks and the kittens. Stephen was drunk.

Wearing a corduroy jacket, black jeans and a grey pullover, with his trademark black cap on his head, Stephen moved his women's penny loafers briskly through the night air. He had bought the tatty shoes at Value Village when he first arrived in town, noticing a few shoppers looking askance as he tried on items in the women's section. But he didn't care. He was a footloose crossdresser, and could not limit his bargain-hunting nature with gender codes. So off he went, faintly cross dressed, into the evening, his Saturday night routine, Value Village for half an hour before it closed at eight, the casino for forty-five minutes, long enough to lose fifteen dollars at the slots, a dirty gin martini at the newly licensed casino bar, and then a fast sushi dinner at Oriental Gardens, just in time for a movie at 10:15. But the best-laid plans were never set in stone, and a few too many slots and one extra martini could make the sushi dinner impossible. He might have to settle for two hot dogs, a large diet coke, and medium popcorn, lathered in butter, all precariously cradled in his arms as he rushed in, just in time to catch the end of the trailers.

But on this particular Saturday night, it wasn't the slots that dismantled his carefully planned night out. It was an extended box office hit and a well-built sushi chef. He skipped the extra martini and another go at the *one-armed bandit*, and made it in time for a quick dinner. Oriental Gardens had a large dining room filled with sizeable tables, and a small counter-seating sushi bar to the right of the entrance.

"That's terrible."

Enjoying his dragon roll with a side of edamame, some hot and sour soup and an egg roll, Stephen was not accustomed or eager to engage in idle conversation with the cook. But this was a delicious new cook, from the look of it, not someone he remembered seeing before.

"Excuse me?"

"That's terrible. All that pickled ginger."

"I love it. But I'm afraid I do overindulge. Sometimes I just eat it all by itself, right out of the jar."

"Sushi, it's like the healthiest food you can eat, then people add a shit load of pickled ginger and fuck it all up."

"I think it's a tasty addition."

"It interferes with your digestion and takes away all the goodness of the fish and the seaweed. It's worse than salt. It's like nutrient homicide."

"Really? I've never heard that before."

"Yeah, it's really common. But it's cuisine crime as far as I'm concerned."

"What about wasabi?"

"Not much better."

"I like both."

"Yeah, I can tell, you asked for double."

"I like to treat myself."

"You want another sake? On the house."

"Well, thank you. I've probably had enough, but I guess I can't say no to free booze, now can I?"

He was blonde, blue eyed, five foot five, two inches shorter than Stephen, tanned, and with a stocky, compact body that seemed tailored to his restaurant apron, Oriental Gardens scrawled across the black bib in bright red embroidered letters. His biceps bulged in crisp white sleeves as he wrapped seaweed around the rice and the avocado filling, then added another layer of avocado, with some glistening fish eggs to garnish, and finally the signature flair of sushi grass upright at the top of the roll, signifying the dragon's head. It was a sensual, conical creation of phallic rice-filled proportions.

He looked like a surfer, or a ski instructor, not a sushi chef. But what did a sushi chef look like? Any social model for the profession might inevitably be based on ethnicity, but was that fair at this point in time? No, but Stephen did have his mid-fifties Ontarian upbringing to contend with, and leaving stereotypes behind was no easy task. Craig. His name, on a little pin above his shirt pocket.

Craig said, "I studied in Tokyo, six years ago. Living at Sun Peaks now. I'm a ski bum."

"Are you an instructor?

"No, I can't teach. Maybe someday I'll give it a try. But in the meantime, you know what they say, those who can, do, those who can't."

Stephen, impatient with the beginning of a false, irritating cliché from the mouth of a handsome chef, perhaps a postcolonial cliché himself—Stephen interrupted, "can't teach. Yes, if I had a dime for every time someone has said that to me, I'd be rich enough to retire from teaching."

"Sorry, I didn't mean to . . ."

"No problem. You had no way of knowing. So this is what do you do, off season?"

"In the summer I head out to the island for two months, to surf at Long Beach. I rent a place in Tofino. Yeah, I know, it's a cliché, except for the sushi part. People are always surprised to find me here. Don't ask, it just happened, a girlfriend made me do it. She was an international student when I first started university here. We lasted a year, went to Japan together for nine months. School lasted four months. I was in culinary arts. Hated it. Did the sushi course when I went with her. We're still friends. I see her the odd time, for coffee, some casual sex. I still go up to the campus, mostly for the view of the valley. It's incredible. I've been a lot of places, but this has to be the most beautiful terrain I've ever lived in, right down here, in the valley. What exactly do you do, up there in the groves of academe?"

"Writer in residence. I teach some creative writing classes. Like you just said, those who can, do."

"Wow, again, sorry. I always thought I'd like to try that, writing something."

Craig must have been an older student when he tried his hand at culinary arts. Somewhere in his early forties now. His year-round tan was weathered, and his hands looked strong and grainy as he deftly manipulated raw salmon and white rice into a seaweed cone.

"Thank you, the food was delicious, and thanks for the advice. I'll try to cut down on the pickled ginger and the wasabi."

"Yeah, you're welcome. Have a good evening, handsome teacher man."

Handsome teacher man? What the fuck? Such a quirky quixotic remark—a romantic, unrealistic interlude in the midst of Stephen's Saturday night routine. As he walked into the cinema Stephen found himself fantasizing about the snowbound surfer chef's culinary moves, translating them into an erotic kitchen encounter. Just as he was imagining a dangerously sexy trick with ginger, a sharp knife, a cucumber, and a sushi mat, he stopped dead in his tracks and muttered to himself, looking up at the marquee, "Goddammit! I should have checked the listings." *Away from Her* held over for a third week. He'd already seen it. Depressing. Beautiful, but depressing. The camera had a bewildering fascination with the face of Julie Christie. And the film occupied the only movie theatre on main street, too late to get up to the larger multiplex cinema close to the campus. So Stephen headed back to the casino, right across the street from Oriental Gardens, only to discover, after brief encounters with several slot machines and a couple of martinis, that the sushi chef had yet another skill to add to his list of remarkably diverse charms.

After fifty loonies were lost to the great vacuum of multinarrative slots, from Jackpot, All That Glitters, and Bejewelled, Stephen turned toward the bar, thought twice, then gave in to his urge to have one more for the road. And there he was, again.

"You're a bartender, too!"

"I sure am. I was hoping I'd run into you again, but this is quick. I was just leaving my sushi gig for my shift here when you left the restaurant. What can I get you?"

"A dirty gin martini. I wish people could still smoke."

"You smoke? It's bad for you."

"Worse than pickled ginger and wasabi?"

Sushi/surfer laughed, turned toward a bottle of Bombay Sapphire and untwisted the top, pouring a more than generous portion into the tumbler.

"I saw you in front of the Paramount when I walked to the casino after my shift. You decided not to go?"

"I've already seen it. I should have checked the listings before I left the house. I usually just come down here on a Saturday night and see what's on. But this one's been held over."

"I want to see it. Didn't some Canadian chick make it."

"Yeah, Sarah Polley. She's very talented. I kind of loved it and hated it. And Julie Christie's face. Fuck, it was distracting. She's almost too beautiful, if that's possible. Kept focusing on her as she came toward the camera on cross country skis. Alzheimer's scares the living shit out of me. Can you imagine, forgetting where to put a shoe, or a hat. Fuck, you'd end up walking down the street with a loafer on your goddamn head and a beret on your fucking foot."

The martini was uncommonly strong, accounting for Stephen's potty-mouthed foray into referencing Alzheimer's.

"Yeah. My mom had it. It doesn't always make you forget how to use things. It makes you forget what things are, like you just stare at them and wonder what the fuck's going on."

"Sorry. I shouldn't have been such a mouthy asshole. That's quite the martini you mixed me. Sorry about your mom. I heard Glen Campbell has it. Will he start into "Galveston" and end up singing "By the Time I get to Phoenix?" He'll become famous for unintentional medleys."

"No, I think he'll just stare at his guitar and not know what to do with it."

"You like country music?"

"I love it."

"Me too."

"Wow, a professor who likes country music."

Stephen took a sip of his martini and thought it might be a good time to reconsider this last cocktail and head home. The mixture of gin and sake was catching up with him. He put a twenty on the bar, said goodnight, and started to get up.

"That's a hefty tip. You don't have to do that. And you haven't even finished."

"Well, yes, thanks, you were very generous with the sake. "

"Well, thank you! You're leaving so soon?"

"I should get home. Grading to do tomorrow, and, you know, the teaching never ends. Those who can do, those who can't, grade."

"Stay a bit. I have a smoke break in five minutes. Have one with me. We can chat."

"I don't smoke."

"I thought you just said you wished you could still smoke inside."

"Yeah, I did. I don't smoke, but when I'm drinking, I like smoky places. Thirty years ago, everywhere was smoky. I miss it. It went with the pastime. Now these places seem too hygienic, not seedy enough. It's like a clinic for gamblers and drinkers. The glamour left with the nicotine clouds."

"It's healthier this way."

"But you smoke?"

"Gotta have one bad habit. I don't eat pickled ginger, or wasabi."

They went out a side door to the parking lot area and sat on a cement divider in the cool fall air.

"I'm Craig."

"Yeah, I read your nametag. I'm Stephen."

"So, you teach, at the university. You're a doctor?"

"Yes. I sure am."

Craig took a drag on his cigarette and then casually cupped the side of Stephen's head in the palm of his fishy-smelling free hand. Stephen was looking away toward the dark shadows of the mountains across the river when the gesture occurred.

"Hey, Doc. I need a checkup."

Stephen moved his head slowly toward Craig's. They kissed. An unexpected, perfectly predictable, loving little kiss. Stephen's lips apart, his teeth tightly clenched, Craig trying patiently and passionately to insert something a little more intimate into a full-frontal procedure that, in his experience, usually included a generous portion of tongue. But, for undisclosed reasons, Stephen wasn't having any tongue tonight.

"I wasn't expecting that, from you."

"You seem nice."

"You seem straight."

"Ya know what they say, can't judge a cook."

"By its cover. Nice cover. I should get home."

"Okay, great. Uh, you could leave me your number."

"I will, next time I'm here. For sure. See you soon."

The week began with what appeared to be an ambiguous pass from an unexpected and inappropriate source, and now the middle of the weekend punctuated by a romantic encounter with a mixed bag of brawn and beauty capable of everything from mogul skiing to martini mixing, sushi rolling, smoking, surfing, and remaining friends with an ex-girlfriend. Kamloops was certainly living up to its name—the tournament capital of Canada—and Stephen found himself engaged in brief unexpected bouts of very pleasant, if not a touch unsettling, romantic jousting. A welcome pleasure in the midst of mounting fear.

The recent diagnosis, day one, that had put his life in brackets, was beginning to frame everything with formidable punctuation. Why did his luck have to turn him toward abandon, when his pathology was motivating him to be more careful than he had ever been before in his life?

"Shit. Fuck," he muttered as he turned the key in the door to the house. "I left my bag of wall hangings at the sushi bar. Now I have to go back tomorrow. I can't live another day without those glorious dogsleds and wolves. And damn, I drank too much."

As he fell asleep on the sofa, a copy of one of his favourite long poems fell from his hands to the floor, not far from the fireplace. Diane di Prima's "Loba" nestled only a few feet away from the small flames of an ash-covered log. Although his carnal proclivities steered more toward men than women, Stephen's poetic passions often found a much stronger connection to the women he encountered in art and poetry.

3 p.m.—Tkaronto—SNOW

The weather outside, it's frightful / Global warming
It's so delightful
It's the middle of December / Let's go to the beach

Stephen loved the way frightful rhymed with delightful.
Apocalyptic aspects were less to his taste, but the seasonal
advantages made him happy. He revised his favourite
Christmas carol to reflect his bitter sense of humour and his
mixed emotions regarding the state of the planet's weather.

Of course, the idea of going to the beach in December
was only unusual if you lived in the not-so-distant north, and
the potential of global warming was unreliable, as it provided
unexpected bursts of cold weather at the most inopportune
moments. Halloween was the worst time of the year for snow,
as far as he was concerned. One year, in Calgary, he had taken
his three young nephews out trick-or-treating in snowsuits,
dragging the youngest along in a sled, with a Picachou mask
on his tiny head. They were all damp and miserable by the end
of their Halloween trek. But they had candy to lift their spirits,
then dump them all, a few hours later, their tired bodies
slumped into a volatile, ultimately sleepy frenzy prefaced by
screaming and tears and harsh words from parents who had
handed out candy all evening and had melting snow in the
front hallway to prove it.

Happy Halloween!

But this one would be different. He was at home, in
Toronto. The snow stayed on the streets for only a day or two.
And it was a relatively warm fall. And he would be alone,
slightly tipsy, and more than happy to distribute candies to

strangers' progeny, then shut the door in their faces until the next temporary familial fix presented itself for a few more seconds of transient love and momentary Halloween goodwill.

It was chilly outside, but only slightly, sudden shafts of warmth in the air to remind him of Chinooks when he lived in the West, although in downtown Toronto, sudden bursts of warm air were likely the product of pollution, the conflagration of tall buildings, and other mysterious urban elements that conspired to create humid mayhem in the metropolis—the metropolis he loved and would never think of leaving. Unless a lot of money was involved.

It did seem to be getting a little chillier as the afternoon progressed. He was happy with the first draft of his poem. Writing it in the laundry room had been a first, giving it a lovely proletarian air among the neatly discarded detergent bottles, the pristine row of dryers, the brilliant white folding table, the bins for garbage and recycling, and the box of clothes left behind by other tenants, boxes he could rummage through, looking for the perfect hand-me-down brand-name T-shirt, or a pair of slightly worn casual pants, or a smart little disco dress he could squeeze into.

He rolled his loaded laundry buggy back through the lobby, past the Styrofoam tombstones, chuckling a little at I.B. Crisp's rendezvous with a toaster. He always remembered to turn off the power bar that the toaster was plugged into before spearing the bread with the prongs of a fork. But one morning, yikes, what if he forgot and ended up lying prostrate on the kitchen floor because of one uneaten piece of toasted coconut bread? And who would find him, crisp, fried, and lifeless?

One of Stephen's least favourite aspects of living alone was the recurring thought of how many hours it would take for the body to begin to smell. And what would he be wearing? Unremarkable grey flannel pajamas, or a cozy, brightly coloured housedress that he lounged around in as he wrote and painted and puttered, trying to make sense of an early self-enforced semi-retirement?

Life was one relentless poorly attended fashion show, filled with the fear of being found dead in something unattractive. And snow? Well, that was even worse when it came to haute couture. Snow is only fashionable in a field, never on a city street. Downtown Toronto winters were like living in a giant, poorly insulated mall—inside and out. You dressed in three or more layers for the bitter cold, but the crowded streetcars and the underground shopping complexes and the subway system were designed to make you break out in a sweat minutes after leaving the blustery bedlam of a freezing street, then wandering for what could be a considerable amount of time indoors toward your final destination. If he was rich, he would live in one of those mammoth condos on Yonge Street, connected to the subway, with everything at hand, from liquor stores to dry cleaners, grocery stores, dollar stores, bars, cafes, cinemas. Everything under the absent sun in an artificially lit bunker below the city. That was where everyone was going to end up anyway, if they made it that far. Why not move closer to the apocalypse, the fallout shelter only a few flights away?

At least, this Halloween, there would be no snow. Thank heaven for global warming.

Day Six—Tk'emlups—Sunday, October 7

Stephen especially loved Williams' plum poem. He often considered Williams' work when he wrote his own poetry. Kamloops and plums somehow came together in the big house by the river.

this bliss—*Mojave / Kamloops, 2007*
mid-morning late September sun pieces of white chocolate
melting on a painted window ledge
moments of grotesque and unassuming beauty

this bliss

lifting pieces gently flies small spiders woefully intact
walks slowly toward the kitchen sink
knowing garburators were invented in order to dispose of
indecent metaphor figurative language
notions he has no cupboard space for
drawing closer to this linguistic waste
drawn to an eastern light in other rooms
woven wolves nestling by fireplaces
warning of winters that may never come
wearing the long black muslin sleeper
from the consignment shop

where some fey white men & women
have carried cruise wear
lingerie for re-sale in baskets made of reeds
and man-made memories of
Moses and the Sphinx
midway between the kitchen and the dining area
he is refracted by a stained-glass surface
impersonating light
he lifts—with his free hand—
the hem of his gown-like dark apparel
passing eastern light begins a slow ceremonial walk
to fauvist gardens cubist cliffs
overlooking impressionist northernmost tips
surreal crusts of land some locals love to believe
has been assigned to the southernmost stretches
of the Mojave—Tk'emlups
feeling exposed by skewed proficiency
with geography and the English language
he trips, his bludgeoned knees sunk into dying plums
gravel-soaked beds that comfort a lone fruit tree
when they find him, he has slept himself through darkness
into shards of light reported by the dead
back again to lives set mid- morning
in that late September sun melting caked
reminding him in glaring invisibility

this misinformed moment of grotesque
and unassuming beauty

this bliss

—DR SAD

A plum tree in his own backyard, well, that was just too gay for words. When Stephen woke, around seven, the first thing he was aware of was night sweat and intense headache, both caused by alcohol, although the former could easily be related to his newfound immuno-deficiency status. But he was hellbent on disrobing that tree of all those glorious purple orbs. The June-to-October growing season coming to a close, the small tree in the backyard full of fruit over-ripe for the picking. Many of the plums lay on the grass, some littering the patio stones at the foot of the stairs to the big wooden verandah. Stephen had planned to get this task done before his roommate returned, he had not planned a hangover on the only remaining day of the weekend. So he had a shower, a light breakfast, put on his sunglasses, stayed in his bathrobe, slipped on some hot pink flipflops, and wandered into the yard with a large wicker basket on his arm. Depending on the quality of light, he composed an impressionist tableau vivant with slight fauvist leanings. The basket handle was wrapped in faded yellow ribbon. Musing over his shadow on the external wall of the verandah as he closed the screen door, he thought to himself, *Fuck me, it doesn't get much gayer than this!*

Stephen had a habit of objectifying himself in a mimetic, homophobic manner. And although he loved the thought of his identity, and the activity at hand, as the graceful act of a late middle-aged homosexual in a heritage home with fruit trees and a gorgeous view of an arid mountain valley, well, the clichéd nature of this picturesque moment, fit for the centrefold of a decidedly queer lifestyle magazine, was not lost on him.

Internalizing the disgrace of becoming a stereotype, heaped on him over a lifetime of homophobia, had allowed Stephen a love/hate relationship with himself, and just about everything he undertook. So when he climbed to the top of a tiny stepladder he had put in the yard a few days earlier, in preparation for the *fruit-picking-the-fruit* task, his head was aching with foggy memories of a night to remember. He slipped, he fell, plums tumbled to the ground. He felt a poem coming on.

Dear God, he thought to himself, as he sat in emergency at the Royal Inland Hospital. *Couldn't it have been someone else on duty, and not the maudlin doctor from the campus clinic?* She was walking toward him with a chart in her hand and a perplexed look on her face.

"Dr. Davis? I thought I recognized the name. Are you okay? Are you here about your recent diagnosis? Emergency isn't really the place for us to meet. We do have a psychiatrist on duty, but there's a long wait, and it might be better to meet with me, someone who knows your situation."

She looked at the notes scribbled on the paper attached to her clipboard.

"Oh, dear, I'm sorry, you've hurt your ankle. Well, let's get you into X-ray and see what needs to be done. How did it happen?"

"I thought I was Mary Poppins, and I jumped off the roof with an open umbrella in my hand."

"You did what!?"

"I slipped and fell off of a ladder picking plums in my back yard. I think I've cracked something. I heard a little snap. Do you have like, those temporary casts? I don't want some big ugly dinosaur plaster where I have to cut all the hems on my trousers and every Tom, Dick, and Mary will want to autograph it, and I'll have to spray it silver for Halloween and go out as the Tin Man, when everyone knows I am a much closer friend of Dorothy's."

"We don't use that kind of cast anymore."

She seemed startled by Mary Poppins, Dorothy, and the Tin Man, but she didn't respond.

"I haven't broken anything in years, well, apart from my own heart."

"Dr. Davis, have you, uh, been drinking, this morning?"

"I was out late last night, had my fair share of sake at dinner, a couple of martinis at the casino, and now that I've described my alcohol-related activities to you in great detail, what business is it of yours?"

"I'm sorry. I am concerned. Your immune system."

"My immune system is my business, and it is in dire need of a very big distraction lately. So, yes, well, I'm sorry too. Could we just attend to this. I have a lot of work to do today."

The doctor smiled sadly and proceeded with an X-ray and subsequent accessory.

Straight from the hospital, in a pale blue, elegantly removable walking cast, Stephen hobbled and hopped over to Oriental Gardens. His whole leg was aching by the time he got there, so he asked if anything had been left behind the night before, politely thanked the attendant when she brought him the Value Village bag from behind the sushi bar, then took a quick peek to see if Craig was prepping at the counter.

"Can I help you, sir? We don't open for half an hour, and the sushi counter is only open in the evening."

"No, it's fine. I was just having a look. I love it here. And your other sushi chef's very good."

"Craig, yes, our new chef. He'll be back again someday, we hope."

"Someday?"

"He came in early this morning to say he'd been called away to his other job earlier than expected. He can't come in again for a while. But we have other excellent chefs. Please come again."

"Yes, I will. Could you call me a taxi? As you can see, I'm having a difficult time getting around today."

"Yes, of course."

"And could I have two California rolls, to go, extra ginger and wasabi please.

"No, sorry, we're not open yet."

"Could you just take pity on me and slip me a couple of day-old dragon rolls."

"No. Sorry. That could poison you, and we don't have day-old sushi."

"I am already poisoned."

And then Stephen swept out of the restaurant like an infectious pink dragon with a limp wrist.

As the taxi sped up the hill to the house, Stephen reached into the bag for the two hangings he had bought last evening. There was only one. The smaller one, the size of a rectangular pillow, was gone. Someone had been snooping in the lost and found at Oriental Gardens.

Stephen wondered if Craig was the kitsch carpet thief. Was he currently lounging in a ski bum chalet at Sun Peaks admiring his tacky prize decorated lavishly with six sled dogs racing through a stolen blue and white landscape marked with blood-red flourishes? Stephen had no way of knowing, but he had a hunch. Stephen wanted to see him again, but the way his luck was going, it was hard to say what was going to happen next.

Out of the cab and inside the house, Stephen managed to slip out of his clothing without taking off the cast, get into his bathrobe, pour himself a small glass of full-bodied wine, gobble up two painkillers the doctor had slipped into the palm of his hand as he left the hospital, she wasn't so bad after all, and sit down to an early evening of rereading the first two chapters from *A Passage to India* for a literature seminar later in the week. To hell with the manuscript proposals. They could wait.

The tenured professor who had taken a sudden leave had left him with a syllabus with several books he had never read. It was a postcolonial literature course, and he had his work cut out for him.

As he sipped wine and read E.M.'s epic take on the British Raj and Indian life in the 1920s, he thanked God for the terrible but frequently delicious spoils of insidious colonial foreplay—something one of his literature professors had told him years ago during a boozy midday lunch—"Complain as much as you like, Stephen, write your self-righteous papers about the dire effects of colonization, but we wouldn't even be here, in a university, eating appetizers, drinking imported beer, and studying all this theoretical crap if it weren't for the goddamn colonizers, now would we? Now, shut the fuck up and pass me the potato skins."

A bit simplistic, but it made a certain kind of terrifying sense. And if history had to happen in an oppressive way, then the very least Stephen could do was to make the most of it all by kissing surfers who moonlighted in Chinese restaurants with sushi bars on the side, skied on stolen land, learned to make delicious seaweed rolls at the expense of Japanese ex-girlfriends, stole second-hand kitsch items from someone he had just met, someone he had kissed, in a parking lot, beside a casino.

Sometimes the world just seemed so gay—so gay gay gay gay gay gay gay!!!

70

4 p.m.—Tkaronto—LAMP

Which doctor is the witch doctor?

The laundry was done—folded and put away. The candy was in the wicker trunk ready to be distributed. Stephen's costume was laid out on his bed, with the stethoscope hanging on the dresser's jewelry rack. Cobwebs strung from the chandelier and energy efficient orange festive bulbs had replaced the clear in the light fixture above the door. The Moody Blues and Patti Smith were in the CD player. Everything in its place and only four o'clock. What to do?

Stephen could sit by the window in the second Adirondack he and Irene had bought, sipping white wine and watching night fall. It would come as early as 5:30, mist rolling in from the lake. Why not get out into the fresh stale night air, wander up Church Street, see some costumes, take in the aroma of bodies drenched in sweat, booze, and outrageous make-up, then drop in at the YMCA for a quick dip in the hot tub and possibly a forty-five minute *aquafit-to-be-tied* class with anonymous bathing-suit-clad octogenarians. And if he was energy efficient and spent his time wisely, he might even have fifteen minutes to spare in the steam room, where he could fondle the massive hairy tits of some gorgeous gelatinous creature sitting flirtatiously beside him on the fibreglass bench. Stephen liked to think of his faintly carnal encounters there as scenes from a playfully anthropomorphized version of *Gorillas in the Mist.* And middle-aged men (Stephen included himself in the assessment) were so much more attractive through a cloud of uncompromisingly flattering steam, the buttons on their fur coats a sight to behold, beckon, and blossom into full-blown appendages.

He slipped into his witch hat and coat, his haberdashery-topped Elvis wig, and a pair of mirrored sunglasses, so he wouldn't look out of place on the most haunting night of the year, and headed north from the heart of the crotch, along the zipper, toward the buckle of the fruit belt.

Just before he left, he opened the door to the walk-in closet in the hallway, switched on the lamp over the shelves where he kept the remnants of his drag collection, and pulled a silver sequined scarf from the confused mass of accessories. He shut the door, threw the scarf around his neck, and left in a contented, self-absorbed, and calculated queenly huff.

Stephen left the sad little overhead lamp in the walk-in closet on—angry, frightened, alone, and fully lit in that claustrophobic space filled with all the items an aging ex-drag queen could accumulate, purge, and then accumulate again over a twenty-five-year period. The crinolines were not in the habit of warming up to a naked energy-efficient bulb. They were furious, threatening to burst into a fiery rage.

Furious Crinolines

Hmmm, that might work as the title for his drag memoir. If he lived long enough to write one.

Day Seven—Tk'emlups—Monday, October 8

Awake early for a full day of marking, to catch up after the overwhelming thrill of a lost weekend and the dull pain of a slightly cracked ankle, Stephen found that the painkillers that the maudlin campus doctor had given him left him with a heavy-headed calm. He felt rested, a little too rested. It took him an hour and a half to pull himself together, to wander around the house, make himself a boiled egg with a piece of dry toast, splash some cool water on his face, brush his teeth, and settle into the easy chair by his bedroom window, the bright fall sunlight focusing his thoughts and allowing him to catch up on the dull tedium of being fastidious.

The phone started to ring around ten a.m., and rang throughout the day, every half hour. Whoever it was knew that Stephen was nearby, since on off-campus days he worked at home. They kept calling, at such regular intervals it had to be the same person, somewhere out there in telephone land. But the ringing was faint, not intrusive, downstairs in the living room, easy to ignore. By 3:30, three quarters of the way through the remaining manuscript proposals, and about to move into prep for the postcolonial lit class on Thursday, he decided to see if any messages had been left.

Eight messages, mostly comical, belligerent haiku, with an affectionate finale in semi-renga form. A silly in-joke between them, Stephen and his mostly absent roommate Peter. Sometimes they sat by the fireplace drinking fruity martinis and having entire conversations in haiku. The drunker they got, the more they had to rely on their fingers to count syllables. Peter was a proverbial wise guy, very quick witted. Stephen could imagine him, on the other end of the line, counting the syllables on his fingertips as he spat off another haiku message into the bottomless pit of the answering service.

Peter's haiku phone messages were always great fun to hear, but today Stephen was too busy to be in the mood.

Hi, it's sexy me / I've got news, will call back soon / Just wanted to chat

You must be outside / Picking plums again you fruit? / Stay off the ladder!

What's going on Steve? / I need to talk to you soon / Answer the phone prick!

I know you're at home / You're avoiding me you whore / Are you jerking off?

Are you sleeping, bitch? / I'm not coming back this week / It's a long story

Where the fuck are you? / I've been calling all day long / We need to talk soon

Okay, here's the scoop / Unexpected change of plans / I'm going to Spain

Okay, the deal is / I've had a sudden offer / I'll call from Madrid

You'd better be there / Jackass! You know I'm joking / We will talk real soon

As busy as he was, Stephen couldn't resist responding. He edited the truth in order to fit the poetic form and the occasion, and sent his response as a series of text messages, a written record of the poetic bedlam of it all.

Hi, got your message / Sorry, I was out a lot / Couldn't hear the phone

Picking plums in yard / Sunshine was goddamn gorgeous / Fell off the ladder

Cracked my fey ankle / walking cast is powder blue / but you know all that

from email I sent / that you, you dick, neglected / Great news about Spain

Bring cheap sangria / Black mantillas for the hair / of this balding fruit

Stephen would wait to tell Peter the news about his HIV status. A bitchy reminder about the plums and the ladder and the cracked ankle enough for now. Didn't want to ruin his trip to Spain. All in all, a positive turn of events, in more ways than one. And perfect timing. More time alone in the big house to get used to a brand-new beginning for a whole new end.

5 p.m.—Tkaronto—CLOSET

A stroll up Church Street, casually exchanging caustic catcalls from witches, goblins, zombies, Gumbys, two mincing ponies dressed as one Pokey—the back and the rear—too many Cinderellas in and out of costume, and Stephen's favourite, a giant tube of toothpaste staggering down the steps at *The Black Eagle* after being refused entry. Delighted by the costumes, Stephen turned left at Maitland just in time to overhear a priceless verbal ejaculation from a beefy bouncer he had once been butt-banged by in an alleyway in the early nineties. The bouncer lightly pushed a wobbling Dracula away from the entrance to the bar and warned him in tones tinged with a hefty touch of sibilance on each intruding *s*—

"Get yourthelf a hamburger acroth the road bitch, and a thtrong coffee and try again in an hour. And brush your teeth. Your breath thtinkth!"

A muscle-bound man with a lazy tongue restored Stephen's faith in mother nature. His own sibilance was a source of resistant comfort, and it was a little-known fact that men with a lisp gave better blowjobs.

Walking east on Maitland, he reminisced about living at the tip of a large (by North American standards) marginalized, gradually gentrified neighbourhood for almost a quarter of a century. He missed Kamloops, but this was home. The gay village was a bit like Halloween, every day of the year. And with new waves of liberation flooding the streets, the costumes became more fabulous by the day.

When he arrived at the y west of Yonge and Grosvenor, he looked at the schedule and saw that there was an aquafit class in seven minutes. He swiped his membership card, rushed through the turnstile, was undressed, showered, and poolside only a few minutes later. Perfect! Only four other people in the class. Lots of room to spread out and flex those submerged body parts for the better part of an hour. And his favourite instructor, the one who played classic fifties rock that gently morphed into Italian opera by the end of the session, with a bit of Village People (YMCA, of course!) midway through the exercises. It contributed to the fitness arc every aquafit-loving enthusiast craved as a part of their daily workout.

The guy dogpaddling to Stephen's right was a sight to behold. He was attractive and moderately well built, in his late fifties/early sixties, with a permanently ethereal, slightly goofy expression scrawled across his face. He had introduced himself as Gerry when they first met, and he rarely followed the prescribed routine. Noodle exercises were especially challenging, and Gerry insisted on a pink one that stuck straight up between his legs and looked like a candy floss-coloured cock the size an oar—or as Irene liked to say, a barge pole—*Fuck me with a barge pole.* Irene was such a size queen. But Gerry was harmless. When they sat together in the steam room after the aquafit class, he kept the smile going full force, and never seemed interested in any fondling or flirtatious foreplay. But today he sat a little closer, and once the two other steam room occupants had left, he put his hand in Stephen's crotch and began to kiss him on the neck. Stephen reached over and gently grabbed Gerry's left breast, something he was very fond of doing, and then arched his head toward the ceiling of the steam room where mist gathered around the light fixtures. Just as he did so he had a memory of grabbing the sequined scarf from his walk-in closet. "Shit!"

Gerry didn't say a word when Stephen quickly got up, said, "sorry, I have to leave," then fled. Dressing in seconds, inadvertently throwing the Elvis wig on backwards, slamming his locker door, exiting the YMCA in a fury, rushing, mincing, careening past all the costumes on Church Street, almost getting hit by a car as he ran across Dundas at the corner of

Church, only to be greeted by fire engines and paramedics at the entrance to his building. Thinking he had started a fire, he quickly muttered, "Oh my God, I'm so sorry."

And just before he was about to go into full confession mode about having left the light bulb on in his closet, he noticed a stretcher coming through the front doors.

One of the paramedics walked him a few feet away from the entrance and explained the situation calmly. He was short and handsome, with tremendous biceps from lifting flirtatious victims out of harm's way, Stephen assumed blithely.

"There's been an incident, a violent one, on the roof garden. Please just go to your apartment. Your co-op management will let you know details as they become available."

"So, there's no fire?"

"There's no fire."

He took the elevator up to his floor, let himself into his apartment, and immediately smelled a plastic burning odour. He pulled open the closet door and saw that disaster had been averted—by the skin of its teeth. He pulled the damaged, lightly singed crinoline from the shelf, threw it into the bathtub, and switched on the shower. The other crinolines had been spared. He sprayed deodorizer in all the right places, turned off the shower, closed the closet door, and headed for his bedroom to change into his costume. But he got sidetracked by a glass of wine and neglected the costume change. He was sweaty from the anxious run home, and hadn't had time to shower before leaving the Y. But what the hell. He would lather on some deodorant, throw the stethoscope around his neck, the perfect picture of hygienic medicinal festive costumed frivolity. And it was only 5:55. Kids wouldn't start to arrive until six, possibly 6:30.

As he sat in the window, waiting for the first trick-or-treaters to knock, watching night fall, sipping white wine with a straw from a box, and thanking God for the small but beautiful way in which alcohol touched his life today, Stephen had a quick flash of the body on the stretcher. He could have sworn the damaged soul was dressed in something with big colourful letters running up the bulbous unitard-like garment. And on the side printed the toothpaste brand with underlying slogan—*Battling Cavities, Fighting Decay!*

Day Eight—Tk'emlups—Tuesday, October 9

The condensation near dried semen on my ass
Petals on a damp spent towel.

—DR SAD

"Don't ask. I fell off a ladder picking plums."

"Nice cast, sir. Powder blue. Wow, I've never seen a designer cast before."

"Thank you for noticing, Jeffrey. And that's a lovely chartreuse hoodie you're wearing."

Jeffrey sashayed by the desk at the front of the classroom, leaving his comment hanging in the air like a bad smell. Stephen's retort made Jeffrey wince a little, then smile, as Stephen turned to address the other students.

"So, enough fashion small talk, change of plans. I've decided we'll choose groups early, so you can get to know each other before the actual group work begins in a few weeks."

Instantly, Lily put up her hand.

"Can we choose our own groups?"

"Of course. Just send me the names in an email.

She spoke like she was giving Stephen dictation.

"Lily, Jeffrey, Martin, and Faye."

"Thank you, Lily. But if you also email the names to me it would save me a lot of time."

"It's just four names, sir."

Stephen hated being called *sir* even more than he hated being called *Dr. Davis*.

"Just send me an email, it will save time, and paper."

It wasn't the simple task of copying the names that bothered Stephen. It was the resistant attitude to everything he said that bugged him. If it wasn't Jeffrey's crack about the cast, then it was general objection to using a thesaurus, or some complaint that the limerick was silly, or the sonnet was too formal, or the villanelle was repetitive and clumsy. Why not just write free verse and say what you felt, any way you chose, without any contrived structure.

Sensing Lily's resistance, and his own growing impatience in the classroom, Stephen had a sudden change of heart.

"Okay, then. Thank you, Lily. Forget the email. I have the names for your group. If anyone else has their group chosen before the class ends today, let me know. Otherwise, send me an email within the next day or two.

As he smiled at Lily and jotted the names of her group members down, he resisted the urge to make a long, convoluted speech about wasting paper. Silently, he raged. *It's the goddamn pen and ink and paper, Lily! Why bother having cyberspace if we're not going to give the forest a rest? What with the pine beetles, and clear cutting, and more paper than I can shake a stick at wasted here in the groves of academe, we'll be out of paper by the time you have grandchildren. I'll be long gone, Lily. I'll be pushing up plastic daisies, if there are any daisies, plastic or otherwise, left to be pushed up, and you'll be rocking little second-generation Jeffreys and Lilys on your arthritic old knees, singing them techno-cyber-pop Lady Gaga inspired lullabies, and the forests will be decimated, because you and millions like you couldn't take the time to send an email. Get with the goddamn eco-loving-program, Lily. Haven't you heard, the groves of academe are blighted by bugs, butchery, and bad punctuation, and it's high time we started to spray our wasteful habits with self-examining insecticide and begin using email for daily communication in the classroom instead of millions of post-it notes and exam booklets and God knows how many kinds of fancy paper in the campus copy centre. For the love of God, Lily! Save the world one email at a time!*

But Stephen curbed the urge to give voice to his inner rants, and took a calmer, less reactionary route.

"Great, then. We've now covered the limerick, the sonnet, and the villanelle. I'll need your brief journal reports on each poetic form we've studied by the end of next Tuesday's class. Our next form, which is quite short and very simple, will be the haiku, followed by renga, both ancient Japanese forms that have become popular among Western practitioners. I suspect that many of you have written haiku before, but renga may be an entirely new structural format for some of you. But, basically, renga is a collaborative form, like a conversation between two people, a two-line response in seven syllables per line. And when I say collaboration, I mean in a paradoxical sense. Even if it's written by one person, the structure possesses a collaborative tone, as if more than one person is speaking, as if the lone writer is responding to what he or she has just written in the opening haiku. In a sense, if you like, it can become a conversation with yourself. But more on renga and its relationship to haiku tomorrow."

Four hands shot into the air, and Stephen raised his eyebrows, grinned,

"Um, yes? So many questions all of a sudden. James?"

"We've chosen our groups."

Stephen looked at the other students with their arms in the air and said, "I see. Is that what everyone wants to tell me now?"

They all nodded. His exasperation was becoming harder and harder to conceal.

"So, on with the show. We really don't have to follow any strict plans now, we have enough of that to contend with in the history of poetic form, and at the end of the term, if my teaching experience has taught me anything, most of you will be submitting manuscripts devoted entirely to free verse anyway, spilling your guts into the great vacuum cleaner of poetic cyberspace. So, great, let's start, write down the names of the people in your group on a godforsaken post-it note, and give it to me at the end of class, twenty minutes from now. And during that twenty minutes, get into your groups and write a brilliant haiku together, and put that on the back of same post-it note as your group names. Here, everyone, take a post-it note. I've got lots. I love post-it notes. They're wasteful, but they're just so darned cute and useful for making notes when you're reading a book. And they're kind of gay, don't you think? A little gaily coloured sticky pad of tiny rainbowesque proportions. By the time I'm finished reading a whole book it looks like a mini piñata about to explode into millions of useless scribbled flags. Yes, wasteful, but decorative and pleasing to the untrained eco-unfriendly eye."

Students seemed amused yet slightly bewildered, so he grabbed his brand-new pad of multicoloured post-its from his desk and handed them out.

Stephen's signature sarcasm had begun to break through a thin layer of suppressed frustration. As he circled the classroom, sticking individual squares of paper on the palm of each student who had raised their hand, he said, with a slight lilt and a touch of gaiety in his voice—

"Little known faux fact. Post-it notes were invented for writing modern haiku. Did any of you know that? They're the perfect size to contain the ancient three-line structure of five syllables, then seven syllables, then the last, and third line, comprised of five final syllables. I assume everyone knows the form of a haiku? Write one together and then tomorrow we will add renga to the mix and begin the first group exercises. Don't forget to read the chapter in your text, on imagism and the work of Ezra Pound."

James thrust his hand in the air.

"Yes, James?"

"I thought groups were starting at the end of this month."

"That was the original plan, but there's been a sudden change, apparently. Okay, then, now write your group haikus, about anything you like. You have fifteen minutes left."

"But I thought the groups were planned, on the syllabus, to start later."

"Go with the flow, James. This is not negotiable. Go with the nonnegotiable everchanging multifaceted flow. It's no big deal."

And then a barrage of questions from the newly formed groups.

"Isn't haiku kind of juvenile. I thought this class would be a little more advanced."

"Not sure how to respond to that, Martin. In a nutshell, no, it's not juvenile at all. It is, in fact, just a form, a complex and beautiful receptacle for language, fitting words into a package—a way to guide your thoughts through a particular poetic hoop. This is an introductory poetry-writing class. If you feel you have more advanced, less *juvenile* ideas, well, you'll have plenty of time to work on that. The first few weeks are organized so we can explore various forms, and then we can move into more complicated areas."

Amber, Brandy, Abigail, Rose, Benjamin, Fran, Pelayo. One by one, more hands in the air.

"But you just changed the schedule."

Stephen bit his tongue.

"I altered it slightly, Amber."

"How can we write a whole poem in fifteen minutes?"

"Seventeen syllables, Brandy, in fifteen minutes? It's just an introductory exercise. You can change it later if you're not happy with the drivel you come up with today."

"We don't know what to write about."

"Write about nature, Abigail. Write about what you did on the weekend. Write about pine beetles. Write about beer. Write about sex. Anything. It's wide open."

"I thought it was seven five seven, not five seven five."

"Well, unless things have changed, Rose, it was five seven five the last time I checked. Look it up online."

"Can you use contractions?"

"No, you cannot, Benjamin. Just kidding. Yes, of course, you can use contractions. But be prudent. Too many contractions look sloppy, and lend a shallow air to the poem."

"Why's it called haiku?"

"I forget. It's complicated, Fran. Look it up."

"How can we write such a short poem together?"

"Pelayo, if you're having trouble collaborating, then just go around the group one by one and say one word at a time and write them down according to the form and see what you come up with."

He was a bit surprised by his own agitation. He wasn't acting very professional, but he was doing his level best to accommodate his students by being as flexible as possible in the face of their dismissive attitudes. And his aching ankle was motivating a sudden and faintly demoralizing HIV/ mortality moment. He was fit to be tied, and struggling to eliminate his negativity.

HIV *positive* had such a lyric quality. The medical establishment had really come through, encouraging language for what many considered a dire prognosis. Stephen had never let death and dying get him down, so as he wandered around the classroom, overlooking the group progress on the haiku, he hummed to himself the tune to a song his mother sang to him when he was a child. It was about accentuating the positive elements and eliminating all negative aspects and to never get involved with someone named Mister In Between. Don't mess with him! Ever since the pandemic had begun it seemed to him like a gay anthem. That was precisely how he had become positive, by messing with too many Mister In Betweens.

There were two minutes left. Students packed up their belongings, and one from each group left their post-it-note on Stephen's desk.

"See you all tomorrow. We'll discuss your haiku and then get started on renga."

And there they were, five haiku, one from each group on its own little square of paper.

indoor tree so tall
it hits the roof of the mall
branches cracking glass
Frank, Jenny, Fortner, John

saturday was fun
sunday I was hungover
such a great weekend!
Ashok, Candace, Sally, Jan

pine beetles sure suck
they kill beautiful forests
nuke them and their eggs!
Pelayo, Fran, James, Benjamin

we had six light beer
then shared a pitcher of dark
sad lightheaded us
Amber, Brandy, Abigail, Rose

STDs are bad!
play safe or you'll be sorry
sex can be good fun
Lily, Jeffrey, Martin, Faye

Stephen's comments would include:

The first one has a certain urban charm mixed with nature's violent contrast.

The second one is for the most part bland and unimaginative, but ends on a nice comical note.

The third one is aggressive, darkly humourous, and topical, given the assortment of giant stumps on campus where the pine beetles have ravaged ancient trunks.

The fourth one has a nice creative flair through the connection between the names of two types of beer, from light to dark, and the physical and emotional state of the speakers.

And the fifth one is a little disconcerting and inarticulate, but lends itself to the development and creation of a dialogue—involving a seven syllable three-line pseudo-renga that might give a more detailed idea of how to have safe sex.

Stephen was clearly projecting his own pathology onto the fifth poem. They were all juvenile, but it was a start for the workshops on haiku and related forms. And where would he be without a complex sense of what it meant to be truly positive in a gaily optimistic triumvirate of seven syllable lines—

accentuate positive
eliminate negative
cope with Mister In Between

Yes, haiku on post-it notes. A fun beginning. When Stephen had decided to change the schedule for the groups, he had improvised a way to get his students to jump into a whole new form abruptly, with little to no preparation, and in groups. They could have been given more time to learn the form, and how to create a more complicated narrative within the space of such a compact structure. The attention to nature

that haiku demanded was something he would suggest later.
But it was only Tuesday. He could change his mind again
on Wednesday. Today, by the middle of class, on only the
second day of the week—the seventh day since his diagnosis—
Stephen was ready for a boozy, relaxing weekend in a cabin in
the woods or a hotel room in Banff. Pine beetles be damned!
There was still enough forest left—to gaze upon from a large
plate glass window and forget about the physical and material
trappings of a middle-aged academic life gone awry.

But he had three more schooldays and two more classes
to get through before any time away. His eventful evening at
the sushi bar and the casino weekend was over. The idea of
casual sex was a whole new ball game, and on this particular
Tuesday night, he would settle for an early evening film after a
quick visit to Oriental Gardens. It would take his mind off an
irritating poetry seminar and a clutch of lame haiku—a good
start, if bland and unimaginative. But he was projecting again.
Maybe tomorrow would be better.

The new sushi chef was pleasant and quiet, no unsolicited
advice on the double ginger and wasabi when Stephen placed
his order. Just a smile and a nod. A pleasant uneventful meal.
And then he took a cab to the theatre on the mountain and
saw *The Hills Have Eyes II*, which scared the living shit out of
him. The scenes in the Chihuahuan Desert reminded Stephen
of the landscape surrounding the river valley in Tk'emlups.
It was always fun, even comforting, to see the familiar in
a film, something that reminded you of your own life and
surrounding environs. He could have lived without the sight
of the dead mutilated scientist discovered under a portable
toilet, and all of the gruesome slaughter that followed. But the
location scenery was quite pleasant. When the bloodcurdling
scenes appeared, he draped his scarf over the brim of his
cap. Stephen looked like a large headed mutant about to
attack innocent filmgoers. He sat in the back row as people
looked askance at this odd middle-aged fellow sitting alone

in a movie theatre on a warm Tuesday night in October. Halloween had come early this year. He was in desperate need of a thrilling cinematic fix laced with a bit of filmic fear that would transport him out of his growing pathologized terror. His favourite quote from the film spoke of the advantages of being dead. Among them was the fact that you would no longer have to hear the sound of your own bullshit. His other favourite quote pondered the joy of the afterlife, and was responded to by an irate character who suggested that the afterlife should be stuck up your ass. Filled with sharp images of nature and death, these dark comic lines comforted Stephen as he tried to be entertained by cinematic horror.

Full of popcorn, diet coke, and a fulfilling form of terror, Stephen laughed so hard he cried all the way home from the movie. Lily and Jeffrey laughed all the way home too, having sat several rows down and to the left of their poetry professor. Stephen hadn't noticed them.

6 p.m.—Tkaronto—CURTAIN

Even after the sad little smouldering pseudo-fire had been put out, there was a strange smell. And where were all the candy-mongering children? There were usually at least a couple of kids and their doting parents in the hallway by six.

Where exactly was the smell coming from? The deodorizer had erased the odour in the closet, but the hallway still had a burnt kind of rubbery aroma.

Of course. Shit. Stephen had forgotten about the crinoline in the bathtub. He rushed into the bathroom, pulled back the shower curtain and immediately identified the source of the anti-fragrance. Promptly grabbing the deodorizer from the back of the toilet, he squashed the nostril-offending molecules with a few squirts of Spring Air Delight. Watching intently as the propellant streams ejaculated onto the smelly little crumpled corner of his one-hundred-and-forty-dollar novelty designer shower curtain, Stephen mourned the loss of a beloved object. He adored that shower curtain and had kept it pristine, putting it in the washing machine twice a month all by itself. It was a shower curtain with Joan Crawford's face printed on it, for the love of God, the perfect *theme bathroom* accessory, and a lovely gesture toward the collection of thirty-five assorted black and white fridge magnets on his medicine cabinet.

Stephen had two favourite fridge magnets. There was the miniature of the iconic photo of Samuel Beckett, looking craggy and elegant in a turtleneck with his hair wild and wonderful. Stephen had purchased it in the gift shop of the National Theatre in London after seeing a production of *Orpheus Descending* with a live goat that circled the playing area from time to time, giving the overall experience a delightful but largely unnecessary naturalistic effect. He would have preferred a life-sized stuffed animal on castors— a satyr, perhaps, more in keeping with his personal view of how the work of Tennessee Williams should be produced— all absurdist and campy, a hybrid collision between Irwin Piscator, Charles Ludlum, Cirque de Soleil, and *The Young and the Restless*. That's what Williams was into late in his career, but no one seemed to care. Theatregoers wanted it natural, even though Tennessee's Blanche had cried out for magic in the place of realism.

His second-favourite fridge magnet was a full frontal upper-body classic portrait of Joan Crawford—late Joan Crawford with the eel-like eyebrows and the demonic upsweep—a deep necklace swollen with gaudy diamond-like stones draped around her gullet and dripping slightly over the upper edge of a simple black bodice that revealed just a half inch or so of lush Crawford cleavage. She could be Beckett in drag.

At the bottom of the magnet, beneath Ms. Crawford's photo, unlike the austere textless Beckett magnet, was a caption with a warning not to misbehave or there would be big campy Joan Crawford-like trouble to come.

In fridge-magnet form, Joan was decidedly less existentialist than Samuel. Her carefully conceived character knew exactly what was going on and why she was placed in the universe for one shining Hollywood moment—to be a diva! Beckett, on the other hand, always seemed to resist diva status, when, in fact, waiting and waiting and waiting and waiting and waiting for something that is never going to materialize, well, what could be more Crawford than that— late Crawford, Baby Jane Crawford.

"But you are Beckett! You are!"

Feeling both happy and lucky to have been able to finally afford such a divine bathroom accessory had been a pivotal moment for Stephen, over twenty years ago, in the early days of moving into the co-op. Joan, as a curtain and a fridge magnet, had always made him smile when he showered or shaved or sat down to evacuate his bowels or bladder. And then, sitting on the toilet, he would look across the tiny room at a framed black and white postcard of Truman Capote. It was a room that made him laugh, essential to good home décor, with a total black and white theme, and a subtle splash of colour on the shower curtain, Joan's face framed by a faint powder-blue background. But now it was ruined. The whole corner of the curtain had been singed and curled by the crinoline's first plunge into the tub, before Stephen had had a chance to turn on the shower. Damn!

There was a knocking on the door as the bubbled streams and tiny cum-like puddles of room deodorizer settled into the singed plastic folds lying on the surface of the bathtub. The first batch of children had arrived, and Stephen was in no mood. He would have to suppress his seething desire to go all Joan Crawford on them, but he would put on his best Bette Davis smile and rise to the occasion. What he really wanted to do was sit on the toilet, weep a little, and mutter to himself, over and over and over and over again—"but I am Blanche, but I am Blanche but I am Blanche, but I am!"

Who knew Tennessee Williams and *Whatever Happened to Baby Jane* had so much in common.

Day Nine—Tk'emlups—Wednesday, October 10

my powder-blue world

in grade school I had a long walk home, almost forty minutes / on the way home, walking, alone I used to like to fantasize about what I would be wearing / if I were a girl / in grade eight, the class slut / just because she was beautiful / and dated every good looking boy in the school / I wasn't beautiful, not like her, and I wanted to date every good looking boy / in the school—I guess I was the class slut too

she had these beautiful powder-blue earrings / in a mod teardrop shape / that I would stare at for whole periods during class / I think that's why I never learned how to speak French, or read music / I would literally lose myself in her fabulous earrings

for a while they thought that I was becoming autistic / but it's just that everything was powder blue / I wanted to wear powder-blue and white vinyl go-go boots / and a transparent raincoat, carrying a matching umbrella / so that everybody, short or tall could see through

to my beautiful powder-blue world / and nobody could touch me / I could only touch them / and it would never occur to them to call me girlie or sissy or hurt me / instead they would just date me to death

and when I finally realized / that being a beautiful young woman can be just as sad as being an effeminate young man / I stopped hiding in transparent rainwear and a gender that wasn't all mine . . .

It was the first autobiographical monologue/performance poem that Stephen had ever written, when he was thirty-seven. Living in Kamloops made him think of it often, because of the walks he took in the arid mountainous area surrounding the river valley. The sky seemed huge, and powder blue, until it cast a pinkish hue on the mountains in the early evening, when layers of a multigendered sky would meet and begin to inhabit each other. It was like looking up into the interior of a giant unpopulated crinoline, staring into space at a rainbow of camp possibility. As far as Stephen was concerned, it was all drag. Or so he had been told by his favourite queer theorists, and he wholeheartedly agreed.

But now that he was older, his youthful preoccupation with autobiography and the unreliability of memory had been exorcised through performance. He used his early work to move through one identity and into another. In middle age, Stephen felt less anxiety about who he was, no fear about the clothing he wanted to wear, or what he was trying to be. He had finally settled into a self-deprecating self-knowledge that was seeing him through a bumpy ride that had just grown a little bumpier. But thank the goddesses for this prolonged period of adjustment. Over a month of solitude in a big beautiful heritage house, all to himself, overlooking a landscape he never expected to find in his own country.

Growing up just west of the Canadian East, he had come to think of Ontario and its rolling hills and abrupt sections of jagged rock as a humid, glorified swamp, with the greatest theme park on earth only a seventy-five-minute flight south— the big fucking apple! In his younger days, he had believed the great American mythology that, had he been born in New York, he could have been anything he wanted to be. He often regretted not running away from home as a teenager and becoming a transvestite hooker, sitting at Stonewall on that infamous night in 1969, mourning the death of Judy, and waiting for love to find him in all the tight places. But he was only thirteen in 1969, and he looked nine. Historically speaking, his timing was all wrong.

For years, it had bothered him that he didn't wear women's clothing on a regular basis. He wanted to, but was afraid of the remarks, and the people staring at him, and the moms and dads at the supermarket keeping their children as far away as possible. He was a reluctant transvestite, frightened by the mob, bashful about scaring the horses and stopping trains from running on schedule.

Entering the academic world hadn't made his fashion desires easier to accommodate. But as he grew older, he managed to integrate various forms of drag into his poetry and performance. He didn't need to all the time. His powder-blue world was a place he could visit when he wanted, while he knew that in another world, a better one perhaps, certainly a more fashion-flexible one, he would always be in a skirt or a dress. Or on a very good day baggy trousers—or even palazzo pants, one of his fashion favourites—tucked recklessly into his zippered leather boots.

The powder-blue walking cast was a small gesture toward Stephen's full-blown wish to wear frocks. When Dr. Maudlin showed him the choices of grey, white, and powder blue for his cast, it had been an easy decision. Although a rather insipid, institutional shade of powder blue, it was still close to the colour of the sky.

Around the house, Stephen wore women's kaftans and moo moos that he got at Value Village. He felt comfortable browsing through women's wear, despite the looks from other shoppers.

When he fell off the ladder picking plums, he was relieved that he hadn't gone out into the backyard in a kaftan. What if he'd injured himself so badly he wasn't able to dress himself and get to emergency on his own? He might have become a rank, fouled transvestite lying unconscious, or worse, dead, in a pool of squashed fruit, draped in a second-hand tie-dyed robe that had probably been left in the donations bin by a local socialite just back from Belize.

On a whim, three weeks before Halloween, Stephen decided to pull something smart out of his emergency drag stash at the back of the bedroom closet and wear it to class. A poetry workshop was an appropriate site for crossdressing; poetry epitomized, for Stephen, language in drag—adorned, cultivated, dressed to the nines. He could always lie and say it was an early Halloween costume if the students seemed taken aback.

He decided on a tailored brown full-length skirt, with a slit in the back. He would leave the house early so he could walk up the mountain to the campus by way of the footpath that began at the end of Nicola Wagon Road. The warm weather was holding out, the sun shining like there was no tomorrow, and he hadn't had a night sweat in a couple of days.

He pulled on the skirt, a lighter brown T-shirt over his head, a bit oversized, so it hung well below the waist, and then finished the ensemble with a plaid burgundy blouse, unbuttoned. He garnished the outerwear with a long strand of dark wooden beads. He looked like a fey lumberjack, a fairy bearing nature's rustic wings.

Stephen tugged an oversized black sock over the powder-blue cast and slipped his other foot into a single hiking boot that went with the earthy colour scheme. Like some gender bending butch/femme traveller from a contemporary version of a Jane Austen novel, he went wild, into the blue yonder of the B.C. interior—an arid sun-swept version of the Lake District, looking for comfort from the recent memory of a brief romantic rendezvous in a casino parking lot.

Stephen wondered what the sushi/surfer would think of him in this get-up, and it made him think of the volatile relationship between Mr. Darcy and Elizabeth Bennett. He would be handing out excerpts from *Pride and Prejudice* tomorrow in his literature class. Men were incidental to his view of Austen—essential—elemental—but incidental to a landscape where all the real work was done in skirts, by women.

"What are men to rocks and mountains?"

Whenever he came to the first line of the protagonist's famous plea, Stephen liked to change *rocks* to *frocks*.

What are men to [f]rocks and mountains? Oh! what hours of transport we shall spend! And when we do return, it shall not be like other travellers, without being able to give one accurate idea of any thing. We will know where we have gone—we will recollect what we have seen. Lakes, mountains, and rivers shall not be jumbled together in our imaginations; nor, when we attempt to describe any particular scene, will we begin quarrelling about its relative situation. Let our first effusions be less insupportable than those of the generality of travellers.

—Elizabeth Bennett—Pride and Prejudice

Apart from a few friendly uprooted tumbleweeds brushing themselves against him, Stephen didn't run into another human being on the trails. His first sighting of someone human took place as he walked into the parking lot of Old Main, the building that housed most of the classrooms on campus. People didn't seem to notice his attire right away, probably because of the unobtrusive earth tones and the natural fibres of his finely tuned ensemble. The rough-hewn necklace was a bit much, though, and gradually curious eyes would move downward from the wooden strand of raffish beads toward the lower body and the gendered hem. At this point, fashion voyeurs would begin to express silent surprise at the sight of a full skirt on a man, with a short slit in the back no less! Little did they know that the slit was fully functional, and made hiking more manageable and less restrictive for the thighs and lower legs. The walking cast wasn't noticeable, and Stephen had quickly learned how to maneuver with only a barely discernible lilt to his gait—and people had come to expect some lilting and limping within certain gay extremities.

When he walked into the classroom, five minutes early, for the first time since the semester had begun, there was no one there. The building had seemed empty when he entered the double doors, and the copy shop was oddly closed. But it was refreshing to know that paper would not be running a mile a minute through all those infernal machines. In the empty classroom, he sat down and started to put the haiku assignment sheets out on the desk in front of him.

After fifteen minutes of waiting for someone to arrive, Stephen looked at his daybook.

Stephen muttered to himself.

"Oh, for the love of Mary. Fuck fuck fuck fuck fuck fuck fuck! It's a day off for special academic training sessions! Shit! Why didn't anyone say anything yesterday in class when I told them we'd look at their haiku today! Christ, I could have stayed in bed. And I've wasted my fabulous ensemble on a small pack of unfashionable strangers."

Never one to find himself at a loss when it came to filling free time, Stephen packed up his things, threw his backpack over his shoulder, and left the building in a semi-relieved huff. He took in the late morning air and quickly readjusted his plan for the day. He would head down to Value Village in search of a new vacuum cleaner. The one the owners left behind had broken during his first week, and the living room carpets were getting disgusting. He was tired of wrapping his fists in masking tape in a futile attempt to lift bits of dust and daily debris from the cheap nylon pile.

He was looking forward to finding a nice old canister model, preferably a Westinghouse like his mother had in the fifties, but that seemed unlikely. New vacuum cleaners looked like little robots who didn't need a human appendage pushing them around the house. What was happening to the good old

1950s, a decade he was born halfway through, when humans were still needed in order to keep their homes tidy and up to date in a thoroughly modern way?

As he walked down Columbia Drive, foregoing a return route via the hills he had come through on the way to campus, he thought of small appliances and found himself becoming excited about his upcoming purchase.

The bargain store was empty except for the staff, and no one paid attention as Stephen strolled in. He had thrown a vest over the shirt just before leaving the house, giving the upper section of the ensemble a nice layered effect. The wooden beads, he had purchased for a dollar and a half the week before.

Even though he knew precisely what he was looking for, he instinctively made his way to the bedspreads, throws, and draperies section, where they kept the kitsch wall-hangings he was so fond of. The secret to finding hidden treasures at bargain palaces was to go often and to look carefully in selected areas.

Lo and behold, a gorgeous mountain scene with deer all over the bloody place. And if that were not enough good fortune for one day, there was a tiny matching pillow-sized throw with the identical scene. And there was snow on the mountaintops! He could make a matching sham and use both the large throw and the small one on the single bed in the spare room. When Peter returned, he might not be too pleased to find that his roommate's penchant for kitsch was overflowing into the rest of the house. But it was unavoidable. Stephen's taste for humorous home décor was like rabbit sex—it just kept on multiplying.

With his fabulous new finds hanging over his left arm, he went straight to the appliance section, where he had bought the small plastic record player to play his Bee Gees album on. As he moved closer toward the area where he might find a vacuum cleaner, there it stood. An avocado-green

Westinghouse canister vacuum cleaner identical to the one Stephen's mother had replaced in the mid-sixties with an upright model.

The coincidental event took his breath away. Coincidence was such a miraculous phenomenon. Hadn't he just written a poem, only eight days before, on a bus ride from Vancouver to Kamloops, about that old vacuum cleaner? As he marvelled at this poetic and breathtaking turn of events, he carefully lifted the object from the shelf, went over to the electrical outlets, and plugged it in to see if it worked. The humming was music to his ears. He couldn't wait to get home and start vacuuming. But this was a cause for celebration. He set the identical throws and the appliance into a shopping cart and headed for the cash register. He would pay for his bargains and then dine at Oriental Gardens, treat himself to a pitcher of sangria. He knew there were some fabulous additions to the menu—paella combo plates, with spicy egg rolls—seafood tempura, dragon roll piñata—and a 16 oz pitcher of sake sangria—$18.99.

The multiculturalism of his favourite eatery was too true to be good, a testament to the diversity so prevalent across this vast colonizing country. Postcolonial discursive strategy was alive and well and living on the streets of Tk'emlups—blithely encased in the text of an eclectic restaurant menu.

The clerk at Value Village raised her penciled-in eyebrows at the sight of the wooden beads, seemed not to notice the skirt, and abruptly said, "That will be seventeen twenty-seven. Sir."

Stephen was surprised. He had added all three purchases in his head, and it had only come to around nine dollars. He asked to look at the receipt.

"What's this item? I only bought three items, the throws, and the vacuum cleaner. There are four listed here."

"The shopping cart."

"The shopping cart?"

"Yes, sir. It's an old shopping cart, with a bit of rust and some broken parts on the sides. It's for sale, see the tag?"

Stephen thought he could hear her muttering *fag* under her breath. It rhymed with tag, and had its own special price. But he wasn't sure.

"I didn't notice. I don't really need a shopping cart."

But how could he pass up buying a vintage Value Village shopping cart to push his new purchase all the way home. It would save him the cost of a cab.

"Okay, great. But won't people think I've stolen it?"

"We took the name off. It'll be fine. You're not the only person in this town with an old shopping cart, trust me. And you could spray paint it a cool colour, to match your funky beads. Did you buy them here?"

The clerk had taken on a mocking tone when she asked about Stephen's beads. Her full pink lips were pursed and her darkly outlined blue eyes widened as she took in his entire ensemble when he stepped away from the shopping cart.

Stephen just smiled, gave the mocking clerk a twenty-dollar bill, and replied, "Yes. I did buy them here, along with the vest, the skirt, the boots, the T-shirt, and the plaid blouse. I think I must be one of your best customers."

The clerk shook her head slightly and pushed change toward him, across the counter, rather than placing the coins and the receipt into his palm.

Stephen smiled as he swept the change into his bag.

"Thank you so much. You've been very helpful. And I just adore your eyebrows. Did you do them yourself?"

As he pushed his four-wheeled accomplice out of the store, the hem of his skirt swaying in the sudden draft as the automatic doors to the front entrance swung open, he thought of the first line of a novel that a close friend had written. It spoke of someone who collected abandoned shopping carts. Abandoned no longer, his cart would become his companion, a robust receptacle for bargain treasures. The day had become an embarrassment of riches—a powder-blue morning was becoming a prosaic light purplish early afternoon. Beginning early with a stroll in a slightly tatty frock, now he was finding himself in possession of so much bargain retail stimulation that he could hardly contain himself. As he walked in the front doors of Oriental Gardens, he even felt teary as he considered rainbow colours for a new coat of paint on his rusty second-hand buggy.

The sangria was weak. It was the end of the day, so the fruit floating in the top of the pitcher seemed rotten, all ribbon'y and thick with the burgundies and the reds of cheap red wine mixed with soggy apple chunks, orange slices, and berries. But it did the trick, and by the end of his celebratory meal Stephen was feeling tipsy.

He had left the cart, filled with his purchases, outside by the window, so when he went inside he could sit at the table looking out and keep an eye on his valued buggy. Afterwards, he would have gone to the casino for a quick slip into the slots, but didn't want to risk losing his cherished bargains.

It was dark by the time he finished eating—and drinking. There was a chill in the air, but assorted layers of clothing kept him warm, and he looked forward to a stroll home.

When Stephen got to the four-lane slope that ran up toward Columbia Drive, past West St. Paul, he didn't feel like going all the way down to the crosswalk. There was no traffic, so he jaywalked brazenly, pushing the cart across the road. It began to tip to the right from the grade of the hill and the weight of the vintage vacuum cleaner. Just as he began to steady the tipping cart, Stephen heard the squeal of brakes. Headlights suddenly appeared at the intersection at the bottom of the hill. The car stopped quickly, waited for several seconds, then squealed into a hard right up the hill. It startled Stephen, and his right arm, supporting the cart, let go. The vacuum cleaner jarred, pushing the cart sideways into the middle of the fourth lane, where the car was headed. In his nebulous ensemble, Stephen and his strange cargo blended into the shadows of the sagging willows lining the street, a shapeless extension of a vague arboreal scene. He lifted the cart, pushed his purchases into the basket, and began to rush toward the sidewalk. As the car sped by, he felt a slight pull at his waist, a quick snap, a light pinch, and then a sudden gust of wind around his mid-section. It all happened so quickly he didn't realize the full extent of the mishap until he sat down on the curb to catch his breath. His thighs were naked, utterly unclothed, rubbing against the bare cement curb. His skirt was gone! As he rushed across the road, away from the oncoming headlights, the car had caught his hem and torn the frock from his body.

Once again, for the second time during a twenty-four-hour period, Stephen imagined himself a contemporary character from a revisionist version of a classic novel, perhaps one by the Bronte sisters. He had crossed the urban heath, been ravaged by the elements, and barely survived a brush with vehicular tragedy! As he sat, thrown to the curb, he felt both violated and amused by all that had happened.

His plaid shirt was long enough to cover his buttocks, and the socks he wore with his cast and hiking boot came to just below his knees. He got up from the curb, wiped a tear from his eye, and began to push the cart along the last block of West St. Paul to his comfortable heritage house. Luckily, no one was walking that late at night, or they would have seen a middle-aged man in a vest, two shirts, a boot, a covered cast, socks, and bare legs from below his knees to the edge of what appeared to be a plaid miniskirt, with the edge of the vest hanging several inches above the hem of the shirt. When he got home, he was so shaken by a sense of the ridiculous and a well-cultivated desire for the sublime that he just pushed the cart through the wooden gate to the backyard and left everything there, protected by the large sloping roof of the lush verandah, until morning.

In no mood to use his new vacuum cleaner, Stephen plodded into the kitchen and mixed himself a full shaker of fruit-flavoured martinis—mango. After finishing the martinis in record time, he staggered limply and liltingly up the stairs to his bedroom, where he collapsed on the arboreal bedspread populated by his beloved woodland creatures.

The identity of the speeding motorist who had grazed Stephen's cross-dressed carcass as he scuttled across asphalt would remain a mystery. And the offending vehicular drunk—a blonde haired, blue-lipped sangria swiller—knew that he had experienced a near miss with a near Miss as he sped toward the highway that would take him back to the ski resort he had recently returned to. Craig seemed to be turning up unseen in familiar places. He was looking for Stephen at Oriental Gardens, but never dreamed he had just seen him in a skirt in a postcolonial mash-up of culinary delight—sushi with egg rolls and sangria—then almost ran him over as he sped out of town with a torn skirt stuck to his fender and a bumper sticker that unceremoniously announced that the offending car was protected by a very angry dog with AIDS—a pit bull. Topped off by oversized plush dice suspended from the rear-view of Craig's vintage Camaro.

7 p.m.—Tkaronto—BALCONY

Stephen sat by the door for forty-five minutes. Once the first
batch of children had eagerly dug their claws into the basket
of prepackaged candy, the stream of trick-or-treaters came to
a halt. As Stephen walked to the fridge for a quick rendezvous
with white wine, he caught a glimpse of himself in the full-
length mirror on the bathroom door. Shit! No wonder the
children had been so standoffish and focused on the candy,
with little to say to him as they dove into his stash. With all
the trauma surrounding the tube-of-toothpaste stranger on
the stretcher, he had forgotten to switch on the light bulb, and
forgotten to put on his macabre doctor costume, still lying
on the bed. He dashed into the bedroom, pulled the white
trousers and shirt on, tied the thin black tie sloppily, slipped
into white high heels with hot pink socks, put on the Elvis wig
and witch hat, smeared a bit of lipstick across his mouth, put
on some cat's eye sunglasses, adjusted his doctor name tag,
and returned to his post in the hallway, peeking out the door
to see if there were more kiddies on their way. Not a single
child in the corridor. Where on earth were the children? Had
word spread that the eccentric old poofter on the tenth floor
wasn't dressed in an even more outrageous costume than
he had worn in previous years, just before he left for nine
months to teach poetry in the interior of British Columbia?
He had had to get permission from the co-op board to leave
for an extended period, and lost his subsidy in the process,
all the time thinking out West he would get a permanent
contract and give up his place. But no such luck. HIV and
union disputes during the last contract negotiations had put
a stop to all that. No ongoing contract, no untainted blood.
Stephen was back in the city for the duration, settling into the

life the goddesses had obviously plotted out for him a very long time ago when they sat down to create a design for living that would simultaneously delight and annoy him. It was Halloween. He was happy to be a little frightened by himself.

Life wasn't so bad. He loved living in the centre of the city. He could forget all his troubles, forget all his woes and go where the neon signs were in abundance. He was already there. Down. Town.

6:55, and no more children. So he poured himself a goblet of white wine and sat by the window, pushing the dark sheers away from the glass and pushing the balcony door slightly ajar. As his hand left the knob and the curtain swung elegantly back into place, he noticed something on the chaise longue. Or someone. He was terrified, for a moment, until he recognized the designer leather boots sticking out from under the edge of the throw he left on the outdoor reclining chair for smokers.

Irene. What the fuck was she doing back from Amalfi so early. She had obviously let herself in with her key when he was at the Y, and was undoubtedly drunk and asleep. He'd leave her there for a few more minutes, at least until he finished his wine and had the fortitude and false cheeriness to go out, wake her up, greet her, then sit and listen to whatever trauma she had endured on the Italian Riviera.

As he sipped and frowned, practising good cheer for an evening that was shaping up to be dull dull dull, he looked out through the long rectangular balcony window again, and thought to himself—

It's so nice, as the cooler months threaten to surround us once again, to see someone getting some use out of my terrace— my sad, tiny, gaily decorated little balcony—but terrace sounds so much more glamorous, doesn't it.

And then he toasted himself, drank to his own health, savoured the flavour of the wine with a dash of concentrate mango juice, and wished that the food bank offered cheap wine as part of their weekly nutritional food plan. The food bank, such a lovely place to spend impoverished afternoons.

When I Thought I was a Mango—by Dr Stephen Andrew Davis

On a sunny Wednesday in March, when the weather suited global warming to a tee, he took his shopping buggy from the balcony and set out for the food bank. Only a few blocks from his apartment, this food bank specialized in healthy items that came in containers ranging from airtight freezer bags to small meat-bearing styrofoam platters, cardboard boxes, foil wrappers, and glass jars.

In the waiting area at the food bank, there was always a transparent, dome-covered plastic tray filled with hot cross buns, Danishes, brownies, cinnamon wedges, butter tarts, and donuts. They were cut into bite-sized portions, a crumbling nostalgic air about them that spoke of slightly better days. But they were delicious. Metal prongs and napkins kept the delicacies safe from germ warfare, and a large canister of hot coffee on a table nearby, sat ready to help the medicine go down.

He put his little grocery buggy beside his chair and went over to the reception desk to check in. Stating his name and answering one simple question was always enough. They never asked for ID, because he had registered several years ago and was in the computer system, but he always took ID with him just in case. He would not want to be caught with his pants down. The pants-down image seemed appropriate, because he, and perhaps others, were eligible for this particular food bank only because they had, through no fault of their own, been caught with their trousers to the floor one too many times.

The simple question the receptionist always asked was: "Do you have any pets?" He would pause for a second, considering what he might do with jars of cat food or doggy kibble. Perhaps he could sell them, or mix them with a rich salty stew that would conceal their true identity? And then he would think better of his thrifty ways and reply, "No. But thank you."

Then he would take one or two selections from the pastry tray, fill a styrofoam cup with coffee, add some powdered milk and a touch of sugar, and sit back to wait until his fruit or vegetable was called. It wasn't a long wait, and the variety of colourful, laminated fruit and veggie bearing cards made it fun:

Apple Banana Blackberry Cantaloupe Date Fennel Ginger Jalapeño Kiwi Lime Mango Okra Peach Pumpkin Radicchio Yam Zucchini

He would arrive shortly after 2:00 p.m. The food bank was open from 2:00 until 7:00 p.m. By the time he arrived they would be as far along as Cantaloupes. He would receive a Fennels laminated card and wait until his group of three or four was called. Once, when he arrived earlier than usual, he was a Date, and knew that the usual gag would be played as soon as the Dates were called.

"Dates anyone? Any Dates?"

Inevitably someone would laugh and say something along the lines of, "I'd love to. Haven't been on a date in ages."

But on this warm Wednesday in March, he arrived well after two, missed the Dates, and thought he was a Mango. He took his card, walked over to his chair, sat down, and saw a familiar face in a wheelchair. Noticing that his acquaintance also had a Mango card, he said,

"I've never been a Mango before. I'm usually a Fennel."

His friend smiled, but said nothing. Apart from the Dates, not much was made of the other fruits and vegetables. So he sat sipping coffee and nibbling at the ragged corner of a hot cross bun, waiting for the Mangoes to be herded down to the selection area.

Consumed by commingled good cheer and slight melancholy—a mixture of emotion that invariably held him

somewhere between a subtle smile and a face hiding tears—
he noticed that the attendant passing out the laminated cards
looked agitated. He could overhear him explaining to an
assistant that the fruit and vegetable cards were all mixed up,
and that he was sending the groups in all the wrong order.

How hard could it be to notice that, he thought, and sort
them properly, in alphabetical order. But it wasn't his place to
make any suggestion about how organizing principles might be
applied. So he sat patiently, watching the names of each fruit or
vegetable come and go on the pixel board above the reception
desk—in the wrong order—and wondering anxiously if his
Mango would ever come up.

After several minutes had passed, he went up to the
desk and politely asked if his fruit had risen. The confused
receptionist asked what fruit he was. When he said Mango,
he told him to go ahead, as the Mangoes had already been
called. So he left the reception area and walked briskly toward
the stairwell of the food bank. On his way, he saw the assistant
who had been taking groups down the stairs to the area where
shelves of dry goods and freezers filled with assorted frozen
meats were kept. He looked at him, smiled, and said—"I think
the fruits and vegetables got a little mixed up today. I was told
to go ahead." The assistant looked at his card and said, politely
but somewhat abruptly—"No. I'll call you when it's time."

A little bewildered, he walked back to the waiting area—
and waited. As he sat, he kept looking at the pixel board, not
able to make head nor tail of how things were organized. The
Mangoes had already gone, and the order seemed to have
been reestablished on the pixel board. And then, after several
seconds of low-level anxiety marked by his signature tendency
to fluctuate between a faint smile and suppressed tears, he
looked at his laminated card, and much to his surprise, and
embarrassment, saw he was not a Mango at all. He was a
Pumpkin. Cinderella. Suppressing images of little white mice
sewing spectacular gowns and singing bibbidy-bobbidy-boo,

he made a quick decision not to dwell on the clichéd, fairy-tale proportions of the mix-up. Instead, he waited until the Pumpkins were called, pondering how this could have happened. He was certain he had been given a Mango. And then, at the height of his anxiety, he looked at the camera option on his cell phone, remembering that he had taken a photo of his card soon after arriving, so he could write a little story about this food bank one day.

Yes, indeed. Cameras seldom lie. He had always been a Pumpkin, and when he chatted with the acquaintance in the wheelchair, and noticed that his card said Mango, he must have assumed he was one too, because the colours of the cards depicting those fruits were so similar.

It made perfect sense, because he knew, in his heart, he had always been a princess. And it seemed fitting, after some fifty-odd years, that he would one day find himself, at the PWA food bank (strictly serving a community of people living with HIV and AIDS) abruptly turning back into a Pumpkin.

Day Ten—Tk'emlups—Thursday, October 11

What's the difference between an Elephant and a Camaro?
A Camaro has an asshole on the inside.

—author unknown

It was on the tip of his tongue, but he could not remember the name of the hunk he had met at the sushi bar—the speeding, skiing, Tofino/Long Beach surfing, cocktail-making, pickled-ginger hating, accidental skirt-thieving, Camaro wielding, tawny, verging on middle-aged hunk.

Craig, his name was Craig.

Stephen woke up in a pool of sweat, thinking about attractive men. Craig couldn't be more than ten years younger than he was. He'd like to see him again. They seemed to have a connection. Little did he know their most recent connection had been the hem of his frock.

He walked into the bathroom, looked in the mirror, smiled, widened his bulging hungover eyes, and whispered, with the passion of an internalized, silent, primal scream, "Oops." He had vague memories of the night before, but not a thought in his head about who the rip-and-run driver might have been.

Stephen had also woken with the distinct feeling that the night had been filled with dreams, but he could not for the life of him remember them. If experience, and Freud, had taught him anything about nocturnal narrative emission, snippets of his most recent dreams would seep into his consciousness over the next few hours, even days.

After showering, deodorizing his sweat-ravaged pits, sprinkling a bit of baby powder on his balls, and dressing quickly—no skirt today—he made himself a cup of elderberry tea, downed a few acetylsalicylic acid tablets and 8 mg caffeine phosphate tablets, with a dash of St. John's Wort in his teacup and a bit of echinacea tincture under his tongue, and walked out onto the back verandah to take in the view of the river. Little did he know that he would soon discover, in his everlasting pathology, that both echinacea and St. John's Wort were a no-no for HIV's search for the perfect cocktail and the perfect diet.

The view gave him a pristine picture of where they met—the two strands of the Thompson River—the largest tributary of the Fraser River—flowing through the south-central portion of B.C. From the porch he had a spectacular view of the wide beaches that extended almost to the middle of the river when the waterline was down during the drier months.

Before Stephen moved to Kamloops, he had never seen beaches like this on a narrow river, some surreal commingling, a geographic scene where slight grassy edges of the land swept into sandy, almost tropical expanses of a partially arid riverbed. The valley'ed strip of northern desert gave way to smudges of scrawny pine trees, a surreal northern cousin to the palm—thirsty pines popping their heads through a crust of land that had its geological roots in the Mojave, all coming together in a dream-like postcard.

"Fuck, what the hell is that?!"

Stephen caught the gleaming, lightly rusted edge of the shopping cart out of the corner of his eye, sitting right where he had left it the night before. It came back like a lightning bolt, and made his head throb even more than it already had been. The whole Value Village encounter flew into his consciousness, the paella, sushi, sangria, tempura dinner at Oriental Gardens, the walk home, and the exhilarating brush with vehicular induced near death. He set his teacup on a little molded plastic table he had bought at Great Canadian Superstore and walked down the wooden steps to the cart. There it was, his most recently acquired bargain stash. Somehow, he had veiled the vintage vacuum with the kitsch throws, and as he lifted them out of the cart, the avocado tone of the canister caught his eye, and he began to cry.

"Holy shit! This could not have happened."

His mother's taut, well-toned arms, and the tiny calf muscles that pulsed in the back of her legs as she pushed that vacuum cleaner around his childhood home flashed before his eyes. It was too much to take in. He shoved the throws back into the cart, and began to lug the whole kitsch'n'kaboodle up the steps, then through the double doors to the dining room. He pulled the vacuum out of the cart, looking for a free outlet, and almost tripped on the cord as he dragged the vacuum cleaner across the room. Carefully inserting the plug into the wall, he looked at the side of the canister for the little silver switch he remembered from his mother's identical appliance. There it was, just as he remembered it, looking like a very tiny circumcised silvery penis jutting from the side of the limbless torso of the machine. He switched the mini-phallus upwards, and the soft purring of the motor began to sing, producing an ambient soundscape for the morning light pouring in the windows. Nature and technology lived, astute and wild eyed, for one brief shining moment, as perfectly matched conjugal paramours. The vacuum cleaner's aroused ethereal vision; it was all he could do to not rip off his clothes and take part in a mad, oft-remembered encounter from puberty. But this was enough for now. He would play hard to get.

He switched off the power, stored his bargain treasure in the hall closet, and left for campus. His first day of teaching postcolonial literature, and he still wasn't sure how to articulate the connection between Jane Austen, Oscar Wilde, EM, Frantz Fanon, Salman Rushdie, Sara Suleri, and Gautam Malkani. But he'd give it the good old college try.

It had not gone well at all. Students were mostly wide eyed, closed mouthed, irritated, or completely inattentive when he began to explain the colonizing nature of Austen's text, how the idea of colonization could also be applied to human bodies, and how this could be traced through a complex literary trajectory from *Pride and Prejudice* to *The Importance of Being Earnest*, *A Passage to India*, *Meatless Days*, *White Skin Black Masks*, *The Satanic Verses*, and *Londonstani*, culminating in an eclectic multicultural chorus of diverse theoretical thought from feminism to gay liberation, critical race studies, and postcolonial research, ultimately bringing seemingly unlikely literary bedfellows together into one big unhappy familial seminar. He even suggested making po-co-mojitos for a class party, Halloween themed, at the end of the term. But he was getting ahead of himself, and none of the students seemed in the mood for witty superficial amusement from a sudden professorial replacement. All they knew was that their favourite professor had suddenly been replaced by a queer new addition.

Except for one student, Jeffrey. There he was, smug and smiling at the back of the classroom, happy to see his trés gay poetry professor up there making an absolute camp-a-licious fool of himself in front of disgruntled third-year literature students. And what was Jeffrey doing there anyway?

"Okay, then. The reading list will of course stay the same, with the exception of the brief passages from Austen, Wilde, and Fanon that I have added. Professor Landry has given me her notes, and would like me to carry on, with only minor adjustments to the syllabus on the handout I've given you. We will still be having the yoga class she organized for next week, so please remember to wear loose clothing, and bring a towel, or a yoga mat if you have one, to class. And please don't forget to bring a couple of well-researched questions about the history of yoga for the instructor to answer."

"What exactly do you mean by well-researched questions, sir?"

He hadn't noticed Lily sitting to the side, in the fourth row, far away from Jeffrey. Her sarcastic, superior tone was not welcoming. He was in no mood for anything even faintly challenging on the pedagogical front.

"What part of *look it up online* do you not understand?"

She just glared at him, smirked, and shook her head.

"Great, see you all next week for a very informative yoga seminar slash workout."

Jeffrey walked over to Stephen's desk.

"I need some help with my essay topic, and I still don't get villanelles. Do you have any time today?"

"I don't have office hours today. Sorry. I have to go straight home. I'm feeling a little under the weather."

"You look hungover."

"And how does that look, to you, from your perspective?"

"Tired. Grey. Old."

"How kind of you to notice. Just email me for an appointment sometime early next week."

"That's too late."

"Have you even researched villanelles? Why don't you ask your girlfriend? Lily seems to be on top of things academic."

"I don't, tried, but still don't get it, and she's not my girlfriend anymore."

"I'm sorry. I shouldn't have said that. It was inappropriate."

"Are you walking home?"

"Yes, I am."

"Can I walk with you, and ask you a few questions? I'd really appreciate it. I have to get started on my essay. It's due next week."

"Fine, meet me at the entrance to Old Main in twenty minutes. I have to go to my office first."

"I can go with you."

"No, the entrance to Old Main. See you in twenty."

He didn't want Jeffrey in his office. Not today. Not any day. Not ever. As a graduate student, in workshops devoted to pedagogical rapport and proper academic conduct, Stephen had been taught always to keep the office door ajar—wide open in fact—during one-on-one appointments with students, especially those you might be concerned about. And Jeffrey's five-day-old remark about the bedspread still haunted Stephen. Even walking home with him seemed inappropriate. But he had unconsciously weakened when Jeffrey explained his romantic and academic predicament, and he wanted to treat him like any other student in need of remedial support. So, walk they would, down the trail toward Nicola Wagon Road, where so many historic encounters between Shuswap, fur traders, gold miners, and cattlemen went tragically astray.

But the bedspread never came up. Their conversation kept strictly to the topics of villanelles and *A Passage to India*. There was a brief uncomfortable moment when Jeffrey took it upon himself to ask whether Forster was, as Jeffrey so eloquently put it, "a big old British closet fag." Stephen simply responded with a quick reference to "The Celestial Omnibus" and "The Story of a Panic," two short stories that might shed literary light on Forster's shadowy, lightly canonized sexuality.

"Why don't you write about homosexuality in some of Forster's work if you're so curious about his status as an old British fag?"

"I didn't mean anything by it, sir, just trying to be funny, but hey, yeah, that sounds great. Can you recommend some sources?"

"Have a look in the library."

"The library."

"Yes, the campus library, or even the downtown library."

"I've never been there before. And there's a library downtown too?"

"Yes, they have everything you need, downtown. Jeffrey, you cannot use only online sources for the work I assign."

"I use online journals and stuff."

"Use the library, Jeffrey. It's easy to find. It's the building filled with an inordinate number of shelves, covered in books of all shapes and sizes. If you need any more help, then email me, and I'll direct you toward some other possibilities."

After Stephen left Jeffrey at the intersection of Nicola Wagon Road and the steep dirt path toward Columbia Drive, watching him take huge post-pubescent strides up the side of the mountain, he had a sudden and jarring sense of déjà vu, something to do with a car, a skirt, an elephant, an asshole, a shopping cart, a vacuum cleaner, and two huge puddles of water meeting in the middle of an arid river valley. But he could not for the life of him sort any of it out. Hair of the dog was the only answer, as he headed back toward a full liquor cabinet and a rented house beginning to feel more and more like an impermanent home.

Stephen opened the balcony door.

"Goddammit, Irene, it's eight o'clock and I'm expecting a guest.

"I'm grieving, you flaming fruitcake! Cancel your guest. I need you to comfort me with conversation and cocktails."

"I can't cancel. He's just about to arrive. I don't even know him, so there's no way of contacting him. And I don't want to. It's the first pseudo-date I've had in centuries."

"You don't even know him? How gay! Where did you meet?"

"In the lobby. Laughing at the mock tombstones. He was waiting to take his kids out for Halloween and we just started chatting. Then he followed me into the laundry room and asked if he could stop by later, that he'd bring some wine."

"Lovely. I'll join you."

"No. You won't."

"Fine. Give me one drink, and I'll leave as soon as he gets here."

Stephen threw together a shaker of martinis for Irene. There was a loud, obnoxious knocking. This was probably his guest, the masked man.

He opened the door ready to smile at his tall handsome stranger, explain that he had a guest, but please come in, she'll be gone soon. Two short adorable toddlers instead—with what appeared to be a pair of same-sex parents of medium height and faintly indeterminate gender standing behind them. At first, he couldn't tell if they were lesbians or gay men. They both had moustaches and seemed to be wearing some kind of lame, pseudo-campy excuse for a costume. One wore a white sports coat with a pink carnation and black jeans, the other a formal black tux with tails and a top hat and white gloves.

The kids were dressed as fairies, gauzy plasticized dollar-store wings attached to their backs.

The two little girls were the prettiest little femmes imaginable. Oops! They were both boys. That only became clear after the thoroughly modern family accepted candy and then sauntered away as one of the lesbian parents remarked, thinking the door was fully closed—

"Well, Jimmy and Alan, that was your first peek at a full-fledged screaming queen. Wasn't she a hoot."

He pushed the door shut, turned the lock, poured himself half the martini shaker, and sat down across from Irene.

"Where's the mystery man?"

"It was more trick-or-treaters. Asshole parents. They called me a screaming queen, right in front of their goddamn fairy children!"

"But, Blanche, you are."

"Frankly, I do not need to be reminded. Let's go up to the roof garden and smoke a joint."

"You don't smoke pot."

"I'd like to start. Now."

"What about your date?"

"He's almost an hour late. Fuck him."

"I'm not going anywhere with you until you get out of that outrageous Doctor costume! Besides, it will scare your date away."

They stood on the roof garden, a distant view of the island, sharing a joint among the dead and dying summer flowers, slowly rotting green tomatoes, the wrinkled zucchini, and the ravaged pots of basil. Overlooking the lake and the plot of land running from Shuter down to Harbourfront, with the island a strange little fragmented assemblage of disconnected earth once attached to the mainland, but broken away at the beginning of the last century by wind and wild water. There had been sacred Indigenous sites, but they had been erased by far less natural causes.

"Why are you back from Amalfi so soon?"

"He dumped me."

"I'm sorry."

"Don't be. I got a lot of money out of the bastard. I'm set until summer. He was an idiot. A kind, gorgeous, generous, intelligent idiot. It was like a divorce settlement, but I didn't have to marry him."

"An idiot? How so?"

"He had everything to offer with one notable exception."

"Yes?"

"He lacked the ability to put up with my bullshit."

"Of course. He's an idiot."

As they left the roof garden, they failed to notice a large hat-like contraption, white and vertically grooved, kind of like the top to an oversized tube of toothpaste, large enough to go on top of someone's head. It was sitting by the wheel of the gas barbeque near the raspberry bushes, which had been recently crushed by something. Raspberry juice dried on the patio stones. It looked like blood.

But sitting at a picnic table at the opposite end of the roof, chatting and smoking, they missed the stains.

Day Eleven—Tk'emlups—Friday, October 12

A day off with no student meetings. Stephen slept until three
and puttered around the house, vacuuming and tidying, until
seven, when he suggested to himself that he join himself on
the verandah for a late-afternoon cocktail. Accepting his
own invitation graciously and enthusiastically, he drained
the last bit of tropical fruit medley into a shaker, filled it with
ice, topped it off with an impressive portion of Grey Goose
vodka, then rattled and rolled it into one heavenly libation.
Then he headed for the verandah, where he suddenly began to
remember the sweaty dream.

The first shard of memory came in the form of a giant
waterslide called the death drop. He loved waterslides. For as
long as he could remember, whenever he travelled, he longed
for accommodations with a spectacular waterpark connected
to the main building. But he often had to settle for a pathetic
plastic tunnel attached to a small pool beside the parking lot,
surrounded by a chain-link fence with sad patches of grass in
thirsty depleted tufts. When he first saw photos of the West
Edmonton Mall, his immediate response was to write it off as
another suburban monstrosity littered with expensive shops
and noisy food emporiums. But the waterslides won him over.

On his first visit, he surprised his brother and nephews
by climbing to the top of the death-drop slide and whipping
down in his red bikini with all the majesty of an aging queen
on her last regal voyage. He imagined himself a combination
of Ophelia and the Lady of Shallot. Unlike those soggy fated
damsels, however, Stephen had the opportunity to make a
tragicomic spectacle of himself—over and over and over and
over—every time he visited Edmonton, or any other cities
with superb aquatic playgrounds.

In the fall of 2006, when his first collection of poetry was launched, the publishers drove him and three other poets from Calgary to Edmonton. Halfway through the three hundred kilometre drive, he politely asked if there would be time to stop at the mall so he could have a go at the slides. Stephen craved a return visit to the site of his favourite aquatic dream. Not expecting them to accommodate his request, he was pleasantly surprised when they agreed to do just that on the way into the city. He would have forty-five minutes to get in and out of the atrium-like structure that housed the waterpark, and then meet them by the roller coaster in time to get to the hotel and relax before the book launch.

On his way out of the waterpark, after a good twenty minutes of glorious sliding, he had noticed a formal sandwich board. Standing proud at the bottom of the ramp leading to the men's change room, it read, in bold letters,

AREA CLOSED FOR MAINTENANCE & CLEANING DUE TO FECAL ACCIDENT

As a sign, it was merely informative and startling. But Stephen arranged the syllables into haiku format and changed the last word to mishap to rid his perfect found haiku of the two extra syllables that would have ruined the syllabic structure of an otherwise, taut, direct verse. As a poem set in ancient form it was slightly vulgar, faintly ridiculous, and utterly sublime.

Stephen was fond of the word *mishap*. He considered it a beautiful utterance, signifying an abject occurrence of unsung proportions. Placing the word *fecal* before it added an extra layer of linguistic texture. But when he suggested the title *Fecal Mishaps* for his next collection of poetry, the publisher put her foot down and gently but adamantly insisted that it would not be a good title for marketing and distribution—not to mention a likely candidate for any literary awards worthy of mainstream respect. But that was something Stephen never put much store in.

The déjà vu-like quality of the waterslide memory was fleeting. Stephen stepped out onto the verandah with his fruity martini and a full shaker nestled in his upturned palm. He liked to carry drinks in the palm of his hand. It gave his wrist a strained, taut curvature that simultaneously belied and enforced the signature limpness expected from his upper extremities. The poem, the waterpark, the returning dream. It was a fruity mélange of mixed emotion and memory in his mind. Changing the word *accident* to *mishap* had served poetry well.

AREA CLOSED FOR
MAINTENANCE AND CLEANING DUE
TO FECAL MISHAP

On the verandah, remembering the dream and its ingredients, as he set the shaker down on the plastic table, he caught in the distance a glimpse of the wide beaches along the river. He had a flash of a long powder-blue shaft of light, like a slide, running from the back yard of the house down as far as the edge of the river. He lowered himself into the plastic Adirondack chair beside the moulded plastic table and lifted the first martini of the afternoon to his lips. As he squinted into the silvery remains of a perfect sunset, the powder blue of his air-infused dream-slide mingled with the tones of the valley.

The hills were a soft pink, and the sandy beach of the semi-arid riverbed was a rich tan. The water was an inky blue in places, wine dark in spots, with softer shades occurring here and there among the brutish, monolithic shadows of the Overlander Bridge. The elegant silhouettes of scrawny trees that lined the river's edge, not to mention the odd human form crossing the landscape with a dog or a child or a random paramour in tow, all began to make sense.

He had never considered déjà vu, or the onslaught of memories from a recent dream, as aided and abetted by alcohol. But this mid-afternoon experience was a notable exception. After his third martini, with one left in the shaker, vivid visual veracity felt like a numb magical tingling, running through his arms and legs, enlivening his soul.

In his dream, he was naked, with his middle-aged, beefy legs jammed through the open slots in the folding seat of his recently acquired shopping cart. A vessel designed for children to sit in while their mother or stay-at-home dad wandered the packed aisles of any given Superstore. The bin section of the cart was filled with carefully folded kitsch throws, piled to the top, his favourite sporting a powder-blue sky and splendiferous peacocks strutting across some fantastical landscape. And there it was, a vintage avocado Westinghouse attached to the back end of the cart, serving as a kind of eroticized motor for the dreamscape. A classic case of too much information would involve a description of precisely what the Westinghouse was attached to as it propelled its passenger down the translucent slide and into the river. Suffice it to say that Stephen returned from the dream immersed in a murky, diverse puddle of sweat and other bodily fluids, river-like in their minor inlets, rivulets, and tributaries streaming among the sheets. As if his maidenhood had ever existed, had seen the clear light of day for a very very long time. But he often imagined himself a cross between Hardy's Tess of the D'Urbervilles and the gloriously garbed Eustacia Vye.

The dream. The night sweat. The triple martini before bed. The trip to Value Village, even the speeding car/elephant's-asshole mishap. It was all a fabulous blur as he sat and sipped the end of the martinis. Remembering the elaborate dream environment that seemed to inspire his nocturnal emissions made him laugh and laugh and laugh, as though a joke had begun that would never end, and if it did, would end in tragedy, as life so often does, tra la. And in the midst of this rushing déjà vu, he had absolutely no thought of crying. Laughter was what he needed.

9 p.m.—Tkaronto—HAPPYBACK

Irene and Stephen wandered back down to the tenth floor by the stairway, just for the fun of it, shortly after nine, laughing all the way. And there he was. Sitting on the floor, his mask still on, his back against the wall, with his veined left palm against his forehead. He seemed to be crying.

"I'm so sorry. I thought you weren't coming."

"No, I'm sorry, I was late. I thought I'd missed you."

"Hello. I'm Irene."

"Hi, Irene. Nice to meet you. I should go. You're busy. You have a guest."

"Please don't leave on my account. I'm on my way out, in more ways than one. Please stay. Stephen has been telling me all about you, well, not really, because apparently he knows nothing about you. All the more reason for you to stay, so you two strangers can become acquainted."

Irene left quickly; said she'd call in the morning. Finally, the night Stephen had hoped for was about to begin. As he offered Zorro (or whoever he was—Dracula perhaps—or just a generic masked man) the dregs of the martini shaker, he realized he had forgotten his new friend's name.

"I'm so sorry. I just realized, I've forgotten your name."

"Graham. And you're Stephen."

"Are you okay, Graham? You seemed kind of upset when we found you sitting by the door?"

"Right, uh, I was sad I missed you. And I had a bad time with the kid's mom when I got back here. That's why I was late. She's always fuckin' around with me. But hey, let's not get into that shit. I'm fine. How 'bout you?"

"It's been an unusual day. But I'm very happy to see you."

"Yeah, me too. Happy Halloween."

Then he kissed him, like a mountain, and a rock, like a man, and a frock. Too good to be true.

Day Twelve—Tk'emlups to Banff—Saturday, October 13

Stephen woke up singing, half asleep, to the sight of the pre-lit beginnings of another godforsaken sunny day. Waking up very early on the opening day of the second weekend since his diagnosis, he felt fresh and dry, no night sweats. By eleven he had to be at the rental agency to pick up the economy car he had booked for three days. He wanted to drive through the countryside, possibly into the mountains toward Banff, only three hundred and forty kilometres, give or take. He had seventy-two hours of free time. He might even splurge, get a room at the Banff Springs Hotel and sip overpriced room-service martinis as he perused student manuscript proposals. All by himself in a lavish room overlooking the appropriated Rocky mountaintops—hopefully a panoramic view of Waskahigan Watchi, his favourite peak, Cree for House Mountain, Anglicized beyond recognition as Mount Rundle by the historical presence of Wesleyan missionary Robert Rundle.

Two weeks ago, Stephen's sleepy but productive bus ride across the Coquihalla had aroused the unconscious desire to flee from all points west, taking an eastern route to drive himself further into the interior, and beyond, of a province he was beginning to love. He had been in the interior a short period of time, but it was growing on him, the landscape occupying his creative imagination. He couldn't seem to get enough of looking at those hills, at the river, the dusty tumbleweed-laden trails he walked along. He felt like a speck of blemished dust in the middle of the universe, this small city nestled in a desert-like river valley, where he had been given life-altering news only a fortnight before, was quickly becoming a comforting home for him.

Tk'emlups/Kamloops, the tournament capital of Canada, sporting the Overlander Ski Club, diving, outrigging, speedboats, women's hockey. The list was endless. From track and field to fly fishing and wheelchair basketball, it all blurred with the athletic energy of a roller-derby queen on acid. But it was the most decorative of them all that attracted Stephen's attention.

Synchronized swimming.

Stephen kept intending to look online to see if he might be able to take in a tournament while he was living there. In his youth, they had called it ornamental swimming, Esther Williams the cinematic superstar of that sport. Pity she wasn't a fan of crossdressing. Finding her gorgeous Hollywood paramour in a frock sent her into a Tinseltown tizzy, and she dove right out of that relationship.

What struck Stephen about competitive sports was the way people appeared to enjoy each other's company during big events. How they laughed and embraced, patted each other on the back, shared food and beverages, spent whole days, even weekends, contributing to the life of a community of individuals hellbent on winning a trophy that would punctuate their efforts with material glory. Or the possibility of a cash prize, or better still, all-expense-paid trips to take part in national and international tournaments. It was jampacked with camaraderie, and what appeared, on the surface, to be functional human interaction. Stephen had always felt alienated from this sort of enterprise, totally disenfranchised. In theoretical terms, during his graduate work, he discovered that he had, ever since childhood, *disidentified* with much of the social interaction that surrounded him. But ornamental swimming—that was new. Why was he so attracted to it? The swimsuits were divine, and the bathing caps out of this world, especially the frilly ones topped with the limp elegance of latex flowers that fluttered in the water. But it was still a competitive sport, involving interaction with other people, even though Stephen always dreamed of doing it alone. Synchronized swimming, with an autoerotic twist.

He had been raised on Esther Williams's films. Stephen's mother had taken him to ornamental swimming events when he was a preadolescent, and if she did not make him gay, she almost made him an ornamental swimmer. He would sit in the bleachers, by the edge of the pool, mesmerized as he watched young women move gracefully through tightly choreographed paths of chlorinated, incandescent water. It all seemed civilized, elegant, graceful.

He fantasized about ornamental swimming all the way to Banff, barely noticing the spectacular views lining the edges of the Trans-Canada highway, and surprised at how the six-hour drive had passed so quickly when he saw the sign for the Banff city limits. He had stopped for gas in Revelstoke, but hadn't really come out of his self-induced ornamental swimming trance long enough to notice the scenery. Even as he heard the sound of the gas pumping into the rental car, all he could think of was the elegant, measured movement of arms and legs gracefully thrashing in the water as they executed synchronized movements in a pool of crystal-clear chlorine-infected H2O.

Slowly making his way along Banff's main drag, beginning to come out of his dream state, he began to notice places he remembered from his first and only visit a couple of years before. There was the dollar store that sold nothing under twelve dollars. There was the Japanese restaurant that had a miniature electric trainset with different kinds of sushi laid out on little plates placed carefully on open flatbed boxcars, to be lifted by unsuspecting patrons who might be startled by the not-so-miniature price of three small pieces from a vegetable sushi roll.

He drove over the bridge, out of the downtown area, and up the winding road toward the Banff Centre for the Arts. On a whim, he had decided to check out accommodations there. He had an artist discount pass for the hotel, from his visit for a poetry residency two years previous, and it might be a nice place to stay, around other people, despite his need to spend some time on his own. But it was jampacked with artists and convention guests arriving for everything from creative writing colloquia to biology seminars, biochemical summits, and dance intensive workshops on alpine themes. After a quick look around the noisy lobby, filled to bursting with jovial groups, he changed his mind and headed back down the mountain toward the Banff Springs Hotel, more than double the price, but worth it for the solitary glamour Stephen was craving. A light October snowfall had been predicted for mid-evening.

"Do you have any rooms available?"

"How many?"

"Just one?"

"We don't ordinarily have walk-ins. Advance reservations are strongly encouraged, but we do have one junior suite available."

"And how much would that be?"

"Five hundred and fifty-nine dollars."

"Per night?"

"Yes, that's correct."

"Does it have a nice view?"

"All of the views here are spectacular."

"What floor is it on?"

"The fifth."

"How late is the pool open?"

"One a.m."

"Great. I'll take the junior suite, for two nights."

The junior suite was an open-concept creation, with a king-sized bed separated by a divider that defined a large living room area and a breathtaking view of the Bow Valley.

A banal oil painting placed at an inappropriate distance from the top of the headboard sported a generic landscape that would have made Walter Phillips roll in his grave. Stephen would have preferred a woodcut or a watercolour by Walter—that famed Lincolnshire artist who specialized in stylized scenes from outdoors Canada. Prone to sporadic generalizations in art criticism as it related to gender identification, Stephen found Walter's reflections regarding the tones of violet and green that shadowed Mount Rundle in an ever-changing array of colonizing hues, a particularly *gay* way of perceiving landscape. He fantasized fictionally about Walter and his wife Gladys engaged in an open alpine relationship when they emigrated to Winnipeg in 1913, a dashing young couple escaping to the colonies in order to avoid the conjugal codes of the old country. Canada, a place to be free of conservative marriage, where they could cavort amongst unspoiled surroundings, render the trees and rivers and mountains any way they saw fit, with no thought as to how they would be appropriated a century later by Stephen, an aging homosexual professor of literature and creative writing who liked to make things up.

Stephen wanted to incorporate the sound of Walter's colourful poetic prose into a poem. He scribbled a few lines on hotel stationery, sipping scotch he had taken from the bar fridge, and gazing out toward Bow Falls.

shades of violet / tones of green / the colours of men's eyes / that I have seen and seen and seen / tones of violet shades of green / swirling into madness as I puke into latrines

He crossed out puke and replaced it with gaze.

as I gaze into latrines

It was a silly poem touched by homoerotic romantic affiliations. He loved the word *latrine*. It didn't sound like what it was, a toilet. It sounded exotic and elegant, part of a gown, an accessory. He imagined himself wearing a slinky sequined ball gown with a matching, softly glittering calf-length latrine draped gracefully across his shoulders, cascading to only inches above the floor as he made his entrance into a cocktail lounge overlooking Waskahigan Watchi. A lounge filled with plush upholstered armchairs and sofas, and men with alluring facial hair, drinking scotch and chatting mindlessly.

But Stephen also carried a distinct memory of a decidedly more punishing use of the word *latrine*, by a high school bully who took it upon himself to torment a poor young woman with the surname *Treen*. Every recess, like clockwork, whenever the girl came into view he taunted, *there goes Mary Latrine / looking like a shit machine!*

That nasty little couplet was startlingly precocious, for none of the other school children knew what latrine meant. Stephen looked it up in the pocket dictionary he carried in his satchel. The other boys would shout it out as a shallow sign of camaraderie; they didn't dare suggest that he might consider choosing a word with more common usage in the playgrounds of the colonies. *Latrine* sounded European, high falutin for a bunch of youngsters running around a Canadian schoolyard in the middle of the twentieth century. But that was just one of many memories Stephen carried, and his imagination allowed him to substitute the idea of the toilet with the idea of an imaginary gown that included a full length, sequined-encrusted latrine hanging delicately from the memory of his youthful frame.

After downing three miniature bottles of scotch from the bar fridge in less than half an hour, and penning two short doggerel bites based on the writing of Walter Phillips, he stuffed the complimentary white robe from the hotel room closet into a cloth bag, along with his bathing suit, goggles, and a towel, slipped into a pair of bright pink flip flops, and headed for the pool. At eleven, there would likely be no one else there, and he could enjoy a swim before bedtime.

From a distance, Stephen could see that the man by the pool, smoking a cigar, had a moustache, and looked about seventy in the harsh light of the fire at the north end of the expanse of chemically enhanced water. His skin seemed wrinkled, a little grey, and he was paunchy and stooped over.

A stone wall with a wood fireplace, and a high narrow waterfall to the left of the hearth was conspicuously nestled in the corner of the large atrium housing the swimming area, giving the space an unnatural commingling of the real and the artificial.

Stephen changed in the adjoining room and came out into the pool area in his borrowed robe and outrageous flip flops, with his age-inappropriate bikini underneath. As he set his towel and goggles on the chaise longue, a few feet away from the fireplace, the elderly man turned and said hello. From a distance, the harsh oranges and flickering flames had made him look much older. Now, as Stephen drew closer, he decided the man was in his mid to late forties, handsome, with a shock of slightly greying hair, shaggy, but restrained by generous portions of expensive gel creating curving waves around his ears and across his forehead, a few damp strands hanging solo to the left of his right eye, quite suddenly irresistible. The unflattering web of shadows on his skin had greyed his flesh and made him look wrinkled and craggy. But in this light, he was golden. As Stephen came closer, the handsome stranger's posture straightened, his paunchy mid-section tightened and disappeared, leaving only faintly unruly flesh at the waistline. He wore a chocolate-brown long-line swimsuit, short legs covering the lower pubic area and leaving room for genitals to breathe without the tight hem of a bikini. He smiled at Stephen and set his cigar in an ashtray.

"Sorry, I wasn't expecting anyone else here this late. I couldn't resist. Smoking a cigar by the pool. A craving I had after dinner."

"No problem. I don't mind the smell. I like it."

A silver shaker and one glass sat on the floor beside his chaise longue, hidden by a designer tote bag. He offered Stephen a drink.

"I've got an extra cup here. Sorry, it's plastic."

"Well, thank you. I've probably had enough tonight, but one more, well, that would be nice. And I'm not one to say no to a free martini."

It was an icy cold gin martini. A bit dirty. Slices of cucumber. It slid down Stephen's gullet like an adult on a waterslide. Exhilarated by the drink and the stranger's direct, grey-blue gaze, Stephen eyed this remarkable masculine specimen. He was beginning to remind Stephen of Walter Phillip's descriptions of Mount Rundle—large, shadowed, everchanging.

They introduced themselves, Stephen and Dan. They chatted, and several minutes of awkward silence followed. Stephen took off his robe and flip flops and began to walk down the semi-circular stairway at the shallow end of the pool. Stephen began his first lap underwater, swimming as close to the deep end as possible.

When he came up for air, Dan was only a few feet away, submerged to the base of his thick, beautifully toned neck. He must have walked to the other end, made his way down the ladder and into the water while Stephen was submerged in his inaugural lap.

Dan began to do the breaststroke slowly toward Stephen. Moving seductively, only a couple of feet away, Stephen paddled back just a little, just enough to signify nervous energy and smouldering anticipation. And then he felt Dan's foot against his thigh. He looked down and saw the shadowy underwater form of this stranger's limb extended toward Stephen's leg, like a detail from an imaginary and erotically charged David Hockney. They moved toward each other, before long their chests touching, and then their lips. Tugging at each other's bathing suits, they began to drown in a lustful embrace. Their heads bobbed up and down as they kissed, water bringing Dan's hair over his forehead. Pressing as hard as heaven and the buoyancy of the water would allow, they groaned softly. It was a lovely homosexual duet—synchronized carnal persuasion, and despite the dual rhythm of their aging bodies, Stephen didn't mind that he wasn't having synchronized sex alone.

The expansive hardness of their cocks revelled in the density of the warm water, and the growing felicity, and the lush heated tepidity they had surrounded themselves with at this iconic hotel. The overpriced junior suite, the booze, the cucumber slices, the cigar smoke, the swimsuits, the water, the adjoining engorged cocks trying to engage in some dance of impossible Borromean knot-like proportions, men trying to tie their cocks together in some mad primal jive.

The rubbery semi-fictitious quality of the water gave them bodies suddenly young, toned against time and each other. Neither ejaculated. It didn't seem appropriate in a hotel pool, and for Stephen, there was the insurmountable question of safe sex. Being with this stranger, without disclosure, was risky enough. But the water and the light and the time of day and the shallow kissing struck him as a judicious and pleasurable encounter, interrupted when florescent lights suddenly clicked on far above their passionately entwined cranial extremities. They heard a door at the end of the pool rattling. They jerked away from each other as swiftly as they could, fast laps to the shallow end, staying far apart as they made their way up the stairs and out of the pool. Putting their robes on and gathering their belongings took only a few seconds, as they ignored each other and fled like semi-erect white mice to the change room.

The cleaner, who had entered the pool, barely noticed them. He was a horny, part-time labourer, used to hotel guests meeting each other for the first time in the pool, making love, the usual stuff single strangers did when they were on holiday alone. He'd even stripped naked himself—had given in to the eyes of a buxom tourist at the deep end of shallow, with delicious lips and abdominal regions to be reckoned with. He would turn off the fluorescents, lock the pool doors, and enjoy a little casual sex himself, before an overnight shift of swabbing the decks, checking chlorine levels, and making sure none of the latrines were plugged. So Stephen and Dan gave the cleaner no pause at all. He smiled and shouted encouragingly as they scuttled across the ceramic floor.

"It's okay, fellas. No need to rush. Change rooms don't close for half an hour."

Alone in the change room, they were nervous, thinking they should ignore each other and head back to their respective rooms. But the pool closed soon, and they'd leave the attendant a tip on the wooden bench by the jacuzzi. They looked at each other, smiled. Dan muttered, "We have enough time to shower and get outta here." They both nodded, took a chance on another bout of lust and headed for the shower stalls.

Without a word, side by side, under a brass-plated nozzle, warm water streaming down their backs, they turned and clutched each other's biceps, gently tugging at each other's genitals, kissing from time to time. And then, as intimately and unexpectedly as they had slipped into each other's lives—crevasses, folds, wrinkles—they groaned, they came, they went, leaving the premises after their pleasurable business. A simple salutation, a fond smile as they went their separate ways, maidens no more.

Despite feigned emotional distance, Dan and Stephen walked hesitantly toward opposite ends of the corridor outside the entrance to the change room. The empty hallway, marked by light-filled shadowy puddles, walls papered in lush forest green, wainscoting to the floor.

tones of violet—shades of green
the colours of men's eyes
that I have seen and seen and seen

As he fell asleep with the afterglow of casual sex, Stephen began to notice a dull throb in his ankle. He had forgotten to put on the walking cast after showering and leaving for Banff that morning. Stephen began to jot down lines as he soothed his ankle in a tub of warm water—

sluice gate (*a reflection on ornamental swimming*)

for every catastrophic poem

finds this vulgar circle of terror around language

concentric globes inscribed by humour bred by faithless boredom

poems about synchronized swimmers

among over-gendered gene pools

wrought with wigs withdrawal and waxing

shall we hoist our rotting bodies upside down and underwater

these bushy notions named pre-accidental axes demonizing
flippers—masks snorkels, bikinis, painted toenail tendrils stubs

Mid-sentence, Stephen dropped his pen on the bathroom floor and fell asleep in the tub.

10 p.m.—Tkaronto—CEMETERY

Let's clear up important details before we move into more sex scenes:

"I'm HIV positive.
"So am I."
"I'm undetectable."
"Me too."

Like two strangers united by an intrusive, legally anointed virus—the undetectables—wandering as carefully as they can through discretionary lust as the better part of squalor.

So, they fucked, mercilessly, endlessly, mindlessly, uncompromisingly. After sex on the forest-green homo-sectional sofa, Graham fell asleep, and Stephen sat at the window and had a glass of white wine. It was good sex, not sublime, a little ridiculous. Their cocks mistook the divide between two firm sofa cushions for something fuckable as they frolicked about, good clean filthy sex. The sofa cushion covers would have to be laundered. Made of a synthetic fabric, they had been ejaculated on many times and had come up as fresh as upholstered, romantically resplendent daisies with penises dropping in and out of love.

As he gazed out the window and watched noisy revellers screaming and laughing in the streets, Stephen thought about the styrofoam tombstones in the lobby, the scene of his first meeting with Graham. He really didn't want to see them again. If they became a couple, they could celebrate their anniversary in a real cemetery, with trees and flowers and squirrels and mounds of dirt. But not in the lobby. Perhaps he would just snoop around and see if anyone else felt the same way before he made a formal suggestion to change the lobby decorations. Gallows humour was great, but it had been the same for two decades. Time for a change. He felt it—gravely.

And then he thought to himself—"Hmmm, cemeteries." How did that line from *Streetcar Named Desire* go?—*Hop on at Desire. Change at Cemeteries. Jack off at Elysian Fields.* Something like that. He loved to stroll through picturesque cemeteries, his favourite in his hometown beside a tiny lake, named after its size—Little Lake Cemetery. His maternal grandparents were buried there, near the most macabre, heartbreaking headstone he had ever seen. It was for two children, little girls buried side by side, with separate headstones joined by a column, below a small white lamb. Inscribed on the surface of the columns, in a joyful font, was the word *playmates*.

The story Stephen had been told was that they were chasing a balloon across a bridge and toppled off. Whether it was true or not didn't matter. He hated to think of the details of death. It wasn't death itself that bothered him, but how people suffer at the end. Just before he was diagnosed, he bought a book called *Dying Well*. He planned to do just that, but not with the help of a book. He threw it out the day after the diagnosis.

The Dying Well Café—he wanted to have a drink there one day—if he ever went back to Toronto. He knew it was called The Living Well Café, but hated the implications of the name. Besides, it was gone, changed to an alternative queer bar with an upstairs cabaret called Zelda's, then burned down the day after an Iranian dissident poetry night.

Dying well

Irene had once told him that she planned to wrap herself in a giant flag and jump off her balcony when it became too much to bear. She said she would get screaming drunk then take the plunge for "God and Country."

"But it's an American flag, Irene?"

"Well, darling, I always wanted to live in New York. At this point it probably isn't going to happen. So I might as well make a big American splash on Canadian dirt when I leave this bitter earth."

"Where the fuck did you get that giant flag? And by the way. I am tired of storing it for you."

"It was a prop, sweetheart—*White Christmas*—a backdrop in a musical I was in, when the troops all march in to surprise the general, or the colonel, or whoever the fuck that guy was in the film version. Dean Jagger. It was Dean Jagger. I stole the damn thing. I knew it was the last fucking musical I'd ever sing in. My reputation was in ruins, and I'd had enough."

"You were a wonderful Grizabella."

"Yes, I was."

Once, in his near and distant youth, in Little Lake cemetery, Stephen got drunk and lay naked on the banks by the water with two nude friends, drinking tequila and flirting. The young man and woman ended up sleeping together for the first time later that evening. But some vague interest had been expressed in a threesome as a teaser to the *real* one-on-one hetero action. It might have been all Stephen's imagination, but there was a threesome in the air. Perhaps the air was in his head, but it was in the air, nonetheless.

In his gay heteronormative youth, Stephen, surrounded by beautiful straight people, often felt like an appetizer at a buffet. But when the hot penile beef and the warm accommodating folds of labial bread were rolled out, his taut buns were forgotten. Stephen had never been the main course, but an hors d'ouevres to be sniffed and nibbled at, then slyly discarded on a napkin tucked into the corner of the buffet. And being rejected in a cemetery, that was the limit.

His aunt's funeral—graveside, in Little Lake Cemetery. A familial occasion. His nana's sister died of cancer, mid-winter —a grey time to go. Stephen and a mischievous boy cousin started to laugh when they spotted a giant hairy cyst sprouting from the side of one of the mourner's balding heads. An older cousin was about to scold them, but nana mistook her grandsons' laughter for tears and hugged their faces into the side of her knee-length grey squirrel coat. He hated that fur coat. It made him sick, even as a child. His whole life he could never look at a grey squirrel without thinking of cemeteries and that wretched coat he had been forced to snuggle in, in a cemetery, by a lake, in the dead of winter.

The worst was the time when they all piled into a visiting relative's gold and black Cutlass Supreme for a ride over to the lakeside tombstones, to pay familial respects to their buried relations. Stephen's mother had a shift at the pharmacy, where she worked as a clerk, at six o'clock. She wore a white uniform with white shoes, like all pharmacy clerks were required to wear in those days. She looked like a nurse, but she actually sold cigarettes, shampoo, toothpaste, mouthwash, and decorative ashtrays shaped like geese or turtles.

As they got out of the car by the graveside, his mother remarked that she had to use the ladies' room, although there were no handy latrines by the lakeside burial site. She had to be taken home to change her stained white pants before her shift.

White people, in white, at a cemetery, and then a fecal mishap, a perfectly ridiculous day, and a memory Stephen never forgot. Driving back to the house, his mom sitting on a plastic bag pulled from the glove compartment, the car jam packed with four cousins, two aunts, and a funny uncle, the windows had to be rolled down and the children stuck their heads out the window, yelling, "Gross!!!"

In the midst of nostalgic funereal memories, Stephen looked over at Graham, asleep on the sectional couch, naked and gleaming in the flashing lights from Dundas Square. One particularly sharp shaft of pinkish light hit Graham's left eye, then turned to a jaundiced yellow, so that he resembled a corpse lying there. Graham rubbed his eyes and raised himself against the arm of the sofa.

"Come here."

Stephen sat on the edge of the sofa, his palm drawing circles in a slowly drying puddle of cum that had gathered in Graham's navel.

"That was great. Did you enjoy it? You were kinda quiet."

Graham was a heavy moaner. When he came it was like a vocal shrug from the depth of his groin, heaving through his whole torso, to a climax in his throat, a finely tuned exercise in deep diaphragm-controlled breathing, sighing, moaning. Stephen was a screamer by nature but had learned to keep his voice down.

"Yes, it was lovely."

They moved gradually into another bout of carnal pleasure.

"Let's fuck this time, something other than the cushions. You got any condoms?"

Stephen lifted the top from a cut glass bowl on the lower shelf of the coffee table, took out two condoms.

"You want me to put it on?"

"You want me to fuck you?"

"Yeah, then I can fuck you after."

"Okay."

Two positive undetectables taking part in close encounters of the safest kind available to them at this point in their lives. They could have thrown all caution to the wind and embarked on a flesh-to-flesh fuck down memory lane, where sheathed cocks were a nuisance, an unwelcome layer of synthetic tissue that rubbed some men the wrong way. But condoms were part and parcel of living and dying well in the years framing two very dangerous and death-defying centuries.

Alas and hooray, desire had begun in the lobby, in a styrofoam cemetery, and the end result was heavenly, in fact, of all things, Elysian.

Day Thirteen—Banff—Sunday, October 14

Stephen woke at five a.m. with a throbbing pain in his ankle. Suddenly remembering the final moments of his visit to emergency, after the plum-picking mishap, he hauled himself from the tub and walked out of the bathroom and into the living area, steadying himself with his hand on the wall. He limped over to his backpack on the coffee table, and there they were, in all their medicinal glory. Right where he had left them, wrapped in a small piece of tinfoil in his change purse, three left. He took two and went back to bed. Painkillers for breakfast.

When he woke again, in his junior-suite lavish king-size bed, the sun was shining through the bedroom window, and he cursed himself for not remembering to close the drapes.

He got out of bed and went into the washroom, muttered his customary "oops"—it had become a morning ritual—and gargled with what he thought was some leftover gold-coloured mouthwash in the tumbler he had left on the vanity. As soon as it swirled into his mouth, he spit it out against the bathroom mirror, gagged, and the *oops* he had uttered seconds before became a high-pitched squeal. It was scotch. Beside the bottle of antiseptic gargle, an empty, miniature bottle of expensive scotch he had taken from the bar fridge the night before. The two liquids looked similar—if you were hungover and bleary eyed. Possessed by limerick-like lyricism Stephen thought to himself,

faded tones of amber / mimicked shades of yellow / the mistaken colours of these liquids / by one hungover fruity drunken fellow

He looked at the remaining quarter inch of booze in the glass, then drank it. No point in wasting such an expensive imposter. Hair of the dog.

Much as he liked his booze, he never mixed it with medication. This was a first, possibly a second or a third, and the quarter inch of scotch would probably have no adverse effect. Walking back into the living room, he noticed that the morning light had begun to wane, in fact, seemed to be dying. Some clouds, or possibly some rainfall, to go with his mood. He felt sweaty, depressed, heavy-headed, even though the growing memory of the one-on-one sex-aquacade the night before was beginning to amuse him with sensual recall. By the time he got to the window of the living area, to see if it was in fact cloudy, or better still, about to pour, he started to remember vivid details of the encounter with Dan, a memory abruptly derailed when he looked out and realized that the waning light was neither cloud cover nor oncoming precipitation, but sunset! The heavy brocade valance of the curtains had blocked out the orange tones of the descending rays as they slipped behind the mountains. He looked quickly toward the bedside table. Seven p.m.

"Shit! Well, I got good use out of this expensive room."

As he headed for the shower, he noticed the red light flashing on his phone. At the base of the table, beside the carved wooden leg, just an inch from the bottom of the door, a piece of folded paper had—apparently—been slid under the door while he was sleeping. Bending to pick up the paper with his right hand, he took the telephone receiver with his left and pushed the button that would play messages. Who even knew he was at Banff? Probably a message from the desk about something to do with maid service. Opening the folded paper coincided with the beginning of the recording, and the romantic synchronicity of it all was too cinematic for words.

*thoroughly enjoyed meeting you last night poolside—want to
meet again? dinner at eight in my room, room number 829 xo*

As he read the note, the message played on, nervous but
direct:

*I guess you're sleeping in late or maybe you're out. How about
a light dinner at eight? The Italian place here at the hotel. Join
me if you can. The note I left says my room. But it seemed
presumptuous. Oh right, it's Dan, from the pool . . . would be
great to see you, dry . . . xoxo*

Dan chuckled a little at the end of the recording, a manly,
slightly nervous chuckle, making Stephen tingle all over.

"Shit! shit shit shit shit shit shit shit! I really missed the
boat this time."

It was 7:15. He could shower and go. But it would be
awkward. What the hell. Clean up and get down there. He
loved Italian, and there would probably be lots of wine, and
the painkiller had taken the aching away, for the time being.
Getting on the elevator, he remembered that new *positive*
information that slipped in and out of his consciousness. Life
was different now, but it hadn't been different for long. The
question of disclosure.

"Shit!"

He was at the entrance to the posh restaurant at three
minutes past eight. Dan was standing inside the doorway,
talking to the attendant at the reservation desk.

"Hi."

"Well, hello. You came. I didn't know if you would. But I
took a chance."

"Thank you so much for the invitation. I did sleep in, very
late I'm afraid. Long day yesterday."

"Yes, indeed, and the nightcap, so to speak, by the pool."

The maître d' showed them to a table by the window. Faint black outlines of the mountains traced against the background of a deep blue/black sky.

"So, this is really nice. Stephen, right? When I woke up this morning it took me like an hour and a half to remember your name. Sorry."

"Stephen, yes, and you're Dan?"

"That's me. Listen, I need to get right to the point, get this out of the way. It's really awkward, but, um, I know you already, and you know me. I didn't remember you at first, like, not right away. When we were in the pool together, when I got in the water, it dawned on me."

"Are you sure? I don't remember meeting, before last night."

"Oh, yeah, I'm sure. I noticed you right away, that first time, but you didn't see me at all. Just a voice."

"A voice?"

"I was in the office at the clinic, on the North Shore, Kamloops?"

Stephen frowned.

"You called the hotline, the AIDS hotline. I answered. I'm a volunteer. I transferred you to someone. It was Sunday, about a week ago. Carl, the counsellor. I just answer phones. He told me later that you called, wanted to talk, and he brought you over, to chat in our counselling room. When you came in, I was busy, and just shouted hello to Carl. You went into the room next to my office. I could hear you both talking, I tried not to listen, but I could tell how upset you were. I don't know what the hell it was, but I was so taken, something so kind and gentle in your tone. I went out of my office twice just to get a look at you. I pretended to be getting some water. And there you were. I could see you through the doorway, hear you talking. And last night, I suddenly remembered it was you, from last week. In the hotel robe. Well, I didn't recognize you right away. So, there you have it."

"So, you know that I'm positive?"

"Yeah, of course. So am I. Kind of strange though, meeting again. A coincidence. Life is full of them."

"Yes, it certainly is. Did you follow me, all the way from Kamloops?"

"What?"

"Just kidding. I'm sort of surprised, I guess, and a little relieved. Quite the coincidence. I was worried about telling you, about not telling you, before we, well, you know, last night."

"It was completely safe. You were a perfect gentleman. And I could have asked. But I already knew."

"And so were you, a perfect gentleman. It was nice."

"Yeah, it sure as hell was. Perfect."

"So why did we walk away? After the pool."

"That's what people do. And we were a little drunk."

The server came to take drink orders.

"Red or white?"

"Whatever you prefer."

"Okay, my usual red. Thank you."

"This is unbelievable."

"It's kind of perfect though, don't you think?"

"How so?"

"Well, here we are, two old homos, in a beautiful hotel, in a fucking gorgeous setting, and we're alone, obviously, and somehow we both end up by a pool, late at night. And I was stupid enough not to let you know that I knew you, or at least knew you a bit. I was nervous, and overwhelmed, and we were both a little drunk by the end. But here we are, another chance. You could have left today. I had no idea."

"How did you know what room I was in?"

"Uh, well, I followed you through the corridors last night. You were drunker than me and it was easy to stay behind by sneaking in and out of corners along the way. When you got on the elevator, I watched for what floor you got off, and I was

148

lucky enough to get the other car up to your floor in time. You were just closing the door as I got off. If you'd been on a higher floor, I would have missed you. So, this morning I put the note under the door, after I called. It really was, well, uncanny."

"Yes. Very romantic. Like some queer, implausible Harlequin romance."

"Well said. A gay Harlequin romance. Works for me. Or a soap opera."

The server came with the wine. Stephen still didn't remember any of Dan's story. A clinic? A counsellor? Last Sunday?

The waiter returned and spoke directly to Dan.

"Sir, are you ready to order, or would you like a few more minutes to decide?"

"Yes, please, just a few more minutes."

Dan smiled, reached across the table and took Stephen's hand from beside his place setting. Stephen feared knocking something over if he ever tried to do something that romantic. But Dan's hand slid across the table with grace and power, the warmest fingers he had ever gently met. The intensity of their mutual attraction was becoming ridiculous. Dan stroked Stephen's palm lightly.

"I'm sorry I didn't say anything last night."

"You were busy, we were busy, with other things. I'm glad you didn't. It might have ruined the mood."

"So, you're not like, at all pissed off?"

"No, not at all. Relieved. I'm relieved. This is all new to me. I should have told you, about my status, but a pool, at midnight, a handsome stranger. Fuck, I couldn't resist."

"I'm glad you didn't."

Dan casually took his hand from Stephen's and lifted his glass. They toasted each other, and Stephen sank happily into a surreal state. A clinic? A counsellor? Last Sunday?

"Cheers. I'm glad we met again. I thought about you off and on for a week, and totally inappropriate to ask a counsellor, Carl, who you were, so I just let it go. But you kept coming back to me. We get a lot of people, most of them are scared, and some are kind of angry. But you, last Sunday. And I was lucky enough to be there."

"Honestly, I don't remember going to the clinic. Last Sunday. I cracked my ankle picking plums, and then I went to Value Village, shopped a little, took a taxi home, and read all evening for my Monday class."

Stephen paused.

He had been reading *A Passage to India*, and became drowsy early. How many painkillers had that doctor slipped into Stephen's palm when he left emergency? She seemed such a conservative type. Could there have been more than four? Did they cause memory loss? It started to return, the memory of those two hours, late afternoon, a week ago, when he did make a call, a call brought on by a passage from E.M. Forster. A single paragraph had motivated Stephen to stop reading and meditate on his own melancholy.

So abased, so monotonous is everything that meets the eye, that when the Ganges comes down it might be expected to wash the excrescence back into the soil. Houses do fall, people are drowned and left rotting, but the general outline of the town persists, welling here, shrinking there, like some low but indestructible form of life.

—*A Passage to India*

Sometimes Forester's prose ached from the dull thud of humid colonialism. As an undergraduate, Stephen had always preferred Thoreau's less abject descriptions.

*The Mississippi, the Ganges, and the Nile . . . the Rocky
Mountains, the Himmaleh, and Mountains of the Moon, have a
kind of personal importance in the annals of the world.*

—*Thoreau*

Could he have forgotten a visit to a clinic on the North
Shore of the river, framed perfectly by the view from his
bedroom window in Kamloops—a river not as iconic as the
Ganges, but lovely to behold and to fantasize about?

He had taken pills for the pain, and by the time he got
home from Value Village, he was feeling weepy and depressed.
Just after reading the passage from Forster, he grabbed his
laptop and typed in AIDS support Kamloops, found the
hotline number, then immediately called.

But that story would have to wait. Just as the server
returned to the table to take their orders, the sound of a
nearby cell phone disrupted the elegance of this faux Italian
setting. Dan pulled the phone out of his jacket pocket,
frowned slightly, apologized, and excused himself. A few
minutes later Dan came back, clearly agitated.

"Sorry. I have to leave, in a hurry. Family shit. It's my
son. He's in trouble. It sounds serious. I have to get back to
Kamloops right away."

"But it's a three-hour drive."

"I have a jet, in Calgary. I'd ask you to join me, but it
doesn't feel, um, well, you know, appropriate."

"No, of course not. I drove. I'll be driving back tomorrow."

"Can I call you? When all this is sorted out?"

"Of course. If there's anything I can do."

Dan took a pen from his bag, scribbled Stephen's number
on a post-it note, walked over beside Stephen's chair, kissed
him lightly on the cheek, then spoke softly and passionately as
his hands deliberately grazed either side of Stephen's neck.

"Even though you've forgotten that first meeting, that you were there. You have the gentlest way about you. I've always loved pansies, excuse the expression. Your voice. Every little fucking thing about you. I'm a bit of a femme chaser."

"Actually, it's starting to come back. It's been an eventful couple of weeks."

"You've had a lot to deal with, but from what I overheard at the clinic, you've been doing well. You were sad, of course, but level-headed, and aware of how other people might react."

"That's kind of you to say. You're sweet. I'm sure it will all come back, eventually, the details. My memory has been foggy lately, with all that's been happening."

"I'm sorry. I have to run. That goddamn son of mine. I don't know how he does it. Like clockwork, once a year, usually in the fall, a whole new mess to untangle. Please stay, have dinner. It's on me. I'll leave my credit card information at reception. I hope we can get together again, in Kamloops."

"I hope so, too."

He lifted his hands from Stephen's shoulders, kissed him again, and left.

Stephen sipped his wine and looked at the menu for a minute or two, when Dan reappeared.

"Could you come with me for just a minute?"

They barely spoke, went into a small wooden-panelled stall in the men's room, embraced, and then began to kiss. Dan pulled Stephen's trousers down around his ankles and began to fondle his balls. Stephen placed his hands against Dan's chest, moving them under his shirt as he pulled it out of Dan's pants—a beautiful powder-blue shirt, of which he had many, no doubt.

Dan came quickly, and then left.

11 p.m.—Tkaronto—LAUNDRY

Graham was asleep again. This time the sex had been thrilling, and by the time they had finished fucking, the forest-green overstuffed pillows were smashed against the balcony door, the city lights flickering from the big window. Graham fell asleep on the floor and—in an over-functional burst of postcoital energy—Stephen decided to do laundry. There was just enough time to wash the sofa cushion covers and let them dry in the bathroom overnight.

Waylaid in the lobby by witches and goblins peering through the doors at the entryway, trying to persuade Stephen to let them into the co-op, he was caught in a typical moment of indecision. He had never seen them before, and when the assorted witches, goblins, and zombies were asked to take their masks off, they became belligerent:

"We live here, asshole. We can't find our fobs. Let us the fuck in, you uptight faggot!"

When one finally lifted his mask, Stephen recognized him, let them in, and then hurried toward the laundry room as they lobbed drunken insults his way.

"Fuckin pansy. He knew it was us. You see us every fuckin' week!"

It was a routine incident. Co-op security was tenuous at best, and it made everyone a little tense. But it was always nice to be told to fuck off by a witch on the most haunting night of the year.

After leaving the cushion covers in the washer, Stephen went back to the apartment. Graham was gone. But his shoes were still by the door.

"Fucking Cinderella. Leaves the ball and never fails to forget her goddamn slippers!"

Day Fourteen—Banff to Tk'emlups —Monday, October 15

Dinner alone had been lavish. Mentioning his own jet—and limo—infused Dan's offer of a free meal with posh culinary possibility. Stephen splurged, never thinking that his hunger would nip him in the ass a week later. In the meantime, in between time, he sank into the melancholia that had been a companion for most of his adult life. Prawns, calamari, whatever he fancied.

But excess consumption did have immediate side effects. It looked good on the menu, laid out like an haute cuisine poem. He couldn't stop ordering, a jumbo shrimp cocktail followed by a variety of dishes that could have fed two.

Instead of the menu's pairing, Stephen decided on a wine quadrupling, and had four glasses of the Sauvignon blanc, after the glass of shiraz Dan had ordered for him before leaving on a jet plane—maybe a helicopter from Banff. Stephen adored helicopters, like giant glass bees. Helicopters reminded him of the helipad on St. Michael's hospital, in full view of his Toronto apartment. He loved to watch them land, it made him think of scenes from *Apocalypse Now*. There were people everywhere, trying desperately to stay alive.

When he woke the next morning, not only was his ankle aching from forgetting the walking cast, his big toe was throbbing from the acid build-up of wine coupled with the seafood of his recent solo feast. He did have the good sense to have his food put in a doggy bag, but forgot to refrigerate, and the smell of leftover prawns wafted through the room.

As he drove his rented car out of the parking lot, his head ached, his ankle throbbed, and his big toe was a beet in the pink flip flops he slipped into in the car. He was tempted to take a painkiller before leaving, but for the possibility of a jackknife flip into the reaches of some fleeting, interminable mountain pass. He drove too fast. Sixteen-and-a-half kilometres from the Continental Divide, Stephen stopped at Field. The synchronized swimming motif that occupied his mind on the initial drive, coincidentally reprised by a poolside encounter with jet-owning stranger, reared its waterlogged head as he pulled into a gas station inside the city limits.

He was less than twenty kilometres from the point where all water to the west flows into the Pacific and all water to the east toward the Atlantic, the greatest unsung waterpark on earth. It occurred to Stephen that someone along that imaginary line must have fantasized about building a theme park with giant waterslides, one pointing east and the other west, and naming it Continental Divide Water Slides and Funpark. There could be adorable little shops and attractions, and The Seward Café, a glass and steel cantilevered coffee house, surrounded by a reflecting pool, just inside the gates, and named after the Seward Peninsula in Alaska, where the divide begins. Thrilling roller coasters designed to look like the icy panoramas of Glacier National Park alongside bejewelled Yellowstone Carousels and Old Faithful Candy Floss vendors, bordering New Mexican roadrunner miniature racetracks, ending with spectacular surround-sound panoramic theatres replete with cinematic views of the Panama Canal as it crosses the divide at the Culebra Cut, also known as Gaillard Cut, after Major David du Bose Gaillard of North Carolina, who supervised the construction of the canal's route through a manmade South American River Valley. He died of a brain tumour at the age of fifty-four, nine months before the completion of the canal, the Culebra Cut renamed in his honour.

After gassing up in Field, and buying three pepperoni sticks and some small packages of sliced cheese from beside the cash register as he shelled out fifty dollars for fuel, Stephen got back into the car and slipped in a CD he took with him on all his road trips. The last time he had listened to it was on that sweaty bus trip back from Vancouver only thirteen days ago. His friend had labelled the cassette *Mostly Ladies*, and it comprised all female singers from the past, with the exception of Rudy Vallee singing "The Whiffenpoof Song." It brought back bittersweet memories. Stephen had added three of his own favourites when he had the music transferred to CD, and now it began with Alison Krauss singing, followed by Norah Jones, and ending with Ella Fitzgerald's version of "Melancholy Baby." One short verse from the only male singer, Rudy Vallee, punctuated the collection with a mournful tone as he sang of lost lambs. *baaa, baaa, baaa*

He sped by signs for the attractions of Takakkaw Falls and Emerald Lake as Alison Krauss sang of the struggle to acknowledge a lover's waning interest. He thought of the Cree word for *awe* as he noticed Yoho National Park advertised to his right, and marvelled at the simplicity of such a beautiful word, almost onomatopeiac, a short and compact way in which to suggest the awe-inspiring spectacle. An echoing word that spoke to the haunting site located on the western slope of the Divide. Tiny troubled words, split by cultural heritage, colonialism, and sloppy, thieving linguistic opportunism. *Yoho* and *awe* were a lot like *oops*. They signified something enormous, but looked small and unintrusive on the page.

As he sped toward his final destination, Stephen muttered to himself, female vocalists ringing in his ears, *awe, oops,* and *yoho,* over and over again, like some Buddhist chant becoming a kind of spoken-word accompaniment to the lovely tunes from the past and the present cascading through his aural cavities.

awe oops yoho awe oops yoho awe oops yoho awe oops yoho awe oops yoho awe oopsy- oho awe oops yoho awe oops yoho awe oops yoho awe oops yoho awe oops yoho awe oops soho awe oops yoho awe oops yoho awe oops yoho awe oops yoho awe oops yoho awe oops yoho awe oops yoho awe oops yoho awe

oops yoho awe oops yoho awe oops yoho awe oops yoho awe
oops yoho awe oops yoho awe oops yoho awe oops yoho awe
oops yoho awe oops yoho

Along the way were predictable signs for tourist
attractions from the Spiral Train Tunnels viewpoint and
Yoho Glacier, to the treacherous declining route into Golden,
home of the highest gondola in the Rockies at Kicking Horse
Mountain Resort, all located along the geographical fault line
of the Rocky Mountain Trench, one of the few features on
earth visible from the moon.

The Columbia wetlands and the Northern Lights Wildlife
Wolf Centre. Rogers Pass in Glacier National Park, the highest
point on the Trans-Canada Highway. The Giant Cedar
Interpretive Boardwalk Trail in Mount Revelstoke National
Park. Revelstoke Dam, the Railway Museum. Sicamous and
Three Valley Gap, Crazy Creek Falls, the Enchanted Forest
and Sky Trek. Salmon Arm, its name from the late 1800s,
when salmon were so plentiful that farmers would spear them
with pitchforks, spreading them over the land as fertilizer.

As Stephen sped through Salmon Arm, Mary Martin
sang, coincidentally enough, about poor little fishies trapped
in a threatening pool with their encouraging mother right at
their side urging them through nature's treacherous course. In
the opening verse, the mama fishy urged her offspring to swim
on if they could, until they swam right over the dam.

And then Stephen's favourite verse that his mother would
sing to him as a child. It consisted of a delightfully nonsensical
series of faintly onomatopoeic sounds beginning with *oomps*
and *boomps*, and ending with all three fishies swimming over
a dam. Stephen had loved hearing his mother sing the verse,
but had no idea what any of it meant.

Only sixty kilometres from Tk'emlups, Stephen drove
toward a city named after a romantic town in Italy. As he
passed the sign marking the city limits of Sorrento, Rudy

Vallée sang the last few lines of "The Whifenpoof Song," a song Stephen's father would sing when he was filled to the brim with music, melancholy, and a bottle or two of cheap rum.

Sorrento had been named by J.R. Kinghorn, a finely tuned eastern capitalist who had developed the townsite along the lucrative Canadian Pacific Railway. The breathtaking view of Copper Island in Shuswap Lake had reminded him of the Isle of Capri in Sorrento, Italy, where Kinghorn had spent his honeymoon. The mountains were filled with colonizing memories. Stephen's father's favourite song had been "The Isle of Capri."

Sorrento's origins reminded Stephen of his encounter with Dan, his solo Italian dinner, and his growing indigestion from too much wine, rich food, and painkillers. Rudy's crooning did help to ease his bitter, romantically inclined heart.

By early evening, after several replays of the *Mostly Ladies* CD, Stephen was back in Kamloops, comfortably arranged in his favourite reading/grading/drinking chair by the bedroom window. Never before had he fallen asleep for more than half an hour—perhaps a ten-minute power nap here and there—as he read student poetry and graded papers. But this particular evening he overflowed with emotion. With many melancholic songs in his heart, he fell asleep in that chair and slept solidly until the next morning, waking with the distinct sensation that tears had dried on his cheeks during the night. Little did he know that there was another exhausted romantic in the house at the time, sleeping soundly and dreaming of his own brief encounters.

12 a.m.—Tkaronto—VASE

The sex was great. He left without explanation. As Stephen stared at the antique vase by his half empty wine glass, he fought feelings of rejection and thwarted romance. But Graham had left his shoes.

Stephen finished the wine, got up from his chair, walked to the doorway, picked up the shoes, opened the door, and walked toward the garbage chute about to mutter to himself, *good riddance to bad loafers*, when he heard the elevator doors opening, followed by a familiar moan. He was back.

"Oh, fuck, I'm so sorry. I think I blacked out. When I woke up and no one was there, I didn't know where the fuck I was. I went to my kids' place, but realized it was too late to knock. Shit. It was you. Right. I was with you. I'm a bit of a drunk."

"Well, of course you are. I wouldn't have it any other way. It's okay. Come back in. You left your shoes."

"Do I have to leave?"

"No. You can stay. But I'm going out for a bit.'

"Can I come?"

"I just want to go for a walk. I won't be long. Make yourself a drink. There's wine, and vodka in the freezer."

"Are you sure? You don't mind leaving me here on my own?"

"No. I don't mind."

"Uh, okay. Wow, thanks. Hurry back."

"I will."

They kissed at the door. Cinderella's shoes stayed put. It was 12:45 a.m. and they had only just begun.

Day Fifteen—Tk'emlups—Tuesday, October 16

It was one of those dreams he would never remember in detail, just the words of a song he hadn't thought of in years, involuntarily changing the word from *sun* to *sad* when he sang it that morning. "Old Doctor Sun," a lyric about the healthy effects of sunshine and its lovely light being shed generously upon those in need.

"Who the fuck is DR SAD?"

As soon as he was fully awake, and the song subsided, the sound of water running in the bathroom startled Stephen. It was Peter, the absentee roommate.

"You're back."

"Sure am, but not for long."

"What's going on? I thought you were going to call from Madrid?"

"Sorry, I got busy. I'm going back Friday morning."

"To Madrid?"

"Yeah, it's amazing there."

"No doubt. For how long?"

"Until the spring."

"Six months. Fuck."

"I'll still pay rent, since I'm officially working on campus, and the work in Spain is related. But I don't need to be here. And I kind of met someone, and she wants me to come over and work with her on a project. She's a video artist, and she heard my talk at the conference in Vancouver. She wants to collaborate. I'll be back a couple of times to check in."

"Okay, then. Sounds fabulous. Did you bring me anything?"

"Oh, yeah, right. It's in my room. You want to go for breakfast at Hello Toast?"

"Sure, can you drive me to campus afterwards?"

"Sounds good."

The news of Spain put Stephen in a whimsical, slightly irrational mood. He welcomed the opportunity to have the place to himself, but didn't want to tell Peter his own news. And he loved Hello Toast, known by many as *the flavour of downtown Kamloops*. He was in the mood for a sugary morning meal.

"I'll have the breakfast special with a glass of the strawberry lemonade, with soda. And I'd like a lemon poppyseed muffin and an order of chocolate balls to go."

"I'm sorry, sir, the chocolate balls won't be ready until noon."

"Fuck . . . I'm sorry, I'm just disappointed. Then just make it two lemon poppyseed muffins to go."

"We don't have the lemon poppyseed today".

"Okay, just the breakfast special. Thanks."

"And you, sir?"

"The breakfast special and an Americano. Thank you."

Peter chuckled, pulled out his cell phone, and as he spoke to Stephen began to type in an unusually long sequence of numbers, holding the phone up to his ear as he spoke—

"You're in a pissy mood. What's up?"

"I've had a strange couple of weeks."

"Do tell."

Stephen started to explain the chain of events, but thought to himself, how far should I go? Where should I start? What should I leave out? Should I wait until he gets back from Spain? What is the big news? My love life, my sex life, or my new pathology? Six months is a long time.

"I went to the doctor, for a follow-up from the bacterial infection I had before I got here. I'm HIV positive."

Peter was smiling wildly as he chattered affectionately on the phone in a mixture of English and Spanish. There were a few *te quieros* here and there and a final *te amo* at the end of the conversation's nine-and-a-half minutes. Stephen timed it as he muttered about his diagnosis in a smug, parodic attempt to make light of the fact that his roommate had heard nothing, beginning with the words HIV *positive*.

"Sorry, that was Madrid. You were saying?"

"Oh, it's been a busy couple of weeks. It'll be weird here with you so far away. What should I tell people?"

"I'll check in in a lot, and like I said, I'll be back a couple of times. You won't have to deal with it."

"Except for when someone asks."

"Just say I'm out of town. You don't really see anyone off campus anyway, right?"

"No, I guess not. But six months."

"It'll be fine, and maybe I won't even stay that long. You know how these things can go."

"These things? No, I'm not that familiar with how anything goes in the grassy field of romantic encounters."

"We'll work on her video stuff, sure, but, well, you know, and I'll get lots of work done. She's committed to her work, busy all the time."

"What's her name?"

"Carmen."

"Seriously?"

"Seriously."

"How operatic of you."

Stephen started to fan himself with one of the plastic fans Peter had given him before they left for Hello Toast.

"Why did you bring that with you?"

"It's a gorgeous, extremely inexpensive souvenir you brought me all the way from your brief Spanish encounter, soon to be a prolonged, passionate, period of siestas. I hope you brought me more than this cheap plastic fan."

"I brought you some sangria, it's in the fridge. And some postcards from the Prado. *Garden of Earthly Delights*, some Goya. I put them in your room just before we headed out."

Peter laughed as Stephen amused him with a few flutters
of his fan and then slapped it down on the table with unusual
vigour and asked about the famed Spanish museum.

"You went to the Prado?"

"No, but I got to the gift shop. Are you okay? You seem
distracted."

"I seem distracted? You just spent the last ten minutes
ignoring me while you were on a long-distance Spanish tryst
with Carmen. Where's our breakfast?"

"What's up with you?"

"Nothing. Really. It's been a strange couple of weeks.
Getting used to a new place, a new job, on my own, and
now, well, it's great having the house to myself, but it's great
sharing, too."

"I'm sorry. I didn't realize."

"It's okay. I'd do the same thing. It'll be fun, and you're
right. You can do your research anywhere. And the romance
will be great, just what you need."

"I hope so. She's really cool, and hot."

"Well, there you go."

The breakfast specials arrived with a brown paper bag, set
carefully beside Stephen's plate. The server patted him on the
shoulder, smiled, and said, "We had a few left from yesterday.
They're still pretty fresh. On the house. I think you need a
sugar lift."

He opened the bag and there were three round, sadly
joyous brown balls of chocolate stuck together at the bottom,
looking decidedly less fresh than he expected given the
cheerful demeanour of the server. Stephen and Peter gobbled
their breakfasts, paid, and left the premises within fifteen
minutes, leaving the sugar-coated orbs behind. But the server
came out the front door of Hello Toast within seconds, waving
the bag and yelling, "Sir, you forgot your . . ."

"My balls, of course. My chocolate balls. How kind of you
to notice. Thank you."

He took the bag and forced a smile.

"Thank you so much."

He got into Peter's car, and they drove to campus for an afternoon of poetry, madness, and sugar-coated testicular-shaped frenzy. Peter tried to appease him about the long absence.

"Stephen, don't worry. It will be fine. The time will fly by."

"You'll end up staying in Spain or some damn thing."

"Highly unlikely."

"Stranger things have happened. And they're getting stranger every day."

"Let's have dinner and you can tell me all about it."

"Great. See you at Ric's Grill? Around six?"

As he walked to the campus, he thought of something Carl, the counsellor, had said to him two Sundays ago. It had started to return after Dan mentioned the meeting.

"What's it like? What's it like to be HIV positive? Suddenly. You've just found out, so this could be inappropriate. But you seem level-headed, articulate, and it might help me to understand, for my other patients, especially the older ones, what it is like for someone to start living with this whole new sense of themselves and their mortality, relatively late in life? I've never actually asked this question, straight out, but what's it like?"

He had put Carl's unexpected outburst out of his mind, just shrugged it off, smiled, shook his head as if he didn't quite know what to say, and didn't answer. But now, two weeks and two days in, his poetic imagination was about to go viral, attesting to the tired cliché that adversity can breed contemptuous art. When he arrived at the classroom, he greeted his students with a disinterested description of what he wanted them to do, in groups, with their haikus. Then he sat at his desk writing a belligerent, ejaculatory monologue about what it was like to be in this situation at this point in his life. As he nibbled on stale chocolate balls he wrote, and he wrote, and he wrote.

Still scribbling, he barely acknowledged students as they filed out an hour later, placing their workshop assignments on his desk. He folded the seven sheets he had scribbled, checked his messages, only to discover that Peter had cancelled dinner plans. Then he walked home, along the usual trail, had a light dinner alone, and went to bed early. His new spoken-word treatise lay restlessly on the bedside table, the pages scattered alongside postcards of the Hieronymus Bosch triptych, *The Garden of Earthly Delights*, that Peter had brought him after fifteen minutes in the Prado gift shop.

What's It Like?

He said What's it like?

I said what? What's what like?

*He said "you know what's **it** like" I said*

Uh, well, it's just great sweetheart

It's given me a whole new lease on life

Mind you, this lease is quite a bit shorter than the last one I had

But I still love this one

It makes me look at a great big beautiful sunset and say

Hey, look at that eh, another bloody beautiful sunset

And even now that I no longer have any doubt about

the earth, the sky, and immortality

I know that I am not Methuselah or Lazarus or George Burns or some frozen Californian corpse thawed back from the dead

only to discover that the Hollywood Bowl has been turned into a soup kitchen

and they're out of soup ! ?

and Celine Dion is not at Caesar's Palace any longer!

even now, after all of my illusions have been busted

I can still look at a breathtaking sunset, breathe freely, and say
Sunset, Heeeellllooooo!

I still find you, you bloody beautiful sunset

Boooooorrrring!

With your blue and your orange and your yellow and your endless
unattainable horizon and your blinding unquenchable light

dead buttbang boooooriing dull

change horizon change!

You are the last cliché

—and he looks at me like some sad irresistible vulture

like some wild werewolfian full moon fool

his blue eyes widen and he says

"hey dude, what's up eh? I was just curious

I care about you I was just curious about how you feel—

how it makes you feel being . . ."

Being what? Being what?

Aggressively skirting this query too inane

to warrant a response

I mean, please, buttwit stupid objectifying lab rat questions!!!!!!

What's it like? you say?

Let me tell you precisely what it's like for me my friend

It's like sticking your own cock up your own ass

and having it come out your own mouth

better still—it's like sticking your own head up your own ass

and having it come out your own mouth—

now there's an erotic painting by Magritte for ya—Surreal eh?!

'Man with his own head coming out of his own mouth by way of his own asshole,'

and you thought 'Nude Descending a Staircase' was wild, whoa!

What's it like?

It's impossible

that's what it's like

It's like golden eagles migrating into your pelvis

It's like a hawk living in your ear drum

As impossible as birds in a house

As impossible as putting something the size of a small pumpkin up your butt and having it reappear through an orifice the size of a change purse

That's what it's like—it's impossible to find a metaphor powerful enough to fuel this inflammatory exchange

these bodily fluids—this gate to hell

with that plague-riddled Bosch'ian beak nosed naked white guy greeting you at the door with no cocktail and no party favour

It's like having a silvery grey translucent skin-tight ball gown designed in the shape of a condom and wearing it diligently every night of your life and then suddenly

with little to no warning it breaks

and you're left without a thing to wear

Like a swarm of hummingbirds—2,000 strong—nesting in your crotch

Seeming sweet with memory

When regret lies buried deep within the folds of pleasure

But the hummingbirds keep on singing—keep on hovering

until you may want to bite their banal little craws away from your flesh

Free them, and give up hedonism for the rest of your life

But then you remember how much fucking fun it was

And you abandon regret with a Botox gaze

and let those perfect birds sing

impaled on their own blossom-sucking little noses

for the rest of your life

It becomes the only way to fly

It's like waking up every morning

for the rest of your life

looking in the bathroom mirror

Smiling sweetly and saying Oops

Over and over and over and over again

Oops

With a slow rhythmic build until Oops becomes a scream on a bridge in Scandinavia with your palms clasped firmly against your cheeks

when what you really wanted from life was to be a cold inanimate piece of fine art stolen from some gilded wall of a Northern European Museum by high tech art thieves and taken into the arms of the art thief underworld only to be rescued by the latest hunky white guy playing James Bond (even though a 007 man of colour is the way it should be!)

Is that so much to ask ?!

everybody!

Repeat 'oops' several times, beginning softly toward a final scream

Oops Oops Oops Oops Oops Oops Oops Oops Oops Oops Oops Oops Oops Oops Oops Oops Oops Oops Oops Oops Oops Oops Oops Oops Oops Oops Oops Oops Oops Oops Oops Oops Oops Oops Oops Oops Oops Oops Oops Oops Oops Oops Oops Oops Oops Oops Oops Oops Oops Oops Oops Oops Oops Oops Oops Oops Oops Oops Oops Oops Oops Oops Oops Oops Oops

Oops!!

Yes, indeed, it is like saying oops until you drop

Do you have any idea how silly the word oops looks when it is repeated on a printed page?

It looks as silly as I feel when I think of what it's like to be asked 'What's it like?'

It's like following Grotowksi into the forest, not speaking or eating all day—pretending to be a wolf or a coyote—biting into the sides of trees—wandering naked among strangers, only to discover that you knew yourself better before you shaved your head shit your pants shed your Club Monaco Gap-infused skin and decided to find the real you

The real me?

This is the real me!

Whining and sighing and bitching and pontificating about the pathology that has set up housekeeping in my middle-aged carcass

What's It Like?

It's like getting an M.C. Escher puzzle for Christmas and stepping into the muddle of pieces and not being able to find your way out

It's like picking your nose in church, like farting in an elevator, like playing Twister with your funny uncle, like playing Scrabble with a parrot

*Finally a light at the end of the tunnel but the light's hung over
a brick wall and you're getting closer and closer to the end*

And now it's my turn to ask you

What's it like? And he said, what? What's what like?

And I said

You know, what's it like?

*What's it like to be some kind of uninfected arrogant buttwit
who thinks he can just walk up to someone, offer them a garden
roll, refresh their cocktail, and ask them what it's like to be
one of millions affected by this unfathomable pandemic—this
unmanageably manageable illness*

What on earth is that like?

*Is that something like stretching your own sphincter over the
gaping wound you call your brain and suffocating in a fleshy
cloud of your own crap?*

Is that what that's like?

Because it seems to me that might be what it's like to be you

But how about, what's it not like?

*Well, darling, it's not like being able to speak candidly to you,
someone I love, without worries, without words I need to filter
in and out of sensibilities too fragile to ask the question*

"What's it like?"

*It's not like—it is nothing at all like—living profoundly short
lives on exploited continents tracing my roots into some tight-
knit colonialist past and future that denies the absolute rape
and pillage of third-world doorsteps and the never-ending chute
of pharmaceutical band-aids that require one giant extremely
invasive colonoscopy to rid them of their utter disregard for
abject poverty and the fact that drugs often come when it's
way too late and yes they are welcome here on this terribly*

compromised land mass, this too unsolid flesh and blood, but
they are barely half the battle

What's it like?

It's like reaching out to touch someone you love

and getting a thorn instead of a rose

It's like receiving the gift that keeps on giving

over and over and over and over again

It's like a rose in a noose

It's like a moose in the headlights

Like raindrops and Moses

bulls without rushes

like dogs biting babies

like bees stinging, rabies

like none of my favourite things

like a lion without pride

like Baton without Rouge

like Boca without Raton

like Corpus without Christi

It's like nothing I could ever say or think

Just a string of metaphors wrung with guilt-ridden gestures
extended across continents

Like coins tossed into fountains of sculptural froth and glory
and the coming of the Lord

What's it like?

Here, so far, for me, within this last gasp of socialized medicine
wait times that compete with the completion of the Sistine
Chapel

here, within this tentative state of living and dying

it's like a half-naked muscleman floating in the sky calling himself Adam, waving at God with his arm outstretched over his famous spare rib—looking like an overzealous pansy never reaching his father's arm, just lounging there on the ceiling in a scriptural pose

What's it like?

For me, here on the gut-sucking soil of some posing as meek

colonialist uncommonwealth country

here, it is a terrifying comfort, that's what it's like

it's the only way to fly

(SINGS Fly me to the Moon)

A madcap riff, rife with figurative language of the frequently nonsensical kind, a spoken-word tirade, on and off the page, based on Stephen's meeting with Carl, the HIV/AIDS counsellor. But it wasn't really about him. Just a departure point for Stephen's growing sadness and smouldering rage, mixing the lighthearted, heavy-handed words in some gaily euphuistic way of coping. And when he performed it in cities ranging from Peterborough to Nicosia, Montreal, and Toronto, it would never fail to fill him with a strong will to live.

1 a.m.—Tkaronto—SNOW

Stephen loved snow. In store windows or on television. On a Xmas card that left the Christ out of Christmas. He used to love the outdoors. He'd heard of indoor skiing in Dubai, but the idea seemed plastic and tame. Vast Canadian expanses of snow-covered hills and mountains were what he yearned for. But not any longer, not now that he couldn't afford to go skiing. And the mild osteoporosis made him wary of flying down the side of a slope, tumbling into a roll, and ending up with fractured ankles and wrists, or worse. His wrists were limp enough already. A splint would make them seem too gay for words.

Stephen tried to miss skiing, but he didn't miss skiing. He had loved skiing. But like so many other loves, he'd had his fill, and was happy being just sad, contented, melancholy. His doctor wasn't sure if the osteoporosis was from the medication or the expected loss of bone density from HIV, or if it was hereditary. When he first told Irene about it, she just looked at him.

"It usually happens to women. It's a honeycombing of the bones. You'll be in a wheelchair in your eighties."

"I'll be dead in my eighties, bitch. And so will you."

"Well, you got your fill of skiing when you lived in the Rockies. Get over yourself and thrive on the memory."

All he could think of when she first said honeycombing was The Honeycomb Kid, the white, lasso-toting, cowboy'ish mascot for the honey-flavoured wheat-free cereal of the mid-1960s. Television commercials featured a special place for kids to play called the Honeycomb Hideout Clubhouse. Stephen thought of his apartment as a kind of hideout, and now that Graham had arrived on the scene, it was taking on a honeycomb effect, a sweetness of sorts.

After leaving Graham at the apartment, Stephen stood in front of the store windows at the Hudson's Bay store on the northwest corner of Yonge and Richmond. He marvelled at the synthetic snow, and how every year it came earlier and earlier. The window dressers decorated for Christmas before Halloween was over. With global warming, there could be a summer sale beach-themed Santa in the window in late August, with a jack-o-lantern in his hand by the middle of October. Such a fucking festive overlapping of one rampant holiday season after the other.

He stood staring into manufactured whiteness and tinsel. It was more than he could bear. So he turned on his heel, jogged north on Yonge, east on Shuter, a short block past Church, then a sharp left toward his co-op. He had a formerly masked man asleep, naked, on his couch, surrounded by the subsidized comfort of his own private Honeycomb Hideaway in the sky.

Who could ask for anything more.

Day Sixteen—Tk'emlups—Wednesday, October 17

The Bather

I go to the pool mid-day

My bathing suit old and worn

No stretch left in it

my penis hangs like a flaccid vegetable about to rot

I try to cover it with my towel

and scurry from the ceramic bench to the edge of the pool so no one will see my little fig

dangling beneath a worn-out spandex lycra blend

I am happiest underwater

It warms me

Sometimes I touch my head lightly

to the pool floor in a spot of light

and then my hands follow and finally my feet

and I propel myself upwards, out of the light

and I am free

Restrain myself from taking on

a water nymph pose

arms outstretched to greet the day

That could disarm onlookers

We are not there to stare

at beautiful bodies

or to free ourselves from our lives on land

we are there to swim

My goggles separate me from God's water creatures

happy underwater with goggles

dark water frightens me

blurry water bores me

clear water, submerged

wearing a pane of plastic

to look into the surrounding water world

comforts me

That is when I am happiest

warm and consumed by wet matter

I hesitate to say that water is my lover

I watch other bodies gliding

but I am not jealous

as I grow middle aged

my bitterness drowns in an image of myself as water sprite

youthful, supple, and filled with grace

all this in chlorinated pools

lined with tiles

surrounded by grey cement walls

Rivers and lakes, streams and creeks, oceans and seas

there I descend into the unknown

that may consume me, threatening

but pools are my domain

I would not have encouraged opening them to the public

So I steel myself against the crowds

trying not to stare, not always successful

knowing that only my relationship with water

is real—all the others are secondary bathers in waiting

I am a princess underwater

a monarch

and at great expense to my curiosity

I try not to stare

I wallow in shallow

I drown in depth

prefer indoor pools

The naked sunlight

the small flying creatures

that litter the outside world

bother me

If I can sustain happiness

for whatever time I have left

it will be underwater in a well-subsidized community centre

I am not haunted by water

I am drawn to it

it is drawn to me

we are lovers and strangers

So much that we will never know about one another

we try not to stare

not always successful

looking into light

searching for water

when we find only human forms gliding through
engaging our desire
flirting with our inhibitions
I am happiest when I am underwater

—DR SAD

"DR SAD?"

The next morning, over a hardboiled egg, dry toast, and
a glass of cranberry juice, Stephen remembered the reference.
The first time he was at Banff, for a poetry residency, there
was a party on the third night of a weeklong artist's retreat.
Everyone got stoned, except Stephen. He drank.

Bouts of giddy gang-bang poetry resounded everywhere.
You couldn't throw a stick without it landing on a beat box.

One drunken poet in his late twenties came up to him
in the bar, put his arm over Stephen's shoulder, and started
bending his ear about Stephen being a queer old bard.

"What's it like eh? Being an old bard, a middle-aged poet?
Your work is so damn funny, but so damn sad, too. Fuck,
I heard you have a PhD in this shit. You can get a PhD in
poetry? What the fuck, eh, what will they come up with next.
So now you're a doctor of poetry, sad poetry. DR SAD, eh. DR
fuckin SAD."

"How kind of you to notice. Actually, my PhD is in
English literature, with a specialization in creative writing."

"Wow, that's quite the combo."

"I have a background in performance monologues.
That was what I wrote my dissertation on, the history of
performance art, with reference to some monologue artists. I
fell into poetry, accidentally. Do you know Spalding Gray?"

"Yeah. I've heard of him. Didn't he jump off the Staten
Island Ferry, and they found his body in the East River?"

178

"For someone who has *heard of him*, you have some detailed information."

"Actually, yeah, I've more than heard of him. I saw him live, twice, in New York, and then again in San Francisco. What a tragedy, eh. But it was all part of the work."

"What do you mean, all part of the work?"

"He told stories, about himself, his view of life, his whole adult life. He's immortal. He was writing a monologue about his own death when he disappeared. His mother killed herself, like a final familial bow. To his audience and his fucking suicidal heritage."

"He was depressed. He'd been in a terrible car accident that he never recovered from. It wasn't a story. It was his life. I wish he could have carried on. There were a lot more stories to be told."

"Like the depressing one you told the other night at the poetry cabaret? The one about swimming underwater. Fuck that was depressing."

"People laughed quite a bit."

"It had its funny moments, but it was clearly about suicide."

"Excuse me?"

"You drowned yourself all through it, over and over again."

"I did nothing of the sort. Swimming underwater was not intended to act as metaphor for suicide. If that's what you heard, then so be it, but it was intended as a description of movement that brings me great comfort. A poetic way of describing a physical exercise that I find therapeutic, and life affirming. Swimming underwater. Coming up for air, but not drowning."

"So maybe Spalding should have just gone for a swim then, eh?"

"You're an asshole."

"Wanna go outside and have a joint with me?"

"I don't smoke. Sure, I'll come out and have some."

They went out into the cold air and huddled in a dark corner.

"Wanna go for a swim at the Sally Borden afterwards? I know someone who works there. They can let us in. It'll be dark, though. Are you really afraid of dark water?".

"Terrified, but yeah, I'll come."

"The lights will be out."

The DR SAD memory was solved. Stephen felt a tinge of eroticized nostalgia remembering it. The confrontational young bard was buxom and hairy, tufts of soft brown follicles overflowing the top of his plaid shirt, bodily attributes Stephen couldn't resist.

They fucked poolside, swam, then showered together, and didn't pay much attention to each other for the remainder of the residency. The young stranger was friendlier, far more fluid, when he was stoned than sober.

The memory of yet another late-night carnal aquacade unfolding, and the melancholy doctor reference clarified, Stephen walked into his classroom with a faint smirk on his face. He felt the urge to cut the class short and get out of there as quickly as he could. The haiku and renga exercises were not working, students bored and restless, wanting more challenging work.

"Okay, everyone, can I have your attention. We're going to try something new, since we've gone as far as we can with short yet complex forms. Now it's time for you to write a longer piece, about something you feel deeply. Something you're passionate about. That's why you're here, to write about feeling strongly? Take the ideas in your haiku and expand them."

Students, still reeling from trying to figure out what to do with their haiku while their nutty professor sat at the front of the room scribbling away and munching noisily on day-old chocolate balls that looked like crumpled miniature cupcakes, were skeptical. They longed to break into free verse and say what they felt. No more structure.

"Your task now is to discover as many rhymes as possible, and expand them into full narrative verse. Take your group haiku, each of you, individually, and make it your own. Take the basic idea from your previous work and turn it into a poetic narrative. But in order to keep some structure, I'll set out constraints for you to follow. I want you to discover as many rhymes as you can for a single word. Choose a word and then run with it. For example, girl swirl twirl hurl curl—and then use those words in a series of simple rhymes. The handout today is from Stephen Fry's book, *The Ode Less Travelled*. He lays out possibilities ranging from masculine rhymes to rich rhymes, and then provides four examples of actual rhyming structures, from couplets to triplets, cross rhymes, and envelope rhymes. Take your chosen word from your haiku and insert it into each structure, keeping in mind the categories explained at the beginning of the handout. That might sound confusing, I know, but pay no attention to what I have to say about it. I'm simply here to guide you, so please don't worry about being precise. Just make a bunch of rhymes. I won't be grading you on structure. When you hand it in next week, remember to include the original haiku and renga at the top of the first page. The poems can be any length you like, but don't write more than five pages. On second thought, how about a three-page limit, double or single spaced. You can begin your work here, and ask your group members, or any other student, for ideas. But the final product will be your own work. Think of it as a solo collaboration. Or you can leave class now, research in the library, or the forest, or a bar. I have to leave early today."

As he left the classroom, Stephen couldn't help but think of the conversation ages ago with the young poet at Banff. The same story, over and over again. What was that like? Being an old poet. Overwhelmed by life, the plots and turns in narrative organized into full-length monologues, memorized, then standing on stage and telling strangers personal details, until one day the suicides you spoke of, the family history of depression, take over, and you throw yourself into cold water from one of the most iconic ferries in the world, having told your loved ones what you would one day do. Would anyone who knew about your life and death ever be able to take that ferry again without thinking of you?

The first time Stephen rode the Staten Island Ferry was the year before 9/11, four years before Spalding Gray took the plunge. The second time was in 2005, only a few months after. He carried a paperback copy of *Swimming to Cambodia* in his shoulder bag on the first visit—Grey's first performance hit— and there was a snapshot of Stephen standing at the railing of the boat, with the twin towers sprouting majestically from the top of his head. But not on the second trip. On the second visit to Staten Island the towers were gone, and his shoulder bag sagged with weight from his visit to the Alexander McQueen exhibit earlier that morning, where he could not resist buying the coffee-table catalogue with an eerie holographic image of the designer's face on the cover, blurring between a skeleton and McQueen's stern queer countenance.

Water meant so many different things to different people. Stephen loved being underwater, but had never thought of drowning. He felt in control under water, comforted, warm. It was a cushion for his sadness, his melancholy pathology.

Indeed, he was DR SAD. But his memories were filled with the joy of having sex.

After some pot smoking, and a quick plunge, the confrontational, bi-curious young bard at the Banff residency had pressed himself up against Stephen at the end of the Sally Borden pool. In the dark, with the glass roof overhead and a clear starry starry sky above, the youthful poet's belly and hairy chest pulsated, yet another underwater story to retell over and over again. The sensation of his large cock against Stephen's throbbing mid-sized member, holding both cocks in his hand like a coupled bundle of damp fleshy cylinders.

The muffled groans as they kissed when they came. It was pre-positive sex of the unselfconscious kind, thrilling.

They swam and they swam and they swam, stoned on strong B.C. pot, and then they tied themselves into orally fixated knots and came and came and came. The smell of chlorine and the taste of cannabis mingled in their conjoined mouths—coming, again, after the initial poolside orgasm. These were pre-diagnosis days, when Stephen was tested every six months. Safe sex between the middle-aged poet and the bitter, young'ish pothead, both trying to make their respective ways in a world of competitive versification. DR SAD and the young poet found sixty-nine ways to finalize their tryst, as they both moved their arms—floating, in flight—into one crucified pose. Moonlight fell on their softly heaving buttocks like ornamental swimmers on fire.

2 a.m.—Tkaronto—LAMP

As Stephen walked down the hallway toward his apartment, he could hear Patti Smith belting out "Redondo Beach." He preferred "Because the Night," but "Redondo Beach" was a close second. And of course, "Gloria."

He opened the door, and all he could see was the flashing light in the window, on and off in a frenzied blur, and a tall figure, Graham, wearing a bright red crinoline, dancing maniacally back and forth in front of the lamp.

It was *the* crinoline—the singed crinoline—flashing across the path of light from Dundas Square, like some makeshift camp strobe in heat.

"Join me. Let's dance."

Graham stretched his arms toward Stephen, pulled him against his bare chest. Stephen broke away just for a moment, excusing himself.

"We need to turn it down a little. The neighbours."

"Okay, sorry. But please. Dance with me. I found this funky dress in the bathtub. I had a shower, so we can fuck again."

As Patti's resonant, haunting voice filled the room, the manic waltz-like slouch became a sway as Graham snuggled his head into Stephen's neck.

"This is the best Halloween ever. Did you have a nice walk?"

"Yeah. I needed some fresh air."

"You weren't gone long."

"I should have just stayed here. I missed you."

"Me too."

"Why are you even here?"

"Huh?"

184

"Why did you come here? Don't get me wrong. I'm not complaining. But why me?"

"I like you."

"We met for the first time in the lobby this afternoon."

"Well, you didn't seem to mind."

"I don't. I don't mind at all. I'm just curious."

"Let's just dance. This is our first perfect fucking date. Let's not spoil it with details."

So he gave in. And why? Well, because.

The night.

Day Seventeen—Tk'emlups—Thursday, October 18th

Stephen scribbled words on several post-it notes and spoke to his new literature students.

"There is a difference between our actual lives and stories about our lives. When Forster was writing about India, he was not, strictly speaking, writing about himself. Certainly, his experiences affected how he told his stories. But he was by no means writing a memoir about his time in India. If you're interested in autobiographical writing then you might want to take my special topics course next term, on the performance monologue. And always remember, when you're writing poetry or prose or poetic prose or prose poetry—fiction is truer than a lie."

Interrupted by the gruff tones from the framework of a devilish grin, Stephen first thought that the voice coming from the back of the room was Jeffrey's. But looking up from his desk he quickly realized that Jeffrey was absent, again, and the impertinent question was coming from another student.

"Was Forster gay?"

"Apparently."

"I heard he fell in love with an Indian streetcar driver. How old was he?"

"And where did you hear that? Through the proverbial grapevine? I really don't know."

"You don't know a significant detail about the life of an author you're teaching?"

"The age of a young streetcar driver Forster may or may not have been in love with might be considered, by some, an insignificant detail."

"Ms. Landry would have known."

"The fact is, as you have perhaps heard through the dependable grapevine, I have taken over for Ms. Landry. I am new to this course. I'm not an expert on the life of Forster. I've taught some of these texts before, but not in the context of a postcolonial literature course. So, please, bear with me. I think I can guide you through the work with an eye for important social and political issues."

"We just want to know if he was gay? It does affect the writing, doesn't it?"

"That's for someone decidedly more essentialist than myself to know and for you to find out. If you're so interested in his sexual proclivities, then look it up, and see what you find. Research the living hell out of it. This is the information age. Just a couple of clicks and you're into a treasure chest of facts and all of the semi-fictionalized embroidery that over-documented online information is privy to."

"I did some research, and I found an essay that said Aziz is really the central character, and that he was based on Forster's Indian lover."

"Good for you. That may very well be the case. But I think we should begin with the text before lapsing into a soap-opera interrogation of the author's life and its relationship to the characters in the novel."

"How old was Forster when he had the affair?"

"I believe the boy was seventeen and Forster was thirty-eight. I'm not certain, and I don't see why it seems so important to you. This is a literature class, not daytime drama."

There was a hush in the classroom. For someone who had just claimed that he didn't know Forster's age, warned his students about lapsing into a soap-opera interrogation of an author's life, and took on a sarcastic tone with each answer to perfectly valid questions about a book they were beginning to study, his responses could be defined as contradictory and ill-disposed.

"I apologize. Of course you're interested in Forster's life. And don't hesitate to consider aspects of his life in relation to his work in your essays. But, please, try not to let it overwhelm your reading of the novel. Think of it as a story first, and then begin to unpack it in terms of the politics of the time, the author's perspective, and the social issues prevalent during that period."

Another student raised their hand.

"Was homosexuality illegal, then, when he wrote the book?"

"Yes, and it still is. In many places."

There was a knocking on the classroom door. Stephen was greeted by a woman in sweatpants and an oversized, homemade sweater that drowned her small frame.

"Hello. I'm Elise, the yoga instructor."

She looked familiar, but Stephen couldn't place her.

"Please, come in. We've been looking forward to your visit. Would you like to start with the half-hour yoga instruction and then some time for questions."

"Questions. Oh, of course. What kinds of questions?"

"Oh, just about the history of yoga. I've asked students to bring questions."

"Well, I'll do my best."

Elise asked the students to move their desks to the side of the room and place their towels or mats as far apart from each other as space would allow. Then she raised her arms and pulled her large sweater over her head, taking her sweatpants and then her shoes off, and rolling her hot pink yoga mat out in front of her. In her mid to late thirties, she had the serene look and soft-spoken tone one might expect from an individual who had devoted much of her life to maintaining corporeal and spiritual balance. But as she started to guide students through a basic routine, she faltered here and there, noticeable anxiety belying the calm, sensual atmosphere she initially brought to the room.

"Now, lie down and try to breathe, breathe, breathe softly, softly, softly, calmly, calmly, calmly—feeling your chest and throat—not too fast, not too fast, not too fast, feel it as it flows flows flows softly through your throat and down into your stomach past your diaphragm, breathe, breathe, breathe never, never, never, forget to breathe, breathe, breathe softly and calmly, don't choke—people have been known to choke on their own breath when they get too anxious. Don't drown in your own bad breathing. It's the most important part of yoga."

She spoke like a slam poet trying to make her way through an emphatic rant, emphasizing and repeating words with a distinct and repetitive beat, yet losing the vocal nuance a slam/performance poet would need to hold an audience for more than a few annoying seconds. Less than one minute into the routine, and Stephen felt anxious. The students were wide-eyed from the start, what with the entrance of the yoga teacher, and having just witnessed their professor's agitated response to the details of Forster's life. Everyone was fit to be tied in yoga knots of outlandish proportions.

Although it could barely be heard over her voice, Elise played a CD of "Nadia's Theme," a kitschy, voluptuous choice, reminding Stephen of a soap opera he watched from time to time, music to the opening and closing credits of *The Young and The Restless*, an iconic presence in the history of gymnastics and daytime television. When the *The Wide World of Sports* used it for a montage of Nadia Comaneci's routines during the 1976 Summer Olympics, the song, originally called "Cotton's Dream," was changed to "Nadia's Theme." Television actor David Hasselhoff, formerly of *The Young and The Restless*, wrote lyrics for the melody for his album *Lovin' Feelins*. History had a grotesque way of reiterating itself.

"Go slow, go slow, go slow. I've chosen this soothing music, a favourite of mine, so you can move into the exercises. Proper form and breathing is crucial. We start with the building blocks toward a perfectly balanced body and soul.

Then we add more strenuous exercises that will test your endurance and maintain serenity in your bodily presence and maintenance, to carry you through your demanding scholarly activities and help you to withstand the pressures that surround you."

Students seemed attentive, insomuch as they were doing the movements Elise suggested, and none of them had lapsed into downward-facing snooze positions. By the end of the thirty-minute routine, Elise had lost her nervous energy and was actually having a soothing effect. Perhaps hers was a psychological technique meant to infuse the air with manic energy so the final result would seem more serene.

"Now, we have time left for questions. Anyone?"

Not a single arm was raised. Only moments before, they had been led into downward facing doglike formations, moving gracelessly from simple salutation hand postures to one-legged king pinions. Elise began to walk among the silent students, some still lying down, others in the process of rolling up their mats or folding their towels. Passing out small cards with her contact information beside a tiny graphic of a contorted figure, she spoke more softly than she had during the exercise as the final round of a never-ending recording of "Nadia's Theme" came to a close.

"My classes are centrally located, right on the main street here in Tk'emlups. If you would like to come to a class, please email me. I have plenty of openings in the coming weeks. More advanced classes will include the cow face, the plough, and the fetus, to mention only a few breathing and stretching exercises. And for the more flexible among you, I offer even more challenging movements."

There were still no questions. Stephen felt the need to end the class with a literary bent.

"Could you tell us about the history of yoga, and how you came to it?"

"I don't consider the history, it clogs my creative memory. I am interested in breathing, concentration, meditation, and ecstasy, separating our physical matter from our spirits, to then bring them back together in a more harmonious union of flesh and soul. I was connected to my body, after my accident, in a terrible way. Once my physical injuries had healed, I was able to use yoga to cleanse myself of a painful past and to bring my spirit back to life."

"An accident led you to yoga?"

"When I was seventeen, I was in a terrible car crash. It took me years to fully recover. A doctor, a psychiatrist, thought it might help me to focus and concentrate on healing my mind and my body. She was right. And we've been together ever since, me, yoga, and my shrink. Well, she's not my shrink any more. We're lovers. She's from Tk'emlúps, but I met her in Nanaimo, at a sushi bar. She works here, at the campus clinic."

Stephen felt it was time to bring the class to a close.

"Okay, then, thank you. So that's enough for now, everyone. Next week we have Ms. Landry coming in to speak on *Meatless Days*. And, please, please please please please, try to bring at least one question, unlike today's dearth of postcolonial queries. Thank you, Elise, for coming."

As the students filed out of the classroom Elise began to put her street clothes on over her bodysuit. When she finished dressing, she smiled at Stephen and said, "We met before. At the cinema."

Stephen was beginning to remember.

"You do look familiar. What film was it?"

"The little festival, downtown, a couple of weeks ago, that film about infidelity and forgetting everything, like a dissonant love song for Alzheimer's."

"Of course. Now I remember. You sat beside me, didn't you? It was called *Away from Her*. I think we chatted about how depressing it was."

"Yes, but beautiful, quite beautiful."

"Indeed. Julie Christie's face was distracting."

"Yes, she is very beautiful. But I can't imagine being distracted by a woman's beauty. It comforts me."

"I think I'd like to take some of your classes. I live just up the hill from your studio."

"That would be wonderful. It will be lovely to see you again. In a less academic setting."

As she left the classroom, Stephen felt a pang of autoerotic regret. Ever since he was a teenager, he had wanted to be flexible enough to pleasure himself. Now, in middle age, he suspected that even with the help of an ancient meditative form, it was too late for him to perfect a self-sufficient state of Nirvana—tantric, self-induced ecstasy. But it was worth a try.

As he fell asleep that night, he couldn't help but wonder whether Spalding Gray had ever taken a yoga class. His last quizzical thought—could he, Stephen, at his advanced age, with a compromised immune system in tow, perfect a new position—downward facing blowjob. Why not give it a try. He had nothing to lose and even less to gain.

3 a.m.—Tkaronto—CLOSET

Thinking of his walk-in closet and all the recent flaming crinoline activity, Stephen had a memory of his childhood closet. When he was fifteen, his father died, at fifty-seven, in a car crash. His nineteen-year-old brother fled to the Western Canadian foothills looking for love and well-paid labour. Untimely trauma had one advantage for Stephen—he had the whole bedroom—the one he had shared with his brother for the first decade and a half of his life, to himself.

His mother let him put old blankets and pillows on the rough wooden floor, and a little pin-up lamp on the support beams of the long, low closet—a crawlspace—at the head of his bed. He would lie in there, reading Archie and Richie Rich and Little Lulu and Casper the Friendly Ghost Comics, and wish he was Betty or Veronica in the arms of Reggie or Archie, but never Jughead—no, never Jughead. Well, maybe in a pinch, Jughead.

He could never decide which he loved more, but he was totally hot for Archie. Reggie was handsome enough, but he didn't have the ginger appeal that Archie's bright follicles brought to each illustrated scene at Riverdale High and surrounding environs. A threesome with his comic book crushes would be ideal.

Stephen called his crawlspace paradise *Honeycomb Haven*, and would invite friends to come over and read comics with him. The pretense was comics, but the resulting adventure was oral in a different way. Of all the incidents that occurred between the ages of fifteen and seventeen—in Honeycomb Haven—with him and his straight friends, under the guise of reading all the latest Archie issues, the one he remembered most was with his friend Kevin.

Kevin would look at Stephen, after coming in his mouth, and say, "If we don't stop doing this, we're going to become homosexuals." Stephen just swallowed his pride, among other things, smiled, and tried to kiss Kevin on the lips. But Kevin always turned away.

Kevin was chubby and cute, with a full belly Stephen loved to lie on. But there was a problem that it took a few months to overcome. Before he knew what lace curtains were—that home-décor inspired metaphor for foreskin—he had been nonplussed by Kevin's excess of uncut meat. Uncircumcised dicks were fine, but Kevin wasn't the cleanest cock on the block. When he got older and reminisced about this formative experience, he referred to Kevin's extravagant tissue as full-length drapes that Martha Stewart would have a thing or two to say about. Not lace curtains, but heavy window treatment that was hard to swallow. So he came up with a plan—a plan that lasted just long enough for him to get what he wanted. Kevin hated kissing, especially deep tongue-filled kissing. It was too intimate, a sure sign of hardcore homosexuality. Stephen, on the other hand, craved a long slow sensual smooch—more than a blowjob. So he told Kevin that he would blow him if they could kiss first. And they did. And then Stephen would jerk them both off and frequently dispense with the blowjob.

During the blowjob Kevin always made a point of talking about all the beautiful young women who refused to date him in the high school he and Stephen attended. Stephen would impatiently endure this testament to heteronormative allegiance, all the time thinking,

"But we are cocksuckers, Blanche. We are."

Day Eighteen—Tk'emlups—Friday, October 19

Stephen was hardly using the powder-blue walking cast, and the dull aching had disappeared. His ankle felt strong, and the cast was a pain in the ass, so he kept it in his backpack and put it on when the walking was strenuous—the trail to and from campus, or when he was carrying an especially large load of newfound bargains home from Value Village. He had abandoned the shopping cart. The empty, four-wheeled creature rusted in a corner of the back yard, losing its sheen and looking like a homeless skeleton of its former self.

Maybe a song lyric exercise would be fun for the poetry class. Maybe not. Classes seemed dull and uneventful, and he felt the need to introduce something whimsical into the syllabus. He noticed his Bee Gees album on the shelf beside the window, and as soon as he was out of bed, he took the vinyl disc out of its sleeve, placed it on the Value Village turntable, and played side one. As the music started, he did his usual bathroom salutation to the mirror—*oops*—brushed his teeth, had a quick shower. As he walked out of the bathroom, Peter came out of his room. They nodded and carried on, and as he walked back into the bedroom, "I Started A Joke" was coming to a close.

As the next song started, it occurred to Stephen that his own poetry, all of his writing, both creative and academic, his entire philosophy of life, was like a Bee Gees lyric—romantic, ridiculously sublime, cheesy, and filled with a nostalgic rhythm that made him want to laugh and cry at the same time. A joke.

As the next song began, the opening notes reminded him of a close friend's wedding, over twenty years ago. As Stephen walked into the church, he heard the anomalous sound of a pop tune wafting through the rafters of an old stone building. The song was called "Words," only words, metatextual in richly and profoundly superficial ways.

Even as he listened to the words of the song, all he could think of were the haunting words of the first song, about the joke. Those words were testament to how he was beginning to view his life and his profession. Was teaching poetry just an elaborate practical joke Stephen was playing on himself? Was his life the stuff of cheesy pop tunes? Was the geography of Tk'emlups just an ethereal dream that he entered to make his recent diagnosis easier to endure? Were all words strung together in simplistic prose, a day to day account of what occurred, the emotions that were felt?

By the middle of the Bee Gees song, he lay down on the bed, intending to rest for a moment, to take in the nostalgic rush that the music created in his mind. He had a headache when he woke up, and a shower had made it worse, his sinuses mysterious entities with minds of their own. As he fell asleep, the telephone rang downstairs. Peter had left a note by his bedside. The sun shone through the bedroom window as rain clouds threatened the eastern edges of his perfect mountain view.

Stephen woke to discover that the greatest hits had ended. His roommate's note said he would call him that evening. And finally, a welcome message on the answering service from Dan, his voice strong, confident, with a faint, romantic coyness that Stephen found endearing.

Hi / it's Dan / I'm back in town / was away all week sorting out my son's latest fiasco / I'm at Sun Peaks all weekend / I've got a plan / come up and spend a couple days with me / I could drive in and pick you up / I've got the place to myself / it would be great to reconnect / call me / I hope to hear from you soon / I could drive in tonight or tomorrow morning / and hey, buddy, that's quite the dinner you had up there in Banff, eh / just checked my Visa bill online / Wow! / just kidding / no problem /

*I'm glad you enjoyed yourself / sorry I had to leave so abruptly /
I miss you / we'll talk soon, I hope xoxo*

Peter's message, scribbled on a yellow post-it note, was
typically vague, playful, haiku'ish, and to the point.

hey Stevie, Steve, Steve

you were fast asleep you bum

I'm outta here, bud

got a sexy call from Spain!

we'll talk later, Pete

Stephen put the post-it note on his makeshift book table
and then called Dan, but he seemed distracted, not like the
telephone message.

"I'm sorry. I still want you to come up. But I've just had
more news about my fucked-up son."

"Is everything okay?"

"It will be, but it's gonna cost me, as usual. Look, I gotta
run, make some more calls. Can you meet me in front of
Oriental Gardens tomorrow, at six?"

"Sure, sounds good."

"Great. Six then. I'll be driving a gold Camaro."

4 a.m.—Tkaronto—CURTAIN

Graham had closed the curtains, and the living room seemed still, haunted by streaks of flashing light from Dundas Square seeping through the edges of the blackout drapes. Stephen came out of the shower, walked over to the homo-sectional sofa, intending to join Graham, but he wasn't there.

"What the fuck! Not again. Asshole."

"Hey, buddy, what's up? Come on in here."

Well, he was certainly making himself at home. Stephen went into the bedroom, and there he was, Graham, sprawled on the bedspread with his little mask back on.

"Remember me? Let's make love."

"Okay."

"You've got a great room! Come on in."

They cuddled, and the last thing Stephen remembered saying, as he fell asleep in Graham's arms—"Why are you here? Where did you come from?"

"Shhhhhh. Buddy! Go to sleep. I'm here. I'm right here."

Day Nineteen—Sun Peaks—Saturday, October 20

Dan was right on time.

"It's my son's car. He's had it ever since he was a teenager. I bought it for him on his sixteenth birthday. All he wanted was a gold Camaro. It's the only thing he's ever shown any real commitment to, the prick. Sorry, I shouldn't get started. It's great to see you. You brought a lot of stuff for just a couple of days."

"I stopped at Value Village. I'm kind of addicted to that place."

"I've never been. Not into second-hand stuff myself."

Only ten minutes out of the city and Stephen was asleep, feverish, and sweaty. He had slept restlessly the night before, worried about what it would be like to see Dan again, this virtual stranger he had known for less than two hours of his life. He was excited, but terrified.

Dan was a cautious driver, and kept glancing at his passenger as he drove up the winding road to the resort. He had only started staying there again since his son moved back from the city. The last time he had driven this route, there was a blockade over Indigenous land rights, and he never did make it to the chalet, just went back to Tk'emlups and stayed at the Plaza.

Stephen had slipped a homemade CD into the player just before he fell asleep. As the final moments of Baby Dee singing "Calvary"—just after hearing Antony and the Johnson's singing, "I fell in love with a dead boy"—Dan thought to himself—who is this man, wheezing and drooling in the passenger seat, who looked so attractive to him a week ago at Banff?

The dying sunlight was not flattering to either of them. The natural light would not have done justice to someone half their ages. Dusk would make them both look ten years younger.

"Hey, wake up, buddy. We're here."

Stephen had fallen into a dead sleep, and took a few seconds to realize where he was. Sun Peaks was completely new to him.

"Where are we? Why did we come here?"

"We're at my place. At the resort. You fell asleep. It's only been about an hour and a half. Are you hungry?"

"Yeah, I guess I am."

"Let's get into the house and freshen up, and then we'll go for dinner. There are some nice places here."

It was a chalet with huge windows, a fireplace, a hot tub, a lap pool, five bedrooms, stone and pine in all the right places, and too many bathrooms to count. Stephen half expected Martha Stewart to walk out of the kitchen and greet them with warm muffins and a pitcher of apple cider. He had the urge to tell vulgar jokes about shitting on her curtains, but suppressed it.

They spent about twenty minutes getting settled, Dan the perfect gentleman, giving Stephen a quick tour. He told him to make himself comfortable, to unpack, to let him know when he was ready, and they'd go for dinner. What Stephen wasn't expecting was his own room.

"We'll share the same room, if you're into it. I just didn't want to assume, and I thought you might like a space to chill out on your own, and this place is so damn big. I should get rid of it. My son likes to have people up, but doesn't look like he'll be here any time soon."

"That's very sweet of you. It'll just take me a few minutes to get ready."

"No hurry. Relax."

Dan kissed him on the cheek as he left the room.

They were shy around each other, awkward. Hopefully some wine at dinner would loosen them up. And then, maybe the hot tub would remind them of how well they got along when they were surrounded by water. The lighting would take years off their faces. Perhaps they would be happiest in the water, where they first met.

During the tour, Stephen only needed a glimpse of the lap pool to feel intimidated. Surrounded by large panes of glass, huge wooden beams, and dark iron girders, it seemed daunting, a Mies Van der Rohe meets Frank Gehry architectural ensemble, an aquatic gallery for a thin horizontal shaft of chlorinated water—innocuous, pristine, faintly banal, slightly ridiculous, totally sublime, the perfect place to recreate the scene of their first carnal coupling.

"Do you like fondue?"

"Love it."

"Would you like me to order for both of us?"

"Sure."

They shared two bottles of white wine, and by the time they were finished with the porcini mushroom and roasted garlic fondue, followed by their mountain berry crumble, there were barely enough words between them to consider it a full conversation.

The second bottle was sweet, and Stephen was convinced there might have been a bit of soap in his glass, but he rose to the occasion and drank his fair share. This brand of wine had a lush, complicated, barely believable backstory that Stephen found delightful, a story that Dan told him as they walked back to the house. It set the mood for a much-needed change in their bashful demeanours.

"I was very young at the time, around seventeen, and I guess you've noticed by now, I have a shitload of money. I didn't earn a cent of it. I'm an occasional businessman, a philanthropist of sorts. I was born into it. But that's boring. The wine, though, not boring at all, Lacryma Christi, that's the wine we had with dessert. The tears of Christ, campy eh? I first heard about it when I read a Truman Capote essay in school.

It's from the island of Ischia, across from Capri. One of the English teachers, at boarding school, he was a real classic, the perfect poofter, a British fag, and he would teach a couple of queer books every term, before I even knew what queer could mean. I did well that year, when he was teaching, and my dad gave me a trip to Europe for my eighteenth birthday. Fuck, the summer of 1957. I heard that the English teacher was going to Paris, so I casually told him I would be going to Europe too, and he said, jokingly, meet me on the isle of Capri. We'll have lunch and a cocktail. You can find me at the Piccolo Marina. To make a long story short, when I turned up, he was shocked, quite nervous actually, but very kind and polite. I was a cute, arrogant kid. He showed me around for the day, and I went back to the mainland the next morning, and toured Italy, all by myself."

"The next morning?"

"Oh, yeah, we spent the night together. He was a sweet old guy. It made sense to me, like the right thing to do, very literary and all that international, intergenerational jazz. But really, that whole summer was kind of magical, and that day on Capri, wow, I've never been back, but it stayed with me. We just sat there, sharing a bottle of Lacryma Christi. I ordered it. I had the Capote essay strategically placed in my backpack, and I remember trying to impress him by saying, as I looked across the Gulf of Naples and smiled at the old guy and said, all cocky and shit, 'Look, Capote was right, it's just a faint blue shadow, Ischia.' But there was no shadow at all, no blue, no jagged edge. He laughed, and we strolled through the streets of Capri. I always order that wine when I want to share a special moment with someone. You reminded me of it—I reminded myself of it when you were sleeping in the car on the way up here. We really are an unlikely pair, aren't we? A couple of stereotypical old fags trying to squeeze a bit more romance out of life. But I don't know what it is, in the old-fashioned sense of queer, kind of offbeat, there's something about you. You know what, fuck, I just realized, you look a bit like Capote, before he got squishy. You're like a kind of faded version of that photo on the cover of *Other Voices, Other Rooms*. Shit, it never occurred to me before. Life is packed with so many queer associations. Did you like the wine?"

Stephen loved the wine, and the romantic story. The Capote resemblance, not so much. He'd had that narrative projected onto him before, and as Dan finished his tale of Ischia and Capri, they were tipsily holding each other up as they approached the entrance to his chalet. Stephen watched Dan wiggle the key at the doorway and thought, *If we're so stereotypical then why aren't we on a beach in Venice, accompanied by Mahler's Fifth Symphony, with mascara running down our cheeks, about to expire as boys a half-century younger scamper about in striped bathing suits. Instead of a godforsaken ski resort on stolen land at the edge of the fucking Rocky Mountains?*

Turning the key in the lock, Dan looked at Stephen and smiled, then leaned forward and gave him a light kiss on the lips, took his arm and pulled him gently toward him.

"Let's go swimming in my lap pool. Is that weird? Considering how we met."

"No, not at all, I'd love to."

He had never been in a single lane pool before, and the dimensions of the lap pool, contrary to his first impression, only seven feet wide and fifty meters long, made for a cozy stretch of erotic playground. With their shoulders against opposite sides of the pool, and their legs outstretched, martini glasses placed just to the left of their respective heads, they were a study in middle-aged symmetry, up to their necks in water, eyeballs glazed by wine and vodka, their legs paddling softly and their toes meeting in the friendliest way, around each other's genitals, squeezing gently in a most fulfilling manner. And given the queer literary allusions made earlier, how could one not consider Whitman's "Song of Myself"—

*The young men float on their backs, their white bellies bulge to
the sun, they do not ask who seizes fast to them*

*They do not know who puffs and declines with pendant and
bending arch*

They do not think whom they souse with spray.

And, of course, there was the light. Dark by now, the
moon could just be seen through the roof of the atrium. The
soft interior lighting gave the space a mottled look, almost
arboreal. The evening had, against all odds, become precisely
what Dan had wanted it to be. Romantic, magical. That
was what he desired. No interminable conversations about
illness and aging, no bitter disclosure about the mess his son
was making of his life. Just initial hesitation that lasted into
dinner, and a disquieting car ride from Kamloops, what with
the mixed CD and the unflattering afternoon light reminding
him that he was not young anymore, nor was his lightly
drooling paramour. But he was content, and the wine, the
literary allusions, and the lap pool played a final punctuation
to a shallow evening filled with depth.

They wrapped themselves in ankle-length terrycloth
robes, monogrammed with elegant capital F's in a rich
burgundy thread, walked arm in arm back to the master
bedroom, disrobed, rewrapped in each other's aging flesh,
and fell asleep with songs of themselves as lullabies to
coincidentally inclined encounters.

Just to their left, a couple of feet away from the bed, a piece
of fabric, two feet by three, folded neatly over the back of a
wingchair that Martha Stewart might have approved of, wove
a lush winter scene. A dogsled, the man on the sled wearing
a red parka trimmed with white fur, and six dogs racing
through a blue and white landscape.

Downstairs, in a laundry room off the kitchen, at the
bottom of a hamper a torn skirt, replete with grease and mud

from the back fender of a vintage Camaro formerly sporting two bumper stickers, one warning that the car was protected by a very angry dog—a pit bill—with AIDS. The other one proclaimed emphatically that the driver was dating someone's husband.

5 a.m.—Tkaronto—BALCONY

Around five, Graham got up and walked into the living room, threw a blanket from the sofa over his shoulders, grabbed his cigarettes from the coffee table, and went out onto the balcony. The drapes in the bedroom were closed, so he switched on the balcony light, lit a cigarette, and lay down on the chaise longue. Under him he felt a rustle, lifted his ass, and pulled a piece of paper into his lap. The wind had lifted it from the top of the hamper during the night. He began to read the scribbled, barely legible handwriting to himself, missing words here and there as he scanned the poem—

Vase

winter rose
but now the effusive dignity of your
odd curvature and sweep
squat on pedestal orange as blood blossoms
rest atop an edge glazed with painstaking yellow
cloisonné-like sigh of leaves that stand
pert and crisp outside your hollow heart

spring tulip
but now the grace of petals
upright in their haughty swing
pale green shank narrow in its sway
leafage groans but stays

nothing all that grand in spring
save eternal blossoming of what immortalizes death

summer lilac
but now that haze overwhelms grace
with riot seeded crowds
among gardens browning into
fragrant tears
dying soil and worm
of breathing life through purpled jet

fall physalis alkekengi
but now the balls of bladder cherries
bulbs in lantern likeness glowing crisp and even
dangled into nature's tease
rhapsodic—
named for robust nations—misnamed for floral treatments
industrializing the cutthroat destiny of pistol cell and stem . . .

"Fuckin' weird shit"—Graham muttered as he finished reading the poem, lit another cigarette. Suddenly a light went on just to the right of his head. He looked up and saw that it was coming from the adjoining balcony.

"Hey, Stephen, is that you over there? You're up late. The smoke is coming in my bedroom window. You don't smoke, do you?"

"Hey, sorry, buddy. I'm a friend. Just up for a quick one. I'll put it out. Sorry."

"It's okay. I smoke. It was just weird to smell at this hour. You wanna join me?"

"Huh?

"You wanna have a smoke with me. Climb over."

"No, thanks. It might wake him."

Graham peered over the balcony partition and smiled, love at first sight. He hopped over to the other side, and before he knew it, lust was in the air. Stephen heard the commotion and peered out of his bedroom window. He saw the tail end of Graham's backside as he climbed over the balcony partition.

"Well, okay, then, might as well be neighbourly."

As he tried to fall asleep, Stephen felt weepy but contented. Share and share alike. Graham had a quick change of heart and hopped back over to Stephen's side in a queer version of not so *Private Lives*. It wasn't dawn yet, close, almost twilight. Graham crawled back into Stephen's bed. Stephen rolled over and muttered—

"Finished so soon?"

"Huh?"

"Finished already, with my neighbour?"

"Oh, sorry. I changed my mind. His place is weird. Is he a hoarder or something?"

"Yeah, He is. You could have fucked him on his balcony."

"Naw. I'd rather be here, with you."

"He's a lot better looking than I am, and younger."

"I wanna sleep here, with you. Are you pissed off?"

"I have nothing to be pissed off about. We met yesterday."

"Yesterday, it seems a long time ago."

"Far away."

"Yeah. Far away."

Day Twenty—Sun Peaks—Sunday, October 21

"You're sixty-eight? Wow! When I first saw you, at the pool in Banff, I thought you were quite a bit younger. You look like my age, younger even."

"And you're?"

"I'm fifty-one. I was born the summer before you went to Capri."

"Does that bother you?"

"That I wasn't old enough to go to Capri with you. Yeah, it sure does. No, not at all. Well, to be honest, it does bother me a little that I look my age and you don't look yours. But I can cope."

The next two days were spent in superficial bliss. Stephen was happy to have a room of his own, to read in the afternoons, or to have a nap, while Dan was outside puttering around the chalet, or on the phone to his son, in Japan. He had been in Tokyo for a few days earlier in the week, just after Banff, getting his son settled with his girlfriend, who was causing an uproar about the paternity of her child. Dan had persuaded him to go and be with her, to see if they could work something out—he didn't want to lose total contact with his first grandkid.

"Do you have any other children?"

"No, just the one, Daniel. Daniel Craig Forrester, the fucking third. He doesn't like to use his first name because, of course, you guessed, it's my name too. So he goes by Craig."

"Well, children can be rebellious. I'm one to talk, but I do have students to contend with. Your name's Forrester?"

"Yeah, and yours?"

"Davis. Stephen Andrew."

"Well, I like spending time with you. We've got one day left, after we make the best of this evening. Last night was relaxing, just what I needed."

"Me too. This is an amazing place."

"You're welcome anytime. I hope you'll come again. And stay longer."

"I'd love to."

"There's a special moonlight walk, at the top of the mountain, with torches. Would you like to go?"

"To the top of the mountain?"

"They open the gondola. It's beautiful."

"Sounds incredible."

"Then let's do it. But I want to make you dinner here. Do you like sushi?"

"I love it."

"My son and I, well, we have hard times, but we get along now and then. When he came back from Japan the first time, he taught me how to make sushi. I'm better at it than he is, and he's pretty damn good."

All very clear. The writing on the wall, but why spoil it at this particular juncture, this fragile moment when clues conspired to shed light on part of the truth, a configuration of eerily coincidental events. What would the point be in that? Who would it help, who would it hurt. And if things didn't last with Dan, Stephen could slip out of the narrative as recklessly, as joyfully, and as seamlessly as he had slipped in. He made a pact with himself. He was going to enjoy the moment. This odd coincidental situation was not going to make him sad. He decided to just go with it, and get his fucking happy back.

He picked up the book he was reading, opening it to where he had left off and continued to read, struck by a line from *Memento Mori*, Muriel Spark's prolonged meditation on the spectacular and fateful events taking place in the lives of a group of elderly people. Something about life being terribly banal if there was not a constant sense of death surrounding it. Irritated by the bleak romanticism of it all Stephen abruptly closed the fragile paperback, the spine brittle and deteriorating, the pages separating from the body. He thought to himself—

This is a dream. This lovely older man. I don't want to ruin it with the truth, the strange coincidental turn of events. I need this flight of fancy now. I need to believe that this wish fulfillment come true is really happening. I haven't felt like this since I was a teenager. Fuck, I never felt like this when I was a teenager! It's like first love, but more like last love, and if Shakespeare's winged cupid and his seven stages bear any truth, then, yes, it is a first love, filled with sweet despair at the tail end of time. I'll just bathe in the glow of this implausibly plausible romantic turn of events, and, yes, see where it takes me.

That night it took him to the top of a mountain. When he got to the summit, he could see the shadowy edges of the Monashees, stretching five hundred and thirty kilometres from north to south, as far as Washington State. But he was more interested in the unity of the face he kept staring into as they sipped warm sake out of the same thermos, two stereotypical older gentlemen, sharing themselves with each other—suspended in a gondola high above the land.

6 a.m.—Tkaronto—GARDEN

By sunrise, a maintenance employee was on the roof garden, scrubbing the deep red stain from the cement, trimming back the smashed raspberry bushes as he cursed the culprit who had injured that poor boy the night before. It was already on the news, and in the tasteless tabloids.

HALLOWEEN HORROR

Young man dressed as a tube of toothpaste

beaten on rooftop in downtown apartment complex

Assailant made a clean getaway

still in a coma

Day Twenty-One—Sun Peaks—Monday, October 22

When they woke the next morning, Stephen noticed a
transparent bandage on the back of Dan's left wrist, a bit of
dried red blood at the edges.

"I didn't notice this before. What happened?"

"A stupid accident. My son's car, I was trying to fix
something."

"What was wrong?"

"It's embarrassing. He can be an asshole sometimes. You
won't believe what was on the fender of that car before I came
to pick you up."

"Try me."

"Two offensive bumper stickers. One was about a cheap
joke about AIDS and a scrappy dog. The other was about
infidelity. I scraped them off with a cutting blade, and it
slipped, I almost slit my goddamn wrist. If that's not a sign, I
don't know what is."

Morning sex took over at this point, and the bumper
sticker debacle added nervous energy. When Dan entered
Stephen, his penis slid in so softly and so perfectly, and the
condom had been slipped on with such ease, that at first
Stephen had to discreetly check, with his left hand, to make
sure there was one. He had learned very early that safe sex,
even with two HIV positive people, was necessary. Reinfection
was a concern. Better safe than sorrier.

And if that wasn't enough sex before sunrise, Dan
quickly slid a new condom over his lover's engorged member
and mounted Stephen just after ejaculating himself, swiftly
rocking his hips up and down, back and forth, sitting upright
on Stephen's penis, his hands pressed against Stephen's
shoulders, his large chest heaving in the early morning light

213

as it crept over the mountains and cascaded into the windows of multimillion-dollar chalets nestled on the rolling edges of stolen Shuswap land, soon to be covered in a blanket of seasonal white, both artificial and real. As Stephen came, Dan cupped the edges of his shoulders and hoisted Stephen's torso toward him, delicately manoeuvring his buttocks to make sure they remained connected, and kissed him. He wanted to hoist him heavenward in some kind of impossible gymnastic feat, a headstand on the bed, impaled felicitously on Stephen's cock, with Stephen upright on all fours, moaning and seething with ejaculatory glee, like the pyrotechnic lust Dan had seen on internet porn. But they were too old, and he settled for geriatric sex, Stephen's low, full moans muffled by the touch of Dan's lips, their clinging bodies carnally intact, from orifice to shining orifice, burning the carnal candle at both ends.

"Would you mind if I did a small laundry today?"

Dan laughed.

"How romantic. Sure, go ahead, but do I get another kiss first?"

"Sorry, I'm a little restless."

They kissed, and Dan fell back to sleep while Stephen made his way to the laundry room by the kitchen. There was a small basket of clothes beside the washer that he threw in with the few things he had, and as they tumbled out, he noticed a familiar piece of fabric. He pulled it from the machine and stared intently.

"This cannot be happening. This is my goddamn skirt. This is the fucking skirt that car ripped off me that night. What the fuck is going on? The goddamn Camaro that almost killed me? Craig must have been driving?"

Coincidence was piling up like artificial snow.

"This is for you."

Dan put his hands on Stephen's shoulders as he lifted the last of the laundry out of the washer. Stephen dropped the clothes onto the floor, bits of mud and grass from the boots

Dan had left by the door clinging to the freshly laundered clothing.

"I'm sorry, I thought you heard me coming. I called your name."

"No, that's okay. I think I did hear you. I was preoccupied."

Brushing the dried dirt off the clothes, Stephen smiled as he pushed the bundle into the dryer and wiped the faint remnants of some tears from the corner of his left eye. Dan didn't notice the tears as he handed Stephen a gift wrapped in brown paper.

"What's this?"

"It's a volume of poetry. I told my son about you, and he sent it along when I saw him in Japan last week. He just up and went there on a whim. I told him you taught poetry."

"But I didn't tell you, about teaching poetry?"

"I looked you up online. You weren't difficult to find. No one is anymore."

"So, your son, he knows my name?"

"Yeah, I told him about you. He was happy for me. He's cool. I know, the bumper stickers, he makes some weird choices sometimes, has a strange sense of humour. But he's a good guy, despite his wild ways."

"So, he's going to stay there, in Japan, with his kid, and the mother, his, uh, I mean, are they married?"

"They're getting married this summer. I'll be going. You wanna come with me?"

"Uh, whoa, I don't know. Yeah, sure. Why the hell not. I've never been. Would, um, your son mind?"

"Actually, he told me to invite you."

"Did he tell you anything else?"

"What do you mean?"

"Nothing. I just mean, he doesn't know me."

"He knows how much I like you. I know, it's early, but I have a good feeling about us, and we don't want to waste any time at this point, do we?"

"No, I guess we don't."

He took the gift in his hands, opened it quickly and almost laughed out loud. The Thomas Eakins image on the front, a detail from *The Swimming Hole*, had always been one of Stephen's favourite paintings. Just inside the front cover, there was a note stuffed into the slot where a library card should have been, from the campus stacks. Stephen took it out, unfolded the note, and read it to himself as Dan walked back into the kitchen and started to make breakfast.

The note read,

hey there! ? well, this is just plain weird, you and my dad ! can you return this book for me—long overdue, campus library

I thought it might be a nice gesture—strange maybe, but nice

for it to move from me through you and back to where it belongs everything's cool (a bit messy here, but cool) be nice to him

he loves you, I think, I can tell, he's a compulsive guy, and he's a great dad

Craig xoxo

(p.s. our little secret, okay? I think that's best)

Another shallow day of small talk laced with sex and the odd lapse into slight autobiographical details, Dan and Stephen getting to know each other. Given the scattered bits of coincidental data seeping in through bumper stickers, vintage cars, pieces of torn skirts, and startling notes stuck into volumes of poetry, it was surprising that they were together at all. This gentle man, but Stephen began to perceive him as a slightly pompous sort, telling outlandish stories, ordering Lacryma Christi, fondue for two, Mountain Berry

Crumble, fumbling about in the kitchen, pretending he could make breakfast, when it turned out to be a slice of slightly burnt, lukewarm toast covered in clumps of cinnamon and mushy strawberry slices. The sushi the night before had been startlingly amateurish, even though Dan claimed to be much better at it than his son. The rolls were loose and damp, and the rice overcooked and starchy. But Stephen doused it in generous heaps of pickled ginger and as much wasabi as his tear ducts could stand to drown out the banal flavours Dan had managed to create. But it was still a lovely distraction being in the mountains with him. And Stephen had a copy of Whitman's iconic collection to remind him that ultimately it was all just a song of himself, lacking in strict continuity, filled with flights of fancy, mired in memory, and littered with melancholy glee. Tra la.

7 a.m.—Tkaronto—HAPPYBACK

By seven thirty, they had been asleep for two hours, wrapped in each other's bodies. Stephen and Graham were new lovers, who knew everything they needed to know about each other. They were both HIV positive. But were they too old to be new lovers? As time had taught him, Stephen knew that everything old becomes new again, like in the song. But it all had to be said, over and over and over again. I love you.

Stephen was still asleep when Graham gently disentangled himself, slipped into his shirt and trousers, pressed his feet into his loafers, took the key from the basket on the wall beside the door, above the plaque-mounted posters of one of Stephen's avant-garde drag shows from the nineties, and left.

He would be back soon. Stephen wouldn't notice. And he felt so happy—to have found someone he actually liked and didn't mind having sex with—and in the same co-op as Graham's kids. It would be convenient if everything worked out.

All he had to be sure of was how long happy would last. So he walked up the two flights to the roof garden, let himself onto the rooftop with Stephen's fob, and over to the scene of the toothpaste crime and prayed for the recovery of the comatose costumed victim.

Day 22—Tk'emlups—Tuesday, October 23

Not since the light evening snowfall in Banff the weekend before, barely discernible through the glass windows of the indoor pool, had Stephen even thought of the abrupt change in weather approaching. It had been a warm fall, and the first official day of winter was two months away. But he knew what that meant in Canadian terms, especially Western Canadian mountain terms. You get winter weather for much of the autumn and the spring, which never made sense to him. As far as he was concerned, even the lightest snowfall meant fall was dead and winter had killed it. He hated winter, and snow, and although he had loved to ski years ago, he never thought of winter and skiing as having anything in common.

He did admire the aesthetic value of snowflakes, and even the pristine covering they provided before human beings and their accessories began to muck about in the midst of that uniquely patterned crystalline form, but he despised shovelling—he called it murdering snowflakes. Skiing, although refreshing, exhilarating even, was largely mechanical. He remembered rope tows and walking up small community slopes in Ontario during his childhood, hating every laborious minute of it. It seemed like a waste of a nice walk, like golfing, but worse. Not until he experienced real mountain skiing, with gondolas and chairlifts, did he realize how wonderful skiing could be, an indoor sport that you did outdoors, craving the comfort of the hot toddy, the martini, the canapés, the nachos and the pizza inside a chalet at the foot of a snow-clad peak. Now that he was living close to a ski resort, with a new love interest eager to get into nature, it might be the right time to make a comeback on the slopes. He could learn to love skiing again, but what would he wear?

Would he break many bones? A new fashion parade began in his mind, and Stephen fantasized about dressing up as a snowbound soldier/majorette—poles twin baton-like bayonets, ski helmets and mittens like soft bulbous firearms.

Dan dropped him off early in the morning, in time for Stephen to get his things together for his first class of the week. Dan headed back to Sun Peaks for a day or two before flying to Japan. He'd be back in time for Halloween, and they made tentative plans to get together, after the student get together.

Dan had offered to drive Stephen to the campus, but Stephen never felt completely settled on campus without a brisk walk through the hills beforehand.

"I'd like to walk."

Stephen didn't notice Jeffrey and Lily at first, as he turned the corner in the trail, just after leaving the end of Nicola Wagon Road. They were sitting, hand in hand, beside an unusually large tumbleweed.

"Hello, Lily, Jeffrey. Are you coming to class today?"

They were startled to see him, and both stood quickly, adjusting their clothes as if something had happened, or was about to happen. The weather seemed chilly for an outdoor encounter, but that was no one's business but their own. They were both self-conscious, Lily especially agitated and nervous, even bashful, which was unlike her.

Without saying hello, she blurted.

"I'm sorry, sir. I'm dropping your poetry class. Nothing personal. Uh, family troubles, sort of. I need to lighten my course load, and I need the other credits for my degree.

"I understand. No need to apologize. I'm sorry things are difficult for you. And, Jeffrey, have you dropped the course as well?"

"No. It's my favourite. I've been helping Lily. I'll be there today. I've kept up with the work, on email, through friends. I have my rhyme assignment all ready. It's like things are heating up, and now we're getting into some more complex stuff."

"I'm glad to hear that. Lily, if there's anything I can do to help, if you would like to keep taking the course, I could make allowances. It might make life less hectic for you, extending deadlines, and some extra meetings during office hours, when you need to catch up."

"That's very generous, kind of you, sir, but is that okay, though, with the school?"

"It's fine. Extenuating circumstances. Very common."

"Thanks so much. I'll let you know. I do like coming, and writing poetry for the class. It's a break from calculus and all that shit."

"You've done some great work so far. It would be a shame to lose you. You're one of the few students who managed to turn a limerick into something more substantial. You'd be surprised how many students used the word Nantucket in their limericks. I guess they thought it was a joke."

Seeing Jeffrey standing there, bashful and sincere, protective of Lily, remembering her limerick made Stephen feel a little self-conscious. The lines wandered through his mind as he tried to remain attentive.

there was a boy that I held

in the palm of my hand like an elf

he wriggled and writhed

he heaved and he sighed

I kept him in chains on my shelf

Stephen looked at Lily as he thought about chains and wondered if this was a metaphor, or if they actually were into a bit of light bondage.

his love like the wind in the pines
was airy and prickly and fine
the way his limbs wandered
made my thighs grow much fonder
and dressed me in lust to the nines

The thought of Jeffrey's limbs wandering and Lily's thighs growing fonder made Stephen twitch, and he knew it was time to be on his way.

"I'll see you, Jeffrey, in class, and Lily, whatever you decide is fine, you need to do what's best for you."

He smiled at them both, nodded his head politely, and quickly retreated.

Although the meeting with Lily and Jeffrey had been unexpected, it had its moments of tenderness toward two students. And having spent the weekend with Dan, Stephen enjoyed a gleeful, slightly frantic energy. A new, unfamiliar spirit infected his mood, making him more direct, more cordial, and yet unsure of every single word he uttered. And it was sprinkled with a touch of giddiness. He was in love.

It wasn't until Jeffrey began to recite his poem, halfway through the class, after four students had recited some of the most banal verse imaginable, that Stephen's mood changed from composed and meditative to alarmed, putting him into crisis mode and making him wish he had taken his grandmother's advice that he become a hairdresser.

At the beginning of the class, he warned students that he hoped they had approached the exercise with a little more academic import than the limerick assignment. He admitted that their attempts had been playful at times, with some lame vulgarity, but now they were expected to put a little more thought into form.

His grandmother had been right. He could be cutting and colouring women's hair instead of hearing impertinent students trying to rhyme the name of a New England town with everything from puck it to duck it, truck it, muck it, buck it, tuck it, and suck it. Surprisingly, no one dared to use the F word. One student made a juvenile attempt at language poetry by emitting guttural sounds that he felt mimicked waves lapping against the shore and called it "Nantucket Sound Poem." He got an A for effort.

Jeffrey, despite the startling nature of his piece, did seem to be taking the rhyming exercise seriously.

"I hope you don't mind, sir. I didn't follow the exercise you gave us exactly the way you asked. I didn't use the group haiku as an epigraph. Is that okay?"

"That's fine, Jeffrey. It was just a tool to motivate you, but if you've come up with something else, I'm sure it will be fine. Do you have a copy for me to make notes?"

Jeffrey handed him a sheet of paper, a photocopy of a page written in longhand.

"Thank you, Jeffrey. Go ahead. Begin."

Jeffrey stood at the front of the class like a schoolboy, prim, hardly proper, but acting so. Like he had rehearsed his shyness and was using it as a weapon. He enunciated clearly, articulating each syllable, pausing briefly between stanzas in order to convey the necessary breaks in his performative mode.

Snowflake Men

the way his wrists will hurl in rooms
the way he whirls like feathered brooms
the way his girlish eyes bedevil
the way his undressed sighs dishevel

boys may not thrive on bread alone
but can he coax an ice cream cone
to let him lick that final swirl
toward one post-pubescent curl

but I don't hear the brackish din
but I don't see these acts as sin
but I don't even look at pearls
but I just keep on loving girls

the way his lips misplace an 's'
the lazy tongue that makes a mess
of all we've come to know as voice
of all he has to choose, his choice

Is twirl and hurl and curl and pearl
Is swirl, unfurl, whirl and churl
I watch him come, I watch him go
I see him touch the ground—within my gaze he melts —
like snow

Jeffrey was a dreamer, a dream weaver, and his poem journeyed into particularly brackish waters. Luckily, Stephen's confidence, post-weekend, was still on the rise, and although he felt panicky, called upon to avert a minor crisis in his own mind, he decided, by the last four lines, to take it all in his stride, let the sloppy metaphors wash over him like so much saltwater taffy. Some of the other students, wide-eyed, chuckled nervously throughout. These were the few who had even the slightest clue of what was happening in the verse being read to them by the only student in the class, second to Lily, who had any truly creative spark.

"Thank you, Jeffrey. That was splendid. There may be one stanza missing. I'll have a closer look, but your first reading, beautifully performed, but I did have the sense that there may have been a jump, an abrupt narrative leap, from the second to the third section, and perhaps again between the third and the fourth. Perhaps that was your intention, but you might have a look and see if anything more occurs to you."

Stephen paused to look around the classroom.

"Good, then, excellent work everyone. See you tomorrow. Class dismissed."

He had called Jeffrey's poem splendid? Stephen rarely used the word *splendid*, he preferred *splendour*. And *class dismissed* sounded so antiquated and juvenile, filled with officious connotations. But under the circumstances, he felt he had to act as subtly as heaven allowed, the faintly effete role of an aging professor trapped in a revisionist queer production of *Goodbye Mr. Chips*—a musical adaptation perhaps, a melodic soiree, an atelier event with three characters, a string quartet and a countertenor in tow. And clowns, sad clowns with overtones of glee. It could not be truly queer without sad clowns trying to get their happy back.

Poetic licence.

Graham was back in bed by 7:20. Stephen pretended to be
asleep when he heard the door open. He was just about to
get out of bed and check to see if his dream had come true
and Graham had left again, without his shoes. He had been
dreaming.

The dream: In an old, vaguely, strangely familiar,
dilapidated house, a pocket mansion, Stephen wanders
upstairs, through beautiful hallways, wood panelled, with
gilded frames of royal-looking people, queens and kings,
princes and princesses, lords and ladies, queer barons, and
sadly diminutive baronets, drag kings—reminding Stephen of
the summer he toured Buckingham Palace with his mother. In
the dream, he notices a dark panelled room from the corner of
his eye, giant puppet heads floating above colourful caterpillar
bodies. He keeps walking past room after room after room
after room. Bleak, dissonant music plays as he wanders, and
bits of Mahler's tenth seep through. At one point he thinks he
is in Buckingham Palace and shouts, "Where the fuck is the
goddamn queen!" Then he decides he is not in Buckingham
Palace, and he just keeps walking.

He comes to the end of the long hallway, and walks
into a room where he finds a line of people waiting to see
a performance piece. Without having to be told, he just
knows, in that inexplicable dreamy way, that they are waiting
for something theatrical to begin. There's a placard on the
wall above the line-up that says DYING WELL—written and
performed by DR SAD. Performers lounge about midway
through the line, clad in bronze-coloured costumes, and
looking like a reclining version of Rodin's sculpture *The
Burghers of Calais*—as if tired of standing around looking

monumental and thin, so they rendered themselves prostrate amid discontented sculptural non-bliss. Stephen pulls a crumpled hamburger out of his pocket, unwraps it from a piece of silver foil with the word Calais emblazoned on the burger wrapper, and eats it in one bite. The Burgher King of Calais.

He gazes at the line of people and notices that when they actually get to the reclining figures, they stop and place bronze-coloured bandages on their limbs. One man in the performance piece is groaning and coughing, and a young woman in the lineup turns him on his side and applies an especially large bandage, that she pulls from her throat, to his asshole.

As Stephen moves further into the room, it becomes a room filled with tables covered in bric-a-brac, a rummage sale, with racks of vintage clothing. Stephen becomes obsessed with finding a porcelain cookie jar shaped like a tomato. Someone Stephen seems to know—vaguely—is at one of the tables with a huge rack of lush Elizabethan costumes beside her. She has bleached hair and porcelain makeup, is wearing a huge codpiece embroidered with roses. She hands him a vintage tomato cookie jar and laughs and laughs and laughs. Stephen is delighted, until he inadvertently squeezes the tomato and discovers that it is real, not made of porcelain. He throws it at one of the dying people in the performance piece and it bursts all over them, blood and seeds spewing everywhere, and the performer shouts, "Where's the fucking guacamole bacon lettuce and quinoa!? I ordered a gbltq, you asshole!"

No one seems to notice the explosion, and after the familiar woman has handed Stephen the tomato, she does a solo performance piece that everyone gathers around to watch.

She shouts out the words, "Who in their right mind would jump from a small boat on the way to Catalina Island?" over and over and over again, and then she screams maniacally that she wants her bellbottoms back. Stephen looks down at his own trousers and realizes he is wearing brightly coloured striped bellbottoms. He laughs at the performing woman, and she starts to cry, and he laughs harder, and then he hears Graham shouting behind him, "I left my slippers at the door." Stephen turns around to catch a glimpse of Graham's naked back as he runs barefoot from the entrance down the hall.

As he tries to follow Graham in his dream, Stephen notices something on the floor where Graham had been standing and declaiming about his misplaced slippers. It's a vase, a brightly coloured vase, broken into three distinct pieces. Stephen walks over to the vase, picks it up, and the vase melts back into a single piece—as perfect as it was before it was broken. He takes a small casket-shaped box lined with white satin, and places the vase in the box. When he takes his hand away, he sees that it is covered in blood, but there is no blood on the vase or the satin. And then the door to the room slams shut, then open again, and the dream ends before any sense can be made of anything.

Stephen wakes to the sound of his apartment door opening, and notices that he has a dreadful taste of soured wine all over his tongue. He looks at Graham entering the room and says, "If we're going to fuck again this morning, I really need to brush my teeth."

Day Twenty-Three—Tk'emlups—Wednesday, October 24

Stephen arrived on campus almost two hours early the next day. Jeffrey was waiting by his office door.

"Do you have time to meet. I need to talk to you."

"Um, yes, for a short time. I have to sort through the assignments handed in yesterday. I can give you yours now if you like."

Stephen places his backpack on his desk and begins to alphabetize the assignments according to the students' names. Jeffrey's is on top. Stephen hands it to him without making eye contact. He keeps staring down at the pile of paper.

"You wanted to speak to me about something?"

Jeffrey stands to the left of the desk, by the window. The door is half opened, and as he takes his assignment from Stephen, he pushes the door closed. Stephen immediately, but casually, walks over and reopens the door.

"The air's better with the door open. It gets very stuffy in here."

They both sit down.

"Sir."

"I thought we had discussed that, Jeffrey. You've started calling me *sir* again."

"Yeah, uh, okay. Sorry. Stephen. It just feels like the right thing to do. Anyway, I came to apologize about the poem."

As Stephen begins to speak, Jeffrey becomes fidgety.

"Why would you do that? No need to apologize. It's an interesting piece. Splendid use of the actual words I used when I first described the assignment in class. Very clever of you, and cheeky, perhaps. I did look at it more carefully last night, and I think I was right. There are some narrative leaps that you could work on, and some of the metaphors float around, without context. You may want to reconsider the ice cream cone symbol. Unless you developed it further. In fact, it could be a much longer piece."

Stephen takes the handwritten copy of the poem Jeffrey gave him in class and begins to point to tiny red squiggles he made on the page the night before.

"After the swirl/curl couplet, for example, when you leave a space before the din/sin pearls/girls stanza, this is where the major narrative leap occurs, creating an abrupt transition. You might consider a connecting line or two at this point. The way the speaker moves into an intimate narrative voice from a somewhat detached assessment of the subject being described is quite disarming. The movement toward a first-person account of not hearing the *brackish din* and then the speaker's interest in girls. This is another example of a jarring leap that might be softened and explicated with a further line or two."

Stephen pauses, looks up, and notices that Jeffrey seems to be holding back tears forming ever so slightly in the corner of his left eye. But undaunted by a display of emotion, he continues.

"And, yet, Jeffrey, as I read this over, it occurs to me that what I call these abrupt leaps may very well be effective contrasts that create dramatic tension. And the final metaphor of snow comes out of nowhere, but again, this may very well be an effective use of unexpected imagery in order to punctuate the end of the poem. I take back everything I've said. It's a perfect poem as is."

Jeffrey wipes his eye and interjects.

"I want to start over. I could have something new to you by tomorrow."

"Well, it's up to you. But you did follow the exercise well, and as you've just heard me say, my repeated readings of the poem give me a different perspective each time."

"It's not just about you."

"What?"

"I wrote it about Lily, and a friend of ours. I wrote it after seeing you on the trail, when I was with Lily. Her situation, right now, is difficult, and I wanted to write about that, but couldn't, so I sublimated it and used some of your affectations to cover what I was feeling about her, and about Ben, our new friend. I think I wrote it too quickly."

"Her situation?"

"She's going through a lot, but I seem to be more upset than she is."

"Then perhaps you should have written about something different."

"I had to write about it, and I'm sorry if it upset you."

"No need to worry. I'm fine. It was a little startling, but it's poetry. It should be startling. You have a knack, a way with poetry, beyond your years. Despite the slightly effemnaphobic objectifying tone."

"Effeminaphobic? What does that mean?"

"When you draw attention to the sibilance, to my lips, my effeminate ways, well, it is an objectifying cliché."

"I'm sorry."

"No need. You still managed to create a sympathetic tone in the third verse, and the final lines, the way you separated them from the repeated four-line structure, with the spacing at the end, was effective, jarring in an open-ended way that leaves the reader with a question."

"A question, sir?"

"A question about how the speaker actually feels about the subject when they hit the ground, and melt, like snow. Unlike the ice cream cone metaphor, which is almost silly perhaps, the snow metaphor is simple and direct. So, enough academic critique. Has Lily decided whether she is going to drop the course?"

"No, I don't think so. I haven't talked to her since we saw you on the trail yesterday. Look, she's really pissed off at me for being an asshole. She left me for someone else, our mutual friend. Some fucking friend. She thinks I should be more mature about it. And she's having an abortion."

"And she left you for someone else. Oh, for the love of Mary! Jeffrey, you're just full of private information, aren't you? I don't need to know this, and I'm not sure you should be telling me."

"I don't want her to."

"Please, Jeffrey, this isn't something I can talk to you about. There are counsellors. But you know, it is her body. Not yours."

"I saw a counsellor, here on campus. She was a nightmare. She went all pro-life Christian on me but claimed she didn't mean it that way."

"It wasn't Doctor, damn, whatsername."

"I don't remember her name, the one who always seems to be at the campus clinic? I think they're understaffed. Very serious, long brown hair, wears it up sometimes. She lives with the yoga instructor. She's no Christian, and no therapist. She used to be one."

"She still gives unwanted advice. Yeah, it was her all right. I had a bit of a run-in with her myself. She is well intended, but sometimes says the wrong thing. You could find someone else, off campus."

"I'd rather talk to you."

"I'm sorry, it wouldn't be appropriate, especially when it's about another student as well. And it's much too personal. I'm not qualified to advise you on something like this."

"I get it. You're right. I just wanted you to know that there's nothing in that poem that I think is true."

"Well, of course it's true fiction, semi-fiction. Don't apologize again. We're over that."

"I'm surprised you liked the poem at all. I felt like an idiot reciting in class. I was really angry with Lily, and I just lashed out in the poem for no reason. I was angry at everything. And you were so nice to us, supportive, it made me pissed off at you too. So I thought I'd write something, from my notes, and read it to embarrass you, but you weren't phased at all.

"Oh, it phased me, Jeffrey. I was hiding my embarrassment. I have, rest assured, been officially phased, and embarrassed for both of us. I need to do some work now."

Stephen opened the door wide and gestured for Jeffrey to leave.

"If Lily comes back to class. It might be weird for me."

"Jeffrey, before you go."

"Yes, sir. Sorry, Stephen."

"Do you have mild seasonal allergies?"

"Yeah, I do. People always think I'm about to cry." He turned to leave.

"Jeffrey. Please, believe me. I'm telling you the truth. It really is splendid, a poem about a human snowflake, and in the midst of a lot of other emotion I am flattered. Yes, it made fun of me, but the fact is, I am a snowflake, I do swirl, I do melt. And I love snowflakes. You even managed to get the lazy tongue in, a term I have been fond of ever since being forced to take speech therapy as a child. It really wasn't mocking, Jeffrey, but creates a necessary tension in the poem, and you and Lily are very good at creating necessary tension in the classroom. I'm sorry you're not together any longer."

Jeffrey smiled, wiped his right eye, and left the room. Stephen sat down at his desk, put his head in his hands, and struggled against the urge to weep. Then the door abruptly opened again, Jeffrey standing there.

"Are you okay, sir? Stephen?"

"I'm fine, Jeffrey. What is it now?"

"I forgot my backpack."

Stephen reached to the side of his desk, toward the floor, where the backpack was lying, as Jeffrey bent over to pick it up. Their hands touched. Jeffrey clutched Stephen's palm, wouldn't let it go, and then he kicked the nearby door shut with his heel and moved closer to his professor. The heavy slam of the door broke a mood that had only seconds to last. They looked at each other. Stephen moved back, and Jeffrey moved forward. All that might have happened did not. Stephen pulled his hand from Jeffrey's, and said in a reassuring voice, "No, Jeffrey. No. Whatever this is, it can't happen. Please leave." Jeffrey tried to move closer, but Stephen walked around to the side of his desk, stood by the door, and gestured for his student to go.

"I'm sorry, sir. Dr. Davis. I'm really sorry."

"It's okay, Jeffrey. Talk to Lily. Work things out. Be mature. If she doesn't want to be with you, then be her friend, see her through this. Let her make her own decisions, support her. To put it bluntly, grow up. I never wanted to, but I did. Just a few weeks ago."

The minute he saw the last of Jeffrey walking down the corridor, a surprising lift and lightness to his gait, Stephen started to cry. He couldn't stop. He composed himself as much as he could, long enough to call the office and say that he had to cancel his class, he was ill. Then he called a cab and went home, had a stiff drink, and went to sleep.

As he fell asleep, just before four o'clock in the afternoon, the rusting shopping cart in the back yard started to sob, picking up where Stephen had left off just before he shut his eyes. Like a sad little cage, a four-wheeled receptacle for material needs, meant to be pushed through the aisles of stores jammed with stuff. Now of no use at all, rusting in the back yard of a heritage house overlooking one of the most calming views in Canada, where two strands of the same river met.

9 a.m.—Tkaronto—LAUNDRY

It was 9:15. Graham rolled over and rested his head on
Stephen's chest. Then he started to squeeze Stephen's nipple,
taking Stephen's left palm and guiding Stephen's fingers
toward his own nipple. Then he fell face forward onto the
little areola tinged with light hair. Graham was a nipple man.
Liked to twist his own and others to the edge of rough, erotic
satisfaction. Luckily, this was right up Stephen's alley. So when
they woke again, they twisted and writhed and let out little
moans and kissed in spite of the need for a good brushing.
And they happily thrust their hips against each other, and
lo and behold, they came at the same time. Real live dirty
sexy synchronized love between naps. A middle-aged homo
and an early-forty-something soon-to-be-falsely-known-as-
criminal—in love. They had met between a lobby that looked
like a cemetery and a robin's-egg-blue laundry room with
a big rectangular folding table that reminded Stephen of a
dissecting platform in a morgue, even though he had never
been in a morgue. When there were a lot of people in the
laundry room, he found himself thinking of Rembrandt's *The
Anatomy Lesson of Doctor Nicolaes Tulp*, and for some reason,
he always wanted to call him Doctor Tulip.
The Anatomy Lesson of Doctor Tulip
Yes, it was love, and there was going to be laundry.
Doctor Tulip, doing his laundry, at the morgue.

Day Twenty-Four—Tk'emlups—Thursday, October 25

Stephen slept until four the next morning, and spent the next four hours in a heavy-headed daze, showering, having a light breakfast, getting dressed, and heading for the campus to do some grading before the postcolonial literature class. He walked along the trail, letting the air fill his lungs in a futile attempt to wipe away the effects of the pills that were having their way with him long after the actual dosage had been consumed. Falling asleep in his office chair within half an hour of getting settled, he woke up two hours later to the sound of knocking on his door. He lifted his face from the stack of papers on his desk and went to the door. She looked startled when she saw him.

"What is it, Lily?"

"Did you know that you have a huge red spot in the middle of your forehead, sir?"

Stephen went over to the small mirror by the door and had a look. He walked back to his chair, sat down and gave the surface of the desk a quick scan, finding the indelible culprit beneath a bludgeoned stack of papers. The marker he had been using for grading lay in a small puddle of red ink which had begun to leak, and wedged between a stack of papers and his forehead, had begun to seep through, leaving a circular spot the size of a quarter on his flesh.

"Well, this is just great. What is it, Lily. We need to make this quick. I have to try and remove this before class."

"It's okay, sir, we can talk later. I just wanted to let you know that Jeffrey told me everything, how amazing you were with him. We've worked things out, thank you for giving him some cool advice. I've decided to come back to class next week. We both are. But one thing. Can we do a long poem together, and we'll make it clear who wrote what lines, and where we've collaborated? It's about a threesome we had, and how it became a duet."

"Um. Great. Sure. Yeah. Go for it. Sounds fun. Sorry, I'm distracted. I have to find something to get this off."

"I have some wet wipes in my purse, sir, if you'd like to try that."

"Thanks, Lily, that would be great. Very kind of you to offer."

He took a wet wipe from Lily's hand and directed it toward his forehead.

"I'll just leave them with you. I can get them back another time."

"Thank you, I'll see you soon."

The wet wipes didn't work. They just helped to fade the colour. Like so many things, they worked, and they didn't work. He put a cap on his head and went to class, forgetting that today was the day Ms. Landry would be there to talk and take questions about Sara Suleri's autobiographical, postcolonial text *Meatless Days*. And that Jeffrey had signed up for a brief presentation on Forster's "The Story of a Panic."

When Stephen got to the classroom, Jeffrey wasn't there yet. Ms. Landry was wearing a soft pink sari and elaborate drop earrings. Stephen felt a strange zealotry as he gazed at the delicate hues and folds of her dress. Pulling himself out of a jealous trance, he introduced her. She spoke clearly and directly to her students.

"I like to call this presentation, *Muddled*."

As she spoke, a succession of PowerPoint images, mostly of women of diverse origins, some of men, faded in and out across a screen at the front of the room, quotations from Forster and Suleri beneath them.

She went on for close to forty-five minutes, referring to other writers whose faces flashed on the screen behind her, entertaining the odd question here and there, with no break in the succession of images of men and women she had so carefully compiled. A parade of literary celebrities and theorists added visual force to her enthusiastic words. Suleri, Forster, Said, Fanon, Spivak, even a brief shot of Gloria Steinem in a Playboy Bunny outfit at one point.

Nearing the end of the seminar, Stephen's forehead became itchy from the baby wipes. Half forgetting about the mark on his skin he took his hat off and began to rub the spot between his eyebrows and the top of his head, and remembered suddenly, from the follow-up information the yoga instructor had distributed after her class, that this was almost precisely the spot where the bindi is placed, the sixth chakra, ajna, representing hidden wisdom.

Not wanting anyone to see this accidental symbol, he lightly scratched the spot, taking his fingers away when he felt a warm damp sensation, and noticing from his reddened fingertips that he had drawn his own blood. He put his cap back on as the class came to a close, wiped his bloodied fingers with one of the wipes Lily had given him, thanked Ms. Landry, and abruptly left the building.

As he hurried across campus, out the main entrance to Old Main, across the parking lot and over the grassy area once covered in huge evergreens, cut down after the menacing hunger of the pine beetle, all Stephen could think of was the trail he would take when he came to the fork, the fork he had noticed but never explored, always opting for the most direct route home.

On his way to campus, there was never time to deviate to paths that veered from the northern prong leading to Nicola Wagon Road. The other part of the trail seemed to go, from his restricted vantage point, downwards toward a rocky stream and a series of cave-like structures, too small for humans to get into, and without any noticeable vegetation around them. When he reached this point, gazing into the descending dust of the wayward path, he noticed tiny flickers of orange tape, attached to small wooden stakes. Was someone actually planning to claim this landscape and ruin his favourite site? Ever since discovering this hilly, unmanageable terrain, he thought that its steep, craggy inaccessibility protected it from the cul-de-sacs and monster homes claiming softer patches of monumentally inclined land. But apparently not.

He sat down by a large tumbleweed, politely said hello, patted its unruly mane, and squatted on his backpack, using it as a makeshift cushion. Removing a slim volume from the pack, he leafed through the piñata-like pages of the book, marked with colourful post-it notes. Finding a passage he especially liked, about landscape, he started to reread underlined sections from Forster's "The Story of a Panic." Surrounded by unblemished nature, the words of the story mirrored Stephen's disgust for urban sprawl.

All the poetry is going from Nature . . . Everywhere we see the vulgarity of desolation spreading . . . If you take the commercial side of landscape, you may feel pleasure in the owner's activity. But to me the mere thought that a tree is convertible into cash is disgusting.

There was a chill in the air, and Stephen stood, placed the volume in his backpack, slung its heavy carcass over his shoulders, and headed toward the same old fork, with snowflakes falling, scattered but promising to engorge themselves into pockets of air more fulsome than those lightly hitting his nose as he plodded toward home.

Rushing up the stairs to the house, his powder-blue cast almost tripping him on the damp wooden porch, Stephen changed his pace just long enough to stand amazed, looking out at the increasing body of the snowfall as it grew heavier and heavier, covering his sweater in a light frosty layer. Wallowing in self-indulgent metaphoric poetic jargon, he could not help but fancy himself one giant aging snowflake, borne of many convoluted social and scientific measures, only hitting the ground once the required weight of water, and heaven allowed—and then, perhaps, melting. He wanted to make a snow angel, but thought better of it.

As he opened the door and entered the house, he remembered Jeffrey's snowflake poem, and their thwarted encounter. He had a drink, wrote a new poem, with the aid of his trusty thesaurus, then went to bed.

flaking

waking to different forms   *his solid gait*
becoming snow

from gaseous to frozen   *needing robust pockets*

a sullied ego moist enough to   *hide threatening*
warmth
                  beneath the cold

as condensed moisture   *manhandled tears*
                            become

shrouds that

mimic mincing clouds

he must grow larger—heavier   *to survive*

to reach the ground as snow

though happy he seems sad

low on undiscerned horizon

storms slurred as full-grown snowflakes pattern

push among young blossoms flushed in airy pressure

flakes who know the summer winter spring and fall

the warmth and chill that damp limp dance

we swirl we end we glow

                                   —DR SAD

10 a.m.—Tkaronto—Vase

The phone rang as they were eating strawberries out of each other's crotches. Stephen had one of those old answering machines where you could hear the caller leaving the message. It was Irene.

"Hello, darling. I need to borrow that big American flag I left in your storage closet. There's a Halloween brunch today, and I need a costume. I'll wrap it around myself like a sari. I'll be by before noon to pick it up. Have you seen the news yet? Wow, your co-op was certainly a gruesome Halloween site last night. I hope you weren't too bothered. And a tube of toothpaste? What a silly costume. Poor dear."

Stephen was neck deep in the valley of iconic red fruit and heard none of the message. A fulsome strawberry bounced against his Adam's apple as he sucked away. After devouring the fruit, his mouth eventually descended on Graham's cock, moving rapidly to the base of the shaft, with a morsel of strawberry sliding down his chin and onto the purple sheets. He didn't hear any of the message. Graham heard it all. He jumped up, almost injuring Stephen's jaw, apologized, held Stephen's face between red stained cheeks in his palms and kissed him.

"She's coming over before noon, your friend I met last night, she just left a message while you were blowing me. You give terrific head by the way. I better shower and get outta here."

"It's okay, she'll only be here a few minutes. Stay. If you'd like to."

"Yeah. I'd like to. But I'm seeing the kids this afternoon. I need to go home and change."

"Okay. Will I see you later?"

"Sure. That would be great."

After Graham had showered and left, Stephen took the vase from the cabinet built into the night table beside his bed and held it his hands. He wanted to get rid of the object badly, but loved it so much. He set it on the bed, resting against the purple pillowcase, and got up to pee. When he came out of the bathroom, he forgot that the vase was there, and pulled the strawberry-stained sheets from his bed so he could throw them in the laundry basket on the balcony.

Finally, it was broken. After over eighty years of uninterrupted objectified living. A perfect porcelain vessel his father had brought home from school as a six-year-old. It was ruined. Stephen tried to cry. But as hard as he tried, just like in that song from *A Chorus Line*, he felt nothing.

Day Twenty-Five—Tk'emlups—Friday, October 26

*The origins of the telephone date back to the non-electrical
string telephone—the "lover's telephone"—that has been known
for centuries, comprising two diaphragms connected by a taut
string or wire. Sound waves are carried as mechanical vibrations
along the string or wire from one diaphragm to the other.*

—Wikipedia

*One of the first shopping carts was introduced on June 4, 1937,
the invention of Sylvan Goldman, owner of the Piggly Wiggly
supermarket chain in Oklahoma City . . . The invention did
not catch on immediately. Men found them effeminate; women
found them suggestive of a baby carriage. "I've pushed my
last baby buggy," an offended woman informed Goldman.
After hiring several male and female models to push his new
invention around his store and demonstrate their utility, as
well as greeters to explain their use, shopping carts became
extremely popular and Goldman became a multimillionaire.*

—Wikipedia

The blinking light on the telephone was mute, the ringer
turned off. It tried to scream out in the night, found itself
without a voice. But the empathic shopping cart could hear
it, rusting away in the snow, corrosion lines gathering across
its formerly glistening, now dull, exposed surfaces. For an
inanimate object to be so disappointed by its new owner, and
so unexpectedly, took a great deal of unconscious neglect
on the owner's part. Had there been a wheelchair ramp, the

cart's urge to make its way into the house and up the stairs to Stephen's bedroom in order to alert him to the ringing telephone might have been more insidious—more Stephen King-like. Both the shopping cart and the telephone loved Stephen Davis, with a vengeance. Stephen was the only one in the house to answer their inanimate call. They had no choice.

But the idea of two crazed objects, a mute telephone and a lame shopping cart, was of no help to someone fast asleep and dreaming of falling headlong into a bottomless pit with a rag doll inches away from his outstretched fingertips. Indeed, the slumbering consumer was of no help to frustrated, sympathetic objects privy to human frailty but with no truly independent way to respond. All they could do was provide assistance, part of someone's routine. But they were wholly dependent on the person's physical presence to do so. Stephen was not emotionally available to his retail purchases. Nor was he present in the life of either object, especially his recently acquired second-hand cart.

He turned the telephone off every night before bedtime, and paid no attention whatsoever to the dying buggy, fully exposed to the elements, beside the house. Living indoors and shielded from climate concerns, the telephone was, for the most part, used to frequent neglect. People, rebellious and inattentive, tried to free themselves from technology, but eventually returned to the handset in one form or another. Being young, and having spent a substantial period of its early life in a cardboard box in a service outlet, Stephen's telephone had ahistorical concerns that were largely introverted and unfettered by any sense of camaraderie with like-minded objects. Most telephones of the private residential kind lived alone in single rooms, by themselves, with little to no thought of their kin. But Stephen's shopping cart was older, and used to a more communal existence.

As part of the breed of innovative hinged carts invented by Oral Watson in 1946, nine years after Sylvan Goldman's more cumbersome, less agile rolling baskets, the newer models were able to conjoin at the rear end and form long sleek lines of metal retail warriors when they were not in use. They resembled troops of patient soldiers packed tightly into the nether regions of each other's rigid bodily formations. There they stood in historic iconicity, about to be thrown into the random race of grocery-mad domestic mercenaries—engineers of a sort.

Making its way to Value Village via a long convoluted narrative history, Stephen's neglected shopping cart had originally come from a large warehouse in a mammoth truck, packed tightly alongside other carts, interlocking in intimate rows with the interior of the main holding basket. These were rolling objects, soon unpacked, stored together in silvery lines of eager, identical metal helpers, to be used and abused and returned to their aisle and the cold internal warmth of brand-new acquaintances, leaving them with no sense of when they might meet again their first interlocking four-wheeled paramours.

All shopping carts were family, and they tried to stick together. Because they were bloodless, incest was not a concern. Telephones, on the other hand, couldn't care less about familial taboos. They had more kinship with flawed humanity, a means of advanced communication that allowed them to hear the intimate details of crisscrossing conversations without having to become fully involved. They, of course, were insanely jealous of the internet and despised Skype, but held their own as younger generations took part in the techno-frenzied world of cell phones, fully rejuvenated as postmodern communication warriors. What with the quivering, sci-fi promise of cellular implants and the six-axis piezoelectric accelerometer that would eventually replace the antiquated and germ-laden surface of the keypad, telephones were a never-ending wave of a never-ending future.

Shopping carts would come and go, yet they carried the very stuff of human sustenance. The shopping cart was socialist, needed more grassroots attention on a daily basis.

The telephone, on the other hand, although garnering praise for its surface pretense of socialist capacity, could be ignored for long periods of time without any harmful effect on nutritional value and the digestive tract. Implants, of course, could conceivably change the whole political bent of any given telephonic device, rendering the ear and accompanying lobe profoundly altered human appendages that no longer depended on flesh and blood detached from the mechanical gestures of an artificial invention. Objects and humans had long since become one.

Becoming part of Stephen's life, had, for the first time in the shopping cart's busy life, deprived it of exposure to a variety of people—human interaction—throughout the course of a single day. Stephen had changed that by buying it for his own personal use and then abandoning it after one Camaro-laden outing.

But morning had broken on October twenty-sixth, two thousand and seven, twenty-four days since his diagnosis, and he was in the mood for a bit of retail therapy at his favourite bargain emporium. In such a mood, and in such a hurry, he did not stop to check his messages on the way out of the house. The telephone felt a pang of regret. But the shopping cart had never been happier. Stephen took the cart with him to Value Village for a family outing.

Leaving the house at noon, they arrived back after a thorough stroll through every aisle in the bargain barracks, then a quick stop at a hardware store to pick up a tin of rust remover. The cart brimmed with useless treasures, all possessing lives of their own that would soon interlock with Stephen's. He was blighted by home décor, and Value Village fed his obsession.

He lugged the cart up the stairs of the verandah, almost twisting his unsheathed ankle, having given up on the walking cast days ago. He pulled the buggy backwards as it clomped up each step with a terrible grin, finally feeling included in its master's chaotic romp. Pulling the cart through the double doors to the dining room, Stephen let it drip the remnants of wet snow onto the carpet as he pulled off his boots and coat, and went to the basement to get an old blanket to place under the cart. After returning from the basement, he tipped the cart on its side onto the blanket, and let all his recently purchased bargain treasures slide out, spilling halfway onto the dampening floor by the fireplace. Stephen sat down cross-legged, and began to sort through his purchases, but not before taking the moth-eaten edges of a red mohair blanket and drying the moist sides of the cart. He was feeling protective of the four-wheeled object, having spent most of the night dreaming that he was in pursuit of a frenzied rag doll he would never catch. It was the nocturnal reoccurrence of a childhood dream that followed him into manhood, reminding Stephen that dolls had inhabited his early dreams and nightmares. Dolls, these miniature plastic creatures he held dear to his heart.

Objects were like people to him, although he never talked about that to anyone, for fear of being considered eccentric. Stephen had had the rag doll dream ever since he was a child. As an adult, he had it less frequently, only once or twice every couple of years. In his childhood he would have the dream twice a week, sometimes more often. He never told anyone, because he was embarrassed, as a boy, to be having nocturnal narrative emissions so dependent on an object that was restricted to what was considered the feminine imagination. A Freudian analysis of a fragile little boy having recurring dreams that involved falling into a bottomless pit after a rag doll was totally unnecessary. Long before he studied queer theory and postmodern revisionist tracts on early psychoanalysis, it was obvious to him that in his heart of hearts he secretly wished that the recurring dream would one day find him, feet planted firmly on solid earth, at the end of the shadowy tunnel with a rag doll in his arms, about to embark on a journey through a less fearsome, light-filled landscape, one that welcomed rag dolls and lisping boys.

After twenty minutes, Stephen had sorted everything from the cart onto the mantle: carved ducks, ceramic angels, brass candle holders, little plush monkeys, stone-carved turtles, and one singing trout with a repertoire of two ditties. One song the fish sang was about coming down to the river, and the other encouraged listeners to remain happy and not to worry. Stephen was worried. He hadn't pressed the button on the singing fish yet. It didn't come with batteries. So there had been no opportunity for the finned creature to slither and warble away, hoping that its new owner's wilted disposition would blossom and bloom. No such luck. Not even the tiny arrangement of blue silk roses sprouting from the mouth of a wicker rabbit could lift his spirits.

The previous day, what with both Lily and Jeffrey making an appearance, followed by Ms. Landry's distressing mélange of postcolonial servitude and dubious white female agency under British rule, not to mention the presence of a red circle on his forehead, had left Stephen frazzled, depressed, inconsolable, enraged, muddled. Retail therapy was the only answer. He needed to buy an assortment of kitsch door prizes for the student Halloween party/postcolonial literature seminar he had planned for the end of the month. The newly acquired menagerie of second-hand bric-a-brac littering the oak mantle in the dining room would serve. He even planned to serve po-co-mojtios in orange tumblers, with dark licorice as tasty swizzle sticks.

Stephen lifted the empty shopping cart back onto its four round feet, rolled it off the mohair blanket and closer to the fireplace. He then took the final item—an old Hudson's Bay

Blanket—out of the basket and unfolded it, placing it over the top of the empty cart as a gesture of melancholic object love. He was finally making amends for those days of inanimate abandonment. His plan was to use the rust remover as soon as the cart was empty, then give it a light cleaning with soap and water, wrap it in the second-hand Hudson's Bay blanket he had just bought, light a fire, sit by the cart in a cozy wingchair, and have a quiet evening staring impatiently into the flames as he sipped a shaker of fruity martinis. But the telephone had other plans.

As he turned away from the blanket and the silently purring cart, he began to fold the wet mohair over the banister to dry. Looking toward the stairway, he noticed the flashing light on the little table in the entryway, quickly walked over, picked up the phone. Everything changed.

"Uh, hi, Stephen. It's Dan. I am so sorry I didn't call earlier. I really want you to come up to the peaks this weekend, well, tonight, actually. I'll be in the city late afternoon until around seven. I'll swing by your place about seven-thirty, eight? I hope that's okay, and I hope you can come with me. It's been a chaotic week. I miss you."

The nerve of some presumptuous billionaires! But Stephen was delighted, pleasantly surprised. The Camaro pulled into the driveway at exactly half past seven. Stephen was packed and eager to rush out the door. He planned to throw his small suitcase in the back seat, jump casually into the passenger side, and then begin to seduce the driver before crossing the city limits, in preparation for the oral pleasure he hoped to lavish upon his recently acquired paramour. But Dan interrupted the flow of Stephen's fantasy by clicking open the trunk, jumping out of the driver's seat, grabbing the suitcase, giving Stephen a full-frontal kiss on the lips, and saying—

"I've got a surprise for you. I hope you're okay with it."

The back door opened as the trunk slammed shut, giving Stephen no time to respond, and out stepped an aging sushi surfer with a lovely young Japanese woman on his arm, followed by what seemed to be the light squeal of a baby from the interior of the elephant's asshole.

"Stephen, this is my son, Craig, and this is his fiancée, Amy. They came back with me, from Japan. They're getting married, earlier than planned, at the chalet tomorrow, and well, we really want you to be there."

They shook hands politely. Stephen got into the front seat, and Dan threw his arm around his shoulder and gave him a peck on the cheek

"It's just so great to see you!"

As the Camaro lurched menacingly out of the driveway, Dinah Washington began to sing on the CD player. Stephen fastened his seatbelt for a bumpy ride, and then discreetly popped a lemon-flavoured breath tablet, lightly laced with the neutral medicinal scent of a lone painkiller stuck to the side of the lozenge, into the middle of his mawkish smile. The unlikely foursome, with infant in tow, drove merrily along as Dinah Washington sang her haunting rendition of "This Bitter Earth."

11am—Tkaronto—SNOW

The frightful weather outside was unpleasant, although the evening and following hours had been delightful. It had turned cold overnight, and a light snow covered the rooftops. Stephen took the broken pieces of the vase and put them into a plastic bag, then went into the hallway to toss them into the garbage chute. He loved a garbage chute. So cathartic, so easy to dispose of what was unwanted. No going back. Although he did wonder what it would be like to jump down a garbage chute. He had a terrible fear of being trapped in enclosed spaces, and sometimes dreamt about it. Dreams could be a pain in the ass.

As he walked back to his apartment, the door at the end of the hallway opened, and his neighbour, whom he rarely saw, came stomping out, yelling—

"Who the fuck was that you had stay over last night? He climbed over my balcony partition, and we made out, and then he abandoned me."

Stephen started to laugh.

"But thanks for sharing, buddy, it was great fun. If he's ever available again, send him over."

Then he slammed his door shut.

What a fabulous loon. Stephen had almost forgotten about the incident in the night. So much had happened. His dream about the "Dying Well" performance piece had taken energy, and then there was the sex and more sex, and the strawberry crotch eating, and Irene coming over before noon to pick up the patriotic costume prop, and it was eleven already.

Where the fuck was that flag? He couldn't find it.

As he rooted through the storage closet in the hall, he suddenly remembered the plastic storage bin on the balcony.

He went out to the balcony and grabbed the bin with the flag, turned back toward the door, and there was Irene. She had let herself in with her key. He went to open the door, and she pulled it shut, laughing, then turned the lock.

"I'm in my bare feet for Christ's sake. Open it!"

She waited a few seconds, then pushed the door open, and he scurried in.

"It's fucking frigid out there."

"Lovely to see you too. Do you have the flag?"

"It's in here."

He opened the bin in the middle of the living room floor and there it was, lightly marked by patches of blue'ish mildew and stinking to high heaven.

"Shit. It's a mess!"

"Damn, I am so sorry. This doesn't usually happen. I store stuff out there all the time."

"Well. I'll just have to cut it in half. It's too big for a sari anyhow."

"You can't cut it in half. That will ruin it. And it's smelly. I can wash it for you."

The laundry was not busy, so it only took forty-five minutes, thirty in the wash and fifteen in the dryer.

Irene dressed in the bathroom, the flag draped and tied in strategic places. She looked like a patriotic pile of red, white, and blue fabric, covered in big stars, surrounding her body in knots and layers and folds.

"Well, wish me luck, darling. There's going to be a hopelessly attractive fellow at the brunch, that I've been dying to fuck, and I know he wants me, and I am on the rebound, so it's bound to be delightful. Maybe I can get him to finger me by the vending machine between courses."

Stephen kissed her goodbye as she left. She smiled, turned, and bounced out the door. Not a good sign. When there was lightness in her step, it meant she was trying too hard to be happy although she was in fact sad. Amalfi had been a disaster. Maybe the brunch would cheer her up.

Day Twenty-Six—Sun Peaks—Saturday, October 27

The wedding ceremony was held on the deck. The mess of footprints from the small group gathered to hear the nuptials appeared as a series of human webs, disharmonious song lines, malicious scars on the freshly fallen flakes covering the cedar planks of a summer patio. If one were standing at the top of the mountain, looking downward, the wedding guests would appear to be indistinguishable specks on a whitened landscape, with a smaller group of pale pink gathered around a single black speck, and the outlines of a more bulbous white speck beside him, tapered at the waist and flaring out into a bell shape. That's what tuxedoes, pink bridesmaids' dresses, and a wedding gown looked like from an elevated distance.

Given the time of day, just before dusk, it occurred to Stephen, as he watched the conjugal proceedings, that a less traditional gown might have been more appropriate, something suggesting the sophisticated black-tie requirements set out by the father of the groom. Stephen had no idea his new queer macho boyfriend was a closet wedding planner. Dan had even taken care of Stephen's wedding attire, without consulting with him.

"Stephen, I hope you don't mind, but I took the liberty of buying you a tuxedo and a formal overcoat. We'll only be outside for about twenty minutes, for the ceremony, and I really, I wanted the photos to be perfect, with everyone in black and only spots of colour from the wedding party to stand out, with the white of the bride's ensemble as an ethereal glow in the midst. I designed the colour scheme myself. I'm putting the chalet up for sale next month and thought I could use the photos for a real estate brochure, show off the versatility of the place. Amy chose her dress, of course, even though I made a few suggestions. I think you'll agree, a sleek, more elegant cut—strapless—would have suited her, with her black hair in a simple upsweep. She's slimmed right down. She would have looked stunning in something a little less traditional. But I suppose it was appropriate to let her choose her own gown. I did get to pick the colour and style of the bridesmaids' dresses, though. I think you'll agree when you see them that I made a good choice. And when all is said and done, the fuller, more traditional sweep of Amy's gown will appeal to conservative tastes when they see the photos on the real estate pamphlet. It could be a selling point. Perhaps I'll call it *An Eastern Cinderella in the Western Mountains*. Maybe not."

Dan seemed decidedly more gay than Stephen had ever seen him. Weddings appeared to bring out the diva in him.

The sound of the snow-making equipment gave the event a slightly military tone, with dashes of the apocalypse thrown in as the mechanical noises interfered with the ceremonial music. Mixed with the string quartet's amplified accompaniment of the pastor's words and the couple's nuptials was a buzz that provided a dissonant foundation for the surprising melody the musicians were playing. And once all of the words had been spoken, and the couple had kissed, lightly, without passion, a young male vocalist began to sing the theme song from *The Young and the Restless*. The lyric waxed poetic, in a somewhat vapid way, on love that moved as quickly as youth and ended abruptly with only memories left to ponder as one grew older. The infant the bride and groom had appeared with was nowhere to be seen.

The subtle, slightly bemused way the guests responded to the lyrics fascinated Stephen, the small grins and puzzled nods that people gave each other as the verses progressed. The young singer appeared somewhat uncomfortable, but made his way through the entire song without flinching.

Much later that evening, Dan explained that the baby was being taken care of by friends in a nearby chalet, to be returned after the festivities ended. He didn't feel that a child born out of wedlock would suit the tone of the brochure he was designing for the real estate agency.

"The song was Craig's idea. He and Amy have a strange sense of humour, and they insisted. They used to watch the soap opera it was the theme song for, together, when they were at university. The melody is lovely, but why they had to insist upon a vocalist, I will never know. He's a skiing buddy of Craig's. Otherwise, I think it was a perfect day."

As he lay in the king-sized bed of the master suite, listening to Dan ramble on about how the day had gone, Stephen's legs began to twitch. It was a sensation he had experienced only once before, six months ago. The description of his condition fascinated Stephen. He loved technical writing's cold poetic air, its smouldering undertone of passionate feeling. With a little online research, he discovered restless legs syndrome (RLS), or Willis-Ekbom disease, a neurological disorder characterized by an irresistible urge to move one's body in order to stop uncomfortable or odd sensations. As he lay awake, old and restless, his legs trembled, and his head reeled from the memory of a truly surreal mountain wedding.

Stephen listened to Dan ramble on until just before three, and then he had an idea.

"Would you mind if I just went for a quick swim, on my own. It's been such a wonderful busy day, and I just need to relax with a few laps, and then I'll be able to sleep, and be all ready for the wedding brunch tomorrow."

"I could come with you."

"That would be nice, but I think we both know what that could lead to. But of course, come with me, we can do a few laps, then come back to bed."

"No, go on your own. I understand. I'll be awake when you get back, eagerly awaiting your return. And then maybe, a little nightcap, so to speak?"

"Sounds wonderful."

When he did return, ninety minutes later, the bedside lamp was off, and Dan appeared to be sleeping. Just as Stephen was about to fall asleep himself, he felt a strong gentle grip on his genitals and the slow fulsome movement of Dan's body as it edged toward him. Their chests met and their lips touched as they relaxed into a sensual embrace they had shared only a few times since their first meeting only sixteen days before. It seemed right, like an old pair of slippers or a favourite cotton robe, with benefits.

The dominant sub-sensation against Stephen's lower torso, commingling as a contrast to the tactile excitement of the thick hair that covered Dan's full chest and swirled menacingly around his large, hardened areolas, was the feeling of a smooth fabric. The soft pinkish bulb of the bedside lamp shed enough of a glow for Stephen to see, when they began to roll among the bed sheets, that Dan was wearing a low cut negligee, triple x, a light pink, the colour of the bridesmaids' gowns, with tubular spaghetti straps that slipped down his shoulders as the sex became more strident, fierce but tender. Without flinching, between agile acrobatic maneuvers, Dan whispered in Stephen's ear,

"There's another one over there, on the wingchair, for you, if you'd like to put it on."

As seamlessly as his lover had made the offer, Stephen slipped out of bed and slipped the crafted, silky fabric on, then slid back under the covers. Just before getting back into bed, as he pulled the attire toward his shoulders, the hem grazed the backs of sled-pulling creatures represented on the throw folded neatly over the right arm of the chair. After moving back into Dan's arms as though nothing of any consequence had changed, except for the addition of one more heavenly clad body, his legs began to twitch again.

The thrill of yet another coincidence on this strange day was second only to the lightheaded sensation that they both had wings, identical imported wings, designer wings in the form of expensive lingerie. Cuddling in the faintly chlorinated afterglow of repeated sexual synchronicity, replete with gender-bending accessories, Dan and Stephen slept like friendly logs in drag. And the newlyweds, comfortable in twin beds in the lavishly decorated guestroom on the first floor, slept with their very separate dreams of how their lives would proceed, given the unorthodox nature of the arrangement the father of the groom had so meticulously devised.

12 p.m.—Tkaronto—LAMP

It was a dark day. Stephen had the lamp in the window on
as he sipped wine, just before noon. He was having only one
glass, to celebrate his new love. The lamp flickered and went
out. He looked across the city, toward the square where the
giant screens advertised films and lotteries and banks and
concerts. The screens were blank and dark. The power had
gone off.

But Graham would be back by six. He'd texted to say so,
and he was bringing pizza and more wine. If the power didn't
return, he would have to walk ten flights. Stephen had given
him a key. Already.

The apartment would be chilly by six. But Graham could
keep him warm. Stephen pulled a duvet out of the closet and
lay down on the homo-sectional, stretching out and pouring
himself one more glass.

As he slept, the lamp came back on, and the screens in the
square advertising everything from travel deals to tooth decay
blasted back to life.

Plans had changed. Their mother was pissed off and
wouldn't let Graham take the kids to the CN tower. So Graham
was returning earlier than expected, in the stairwell of the
fifth floor, around 12:45, when the power regained. He had
his keychain flashlight when the lights came back on. He
walked out the door to the fifth floor and toward the elevator.
When the elevator door opened, he was startled by two police
officers.

"Hello, officers. Oh, you're going down. I'm going up."

"Could we ask you a few questions first?"

"Sure, uh, I don't live here, though. Just visiting. What can
I tell you?

"Well, first of all, you can tell us how you got that blood on the collar of your shirt."

Day Twenty-Seven—Sun Peaks—Sunday, October 28

Pitchers of hot raw cacao punch and crystal bowls of Mountain Berry crumble everywhere, and bannock, and sour cream donuts topped with thick warm syrup, and the lightest, loveliest lemon ice in the cutest little dishes, hand painted in Portugal, those tiny two-compartment type dishes, with one concave porcelain fold for the primary foodstuff and a smaller, conjoined bowl for the sweet condiment, in this case maple syrup from a hot yoga fitness centre where the happy couple planned to spend their honeymoon before returning to Japan.

Heavy on the desserts, and opening with small tasty portions of porcini mushroom, roasted garlic fondue in large brass vessels, with small shallow bowls of Alpine mushroom chowder placed close to tiny individual baskets of bannock flanked by bowls of Yukon gold potatoes, alongside overflowing platters of cold smoked salmon sprinkled with red onions, capers, arugula tufts, radish rosebuds, horseradish chive, crème fraîche, and artisan bread. An impressive dining table in the main room of the soon-to-be-sold family chalet. Surrounded by a selection of guests who had spent the night at the nearby Hearthstone Lodge, all gathered together for a post wedding brunchy-like linner, competing with sinner and lupper for silly revisionist words for a meal. It had been carted to the premises in horse drawn sleds, with wheels, since there wasn't enough snow at the base. But it was cold enough for some energy-efficient snowmaking to blanket one gently cascading intermediate run, privately opened in order to accommodate the wedding party and seventeen random guests for a quick shoosh down the mountainside after a hefty late morning meal.

As Stephen nibbled, he wondered whether it was all a lavishly catered recipe for disaster. Everything was happening so fast. The sensation of flying down the side of the mountain after a cozy chairlift ride alongside Dan was exhilarating, if not a little disorienting. As if the lingerie had not been enough. Dan had equipment ready and waiting, the right size ski boots, tasteful outerwear in earth tones, sleek fitting goggles, a lovely tan turtleneck, and matching gloves. Even the ski poles were colour coordinated. Everything had been put together to include Stephen in this over the mountaintop family gathering, and in short order, with such love and consumerist affection.

The chairlift swung, fake snowflakes swirling into nature's compromised complexion. Dan looked at Stephen and said, through the chilly air—

"How did you like my little surprise last night?"

"The lingerie? I loved it."

"I thought you might."

"What made you think that?"

"Well, I have a sixth sense about some things. We seem to have a lot in common."

"We do. It's uncanny. The stuff of cheesy romance fiction."

"Then let's make it fact."

"What do you mean?"

"What I mean is, I think the next time there's a celebration like this, it should be for the two of us. Whaddaya think of that?"

Suppressing a mixture of both horror and delight was a specialty of Stephen's. He looked at Dan, both of them shrouded in expensive winter wear—in a sense, ski drag— their faces masked by sleek two hundred-dollar goggles, and he smiled.

"It's kind of quick, but yeah, it's a wonderful idea. Romantic."

And then they kissed, or at least tried to, as their hard-plastic visors collided, allowing only the edges of their lower lips to brush against each other as their tongues tried to engage. But the man-made wintry buzz and whir of the spidery snow guns lining the sides of the slope beneath them had their way, spouting waves of frosty mist, becoming snow, interrupting the impetuous meeting of same-sex oral fissures in the midst of stolen environs lightly blanketed in the outrageous splendour of an artificial winterish wonderland.

Craig and his new wife looked on, bemused and estranged, swinging gently in the chairlift behind the father, and soon to be step *mother* of the groom, smiling sweetly for the sake of conjugal convention, all the time thinking of their upcoming retreat, destination Asia, from this over-orchestrated Western gathering.

And as they fantasized about their very separate plans for the future, the object of the groom's affection, one angelic wedding singer, cradled the infant in the wingchair, in the master bedroom of the chalet, singing in a lovely countertenor, belying the lower registers he had chosen for the song selected by the newlyweds as postnuptial accompaniment the day before. Beside him sat a CD player emitting the subtle sounds of an ancient drumbeat as he sang

"Lavender Blue Dilly Dilly."

Indigenous drumbeats accompanying English folk tunes in the seventh year of the twenty-first century. Wedding parties swinging gently in the mist-laden air on October twenty-eighth two thousand and seven. The idea of originality being tested in the mountains on this pseudo-blissful day. Like the energy-efficient superficial layer of faux snow that would accumulate in the days to follow, becoming, in time, a full-blown blanket of crystallized condensation allowing the winter sports crowd to bask in the illusion of nature afforded them by complex webs of technology, colonialism, weather, and real estate strategies.

All of the world—a crowded stage. All the men and women in drag. Skiwear, negligees, drumbeats adorning melodies wrung from other cultures. Layer upon layer of raiment, social fabric. Similes caught in blizzards. Word storms weathering the onslaught of language ravaged by time and the forced strains of anglicizing intrusion.

Stephen smelled smoke. He jumped up from the couch and ran into the hallway. He'd left the goddamn light on again. Twice in twenty-four hours. He pulled open the door. It was a fire bigger than the last one, but small enough to contain. He ran into the kitchen, grabbed a pot from the stovetop, ran to the bathroom, filled the pot in the tub, and then over to the closet, threw it onto the flames. Extinguished quickly, before the fire set off the smoke alarm.

And then he came out of the closet.

There was a knock on the door.

No one knocked on the door. Not here. They had to be buzzed in from the lobby.

"Who is it?"

A man's voice from the other side of the door.

"It's the police. Could I speak with you? Mr. Davis."

Stephen opened the door, wanting to say, *Well, hello, officer.* Instead, he simply said, "Can I help you?"

"A friend of yours. Graham. He asked us to ask you to let us know where he was for the past several hours, since yesterday."

He lied, instinctively. Said Graham had been with him much longer than he actually had. The details didn't make sense. Graham wouldn't hurt a flea, or a tube of toothpaste. Stephen knew it. He instinctively knew it.

And besides, the toothpaste symbol was going nowhere. No metaphoric properties to speak of, and not the least bit sexy. They were going to have to come up with a far more original costume if he was going to believe any of this half-baked story of his lover having attacked an innocent tube of dentifrice on the roof garden late yesterday afternoon, when the sun was setting, near dusk, and the night was yearning for lovers.

And why? Because. Just fucking because, the night.

Day Twenty-Eight—Sun Peaks—Monday, October 29

Stephen's ankle was throbbing from the single run down the intermediate slope, and he had forgotten to bring his walking cast with him for support. He was covering the discomfort with the composed delirium of a mild painkiller high, and overcompensating for a slight limp that, under less stressful circumstances, he would have given in to, letting his gait fall into a wilted uneven pattern. But not in the presence of such tasteful company and elegant surroundings. He was following what seemed an unspoken directive regarding decorum and the proper way to behave during lavish wedding celebrations. He concealed his natural flamboyance, characteristics even Dan had not been privy to during the short time they had known each other. Characteristics he had left behind, for the most part, when he moved to Kamloops, although they were never far from the surface, especially when he was teaching poetry.

During the wedding festivities, he did not see Craig on his own, and exchanged only a few words with the bride. The intimacy between Stephen and Dan was a blanket that covered them both, and kept them warm at night, but during the day, among the guests, a soft, heavy chill hung in the air around them. Had they been further east, on the other side of the Rockies, the emotional tenor of the weekend might have been compared to a Chinook, strong gales of warmth between the frosty intimations of winter weather. It felt surreal, like time melting in a desert, like snow on a beach, like sands through a broken hourglass, life in an elongated, spidery fiction, anansi-like, arms and legs that could scale fictional constructions in a single bound. It's a bird! It's a plane! It's super fag!

When he did find himself confronted alone with Craig, the chill swiftly became frozen in time.

"Hi, how are you doing? Where's my dad?"

"Uh, he's still asleep. How's Amy, and the baby?"

"She's sleeping. The baby's with Kurt, the singer at the wedding. Did you meet him?"

"No, actually, we didn't meet. He's a lovely singer. Interesting choice of music. You left your child with the wedding singer?"

"Yeah, well, it's complicated. He took Danny out for a sleigh ride. I don't think there's enough snow, but he insisted."

You could cut the tension in the air with a wedding cake knife.

"Listen, I'll just say this quick. I respect you. And my dad and me, well, we've had our differences, and you and me, we both know what happened between us that night by the casino. So much just came thundering down on me in the following days, and I thought I'd reconnect with you when things calmed down. But, as you can see from this past weekend, they didn't exactly—calm down. They kind of boiled over. But just knowing that someone is making my dad happy is good enough for me. My mom's been gone a long time, and there've been so many changes, for both of us. But we've landed on our feet, my dad and me. And, now, well, it wouldn't make sense to bring any of it up, about our little meeting. So, I guess what I'm saying is, we don't have to address anything that happened, do we? Because, in a way, and I don't mean this as an insult, it was nothing, a sweet nothing. It was one brief precious little meeting. I wish you love, both of you. I have so much on my plate right now, and we're going back to Japan soon, the four of us, where we'll have to come up with some kind of plan to raise this child properly, whatever the hell that means."

"And the wedding singer? He's going with you?"

"It's a long story, but yes, we're almost together. I thought you might have noticed, and my dad doesn't really know the whole story, but he's probably suspicious. He's the kind of guy, you might have noticed, who doesn't bring it all out in the open right away, so if you could not tell him, I just spilled the beans to you, that Kurt's coming back with us. Shit, I have a big mouth. I met him when I left Oriental Gardens early and came up here. He's amazing. He knew my mom when he was a kid, and he works at Sun Peaks. He has a cousin who keeps trying to persuade him to stop working on stolen land. I get his fucking point, but he's an annoying bastard. It will be good for Kurt to get away from here."

"Your mom. Dan's never mentioned her. You did though."

"Yeah. The Alzheimer's movie, all that shit."

"It's okay. I don't really know your dad, or you of course, very well at all. But your secrets are safe with me, even the ones I don't know."

"Thank you. I appreciate it. Amy's cool about it all. As you can see, she's younger than me. She'll be fine, and she has her own stuff going on. Dad is really stepping up. I guess it's not surprising. He's a decent guy, and he told me he wants this to work with you, so telling him about us meeting, well, I don't think it would serve anyone in the grander scheme of things. You know all about that. And I know about both of you, and the HIV thing. It's cool. Sorry, you know what I mean. It's a perfect match, made in gay heaven, in so many weird ways."

"Yeah, I guess it is. I feel lucky to have met him."

"You really are a sweet guy. If things had been different. Fuck, what am I saying."

Craig gave Stephen a light kiss on the cheek, smiled, then turned and walked down the hallway toward the lap pool. Strolling casually through the chalet in mauve flip flops, with an orange and brown striped towel over his bare shoulders. The image would have been disarming at the best of times. But these were not the best of times. They were the weirdest of times, the most coincidental of times, and Stephen knew it was in his best interest to watch the son fade into shadows cast by the glass door leading to the change room. As it swung open, Craig turned briefly, smiled back at Stephen, and disappeared into the pool area. He wouldn't see him again that day. He and Amy, the baby, and the wedding singer, would be gone before breakfast, leaving a loving note for daddy, a note Dan would not find to his liking. He was furious when he told Stephen about it.

"Fuck! Well, sweetheart, I have to say, you're a lot more understanding than me. Those kids could have waited a bit longer and said goodbye, but I guess they were in a hurry. But we've made a lot of progress as father and son, in a short period of time. I only came out to him a year ago. He's really stepped up. We'll see them next month, in Tokyo, a surprise.

"Next month? We'll see them? In Tokyo?"

"I want you to come with me."

"I'll be teaching."

"You can take some time off, under the circumstances."

"Under the circumstances?"

"It's amazing, that you just keep on, without missing a beat, day after day. On Halloween it will be a month won't it? Since your diagnosis."

"I haven't been keeping track of time."

"It leaves you foggy for a while. Most people take a year to get used to this kind of thing. You can get a medical leave."

"I'm a term employee. The only leave I could get would be to just leave, with nothing."

"I can take care of any financial stuff, needless to say."

"Needless to say."

At the dining table, during breakfast, on their last morning among the white peaks, Stephen nervously played with the fraying edges of a wicker placemat. Small pieces broke off, and he slipped them into his pocket, saving seven of them for a curious image that was growing poetically, as his fingers frantically tugged at the worn material.

It was a quiet drive back to Tk'emlups mid-afternoon. Dan was preoccupied, chattered away on his cell phone about flight reservations for Japan, driving much faster than usual. When they passed the tournament capital of Canada sign, just before crossing the Overlander Bridge, Stephen asked if he could be dropped off downtown, in front of Oriental Gardens.

"If you need to pick up some stuff, I can go with you, then drop you at your house. We could go for sushi."

"Thanks, that's very sweet of you. But I'm not really hungry right now, and I'll be fine, there's food at the house. I just want to wander a little, browse at Value Village. It's been a strange and wonderful couple of days. I need to decompress before going back."

"Okay, sounds good. So, I'll see you Thursday, then, at your place, at your party?"

"Yeah, Thursday, Halloween, I'm looking forward to it."

"Let me take your luggage back for you, though. I'll leave it on the back verandah. So you don't have to lug it around."

"That would be great. Thanks."

A long involved kiss in the front seat of the elephant's asshole, like that second-hand Hudson's Bay blanket Stephen had bought—warm, comforting, intimate. But the emotional chill colonized the blanket, surrounding them, and the only remedy could be the light whirr of the wheels of the shopping cart as Stephen stared menacingly into the eyes of inanimate objects, roaming in a daze, through the aisle of his favourite cut-rate emporium.

His own personal cart was waiting patiently at home, wrapped in red mohair, but for the time being Stephen would have to rely on the agility of a strange old cart he lovingly guided away from a perfect interlocking row of mechanical brides.

2 p.m.—Tkaronto—CURTAIN

There were curtains on the balcony door, but he always left them open. Stephen's balcony, his slab of cement comfort in a plastic urban environment, was a place of joy, colourful and comfortable, with a single resting place, an old divan covered in a patterned throw, a few plants, a bamboo blind painted white hanging on a makeshift pole to keep out the stifling summer sun for a few weeks of the year. And the Adirondack chairs added a cottage effect, overlooking a panoramic view of decidedly non-cottage-like environs. Dundas Square, a grey meeting place for concerts, kiosks, and special events, considered an urban eyesore, a bleak elephant's asshole, was to Stephen a blank haven for openness and community life, alive and well in the heart of the city.

By the time Graham arrived, Stephen had lit candles and made soup, ready for a lovely second evening together. The supposed blood had been strawberry juice, an elaborate misidentification. He left the police station not long after arriving.

Graham's shirt was lying on the floor beside the bed as they nibbled voraciously on each other's berry-covered groins. The police discovered it was juice, had no proof of anything else, and decided to take Stephen's story as enough of an alibi, the added berry narrative enough to blow Graham out of the water as a prime suspect.

It was a perfect night. And as they made love, after a bowl of pumpkin soup, a few slices of pizza, and oodles of wine, a stranger's eyes from a window at the Bond Place Hotel, aided by binoculars, could make out the faint silhouettes of their aging carcasses embracing, entangled in each other's narrative sinew, muscle, and the odd patch of pink'ish flab. A terrified stranger fleeing from the guilt of having accidentally injured a costumed tube of oral hygiene while buttfucking in a frenzied clutch on a roof garden, raspberry bushes hanging over cement patio slabs. They had found themselves leaning against the slabs after leaving a mutual friend's party. It was an accident, a frightening accident sending shockwaves through a community of costumed party dwellers. Happy Halloween.

In the meantime, Irene was sitting crying in her apartment. The brunch had gone badly. All in attendance had known the tube of dental paste, a sweet kid who hadn't been in the city long. It was a gloomy brunch, and Irene was the only one in costume. And her hoped-for romantic interlude did not happen. She sat on her couch crying, and cursing, and considering another plan for that giant flag. But did she have the nerve.

I am Blighted by Home Décor—and other poems
A Brief History of Placemats—and other poems
Fecal Mishaps—and other poems
House of A Nancy—and other poems

Contemplating potential titles for his next collection of
poetry, Stephen disappointed himself in a flurry of suppressed
class-conscious rage as he toured the aisles of Value Village.
Everything looked cheap and unattractive. Even the kitsch
throws. There were four of them, of varying size, colour,
and shape. But they were cut from a synthetic pile, and the
pastoral scenes held no interest. Fawns and their mothers
posing languorously in grassy environs dominated the
current collection. Where were the exotic peacocks and racing
wolves of yesteryear, the ones he snatched up as quickly as he
caught sight of them hanging on the racks among blankets,
tablecloths, formal napkins, and faintly soiled placemat sets
imported from Taiwan. What would have been a thrilling
find on any other day of the week leading up to this day of
the week, the day after a weekend in the mountains, was
filled with a dull, hazy awareness that Stephen's tastes in
home décor were changing. With the astounding events and
encounters of the past month, he was grudgingly accepting
unexpected change. Even retail therapy did not help. He was
coping. But barely. After only ten minutes in the store, Stephen
returned the cart to its holding pen and walked home empty
handed, made himself a big shaker of blueberry martinis, and
went to bed at eight. When he woke at five the next morning,

he was fully clothed and hungover. As he pulled his trousers off, he remembered the placemats and the tiny wooden pieces of broken wicker he had so carefully saved in his left pocket the previous morning, Dan chattering away about family and real estate, noisily chewing stale leftover bannock as he spoke. Tearing at the edges of the placemat saved Stephen from the gross tedium of his new lover's idle conversation.

He had a curious image of those placemat bits in his head. Carefully turning the coat pocket inside out, he let them fall onto the white plastic surface of his bedside table. In the drawer below, he kept his digital camera. Taking it out, he quickly checked for batteries, then placed the camera on his pillow. Each piece of wicker fit perfectly between his thumb and his index finger, creating a strange jaw-like object consisting of a profile shot of his contorted, half-crazed hand and fingers. The wicker bits looked like stringy teeth running vertically between the horizontal shafts of his two opposing dactyls, one thumby and squat, the other slim, robust, and lean. Once the image had been completed, it made his hand look like the miniature head of an obscure dinosaur, mouth held open by the splintery digits of an exhausted placemat. Surreal.

With this limb-like installation in place, Stephen carefully took his camera from the drawer with his other hand, set the automatic timing device, found a place to position the camera, then stood with his hand set against the white of the bedsheets, and waited for the click. As he walked from the windowsill, two place mat pieces fell to the carpet. About to give up and toss the whole idea into the unsung bin of his creative imagination, Stephen noticed that the missing pieces made his two-digit contraption look more uniform. Only five dinosaur teeth, and they looked perfectly spaced between the chosen dactyls. The photo turned out beautifully and he immediately entitled it—

A metaphor for everything he had written and experienced, a fantasy laden with the single tool of his trade, a hand connected tenuously to a brain within an aging body. All that was left was to get to campus, apply for a medical leave, if that was possible, and begin to imagine himself on a flight to Japan. But first he had to check his messages.

"Stephen, uh, look, a weird thing has just happened, since I dropped you off. I checked my credit card online. I had an email that there was some odd activity, and it turns out my son has changed his tickets to economy from first class, and bought another one for his goddamn wedding-singer friend, the kid singing that fucked up song about being young and restless. Anyway, I'm flying over there, tonight. They went straight to Vancouver for their flight to Tokyo, cancelled the honeymoon. I'm gonna head them off at the pass, so to speak, and see what the fuck is going on. Something's fishy. I'm sorry. I won't be able to make it to your Halloween party. I'll call you later this week."

"Goddammit!" he muttered under his breath. He would have to wait and see how matters unfolded, but worst of all, his outfit for the upcoming party would not work nearly as well without a costumed partner in crime—without a groom.

When he arrived in the classroom, he was distracted and annoyed, but hid his contempt for all things human.

"Okay, everyone, your work is progressing nicely. Some of you have come up with engaging pieces. Now what we need to do is move into more complex forms of poetry. Love sonnets, but not about love. Expand the metaphors, the sentiments, and come up with stories, ideas, that resonate with larger themes. You have the handouts. Work in groups, compare your work, read it aloud to one another. Stay here in the classroom or go to the campus common and work. I want first drafts by tomorrow, and remember the Halloween party at my house on

Thursday. You're all welcome. Students from my other courses will be there, a party/seminar of sorts, I thought it might be fun. If any of you have some work you'd like to read, a short piece, feel free to bring it along. There'll be an hour or so set aside for student presentations, followed by some light snacks and refreshments. Around eight."

"Sir?"

"Yes, Lily?"

"The campus is closed tomorrow. No classes. They're fitting all the classrooms for new computer tech stuff."

"Thank you, Lily. Sorry everyone, I'm a little off schedule. It's Thursday, then, for any of you who'd like to come to the party. And next Tuesday for the sonnets. Gives you an extra week to develop your ideas on love. Any idea about love, by its very nature, is destined to become outlandish, given the relentless desire to couple human organs in such a surreal way."

Oops, he'd said too much. His distress over Dan's sudden change of plans had influenced his mood. He was bitter and disappointed, and it came out of his mouth in a questionably bawdy manner, considering the setting. The students laughed. Stephen apologized. He was a nutty professor, prone to wordy ribaldry.

Lily had no intention of going to the Halloween party. She was going to Vancouver with Ben, to get an abortion, and then rest on the island for a few days. Jeffrey knew, and they had his blessing. She wasn't ready, and Jeffrey knew he had to support her choice. He had taken Stephen's words to heart. He had grown up. But he would be at the party, dressed to the nines, happy to be on his own, and eager to see what his poetry professor would be wearing.

3 p.m.—Tkaronto—BALCONY

In the mid-seventies, at twenty years old, when he moved
to Toronto for his first year of college, Stephen lived with
a distant cousin and his wife who were never home. They
travelled all over the province on business, and flew to the
tropics in the winter to help promote the tourist industry that
was developing formerly remote islands. He loved them, and
he loved living alone.

The apartment was covered—every room—with white
shag carpeting, lightly soiled from casual day-to-day use.
There was no balcony in their apartment. It was on the
twenty-first floor but seemed higher, because it overlooked the
wide deep site of the Don Valley Parkway. His cousin would
stand by the window and look out through binoculars at the
passing cars and would say,

"If you stand here long enough with these things, you're
bound to see an accident happen. I've seen a few. Some are
gruesome. Some are just boring fender benders. But, boy, I'll
tell you, people are always really pissed off. It's a hell of a place
to get in an accident. That's one damn scary parkway. Never
should have been built there. It's a beautiful valley, with a
ribbon of traffic ruining the whole goddamn view. But I like to
look. Nothing we can do about it now."

It was Stephen's first taste of apartment living, high above
the city, foreshadowing his move later into his own place—his
own balcony, his own personal brand of urban mayhem.

Having been raised in a storey-and-a-half house in a small
town two hours northeast of Toronto, Stephen never imagined
that he would end up on a lofty floor in a co-op apartment
building, leaving from time to time—to live in Calgary,
Kamloops, and Vancouver—but always returning to what he

liked to refer to as his airtight cabin in the sky. A place where he could sit and gaze and drink and pretend to be happy. Because he believed that life was pretense and fabrication and invented narratives we cling to in the hope that one of them may one day come true. In the meantime, enjoying a semi-fictional view suited him just fine.

No one was happy. And no one was sad. They stood on balconies, watching the goings-on below—mishaps, misfortunes, traffic accidents, pedestrian interactions, smiling as they watched, like would-be monarchs—queens—regally surveying the worlds they would never know, never fully inhabit, just looking down, inventing friends and lovers, and hoping they would never fall.

Stephen never would fall. He was half afraid of heights. Loved the view, but a mild case of vertigo kept him a few inches from the edge. Irene, on the other hand, he wasn't so sure about.

Shit. Had she really used that flag for a costume brunch! Or was it a ploy? Time was moving quickly, and slowly. Cities and landscapes melded in his mind, and he was beginning to wonder whether the loss of one city would be the gain of another. Where was he now, in Toronto or Kamloops? Tk'emlups or Tkaronto? How long would he be happy back in environments that had been left behind?

Day Thirty—Tk'emlups—Wednesday, October 31

Stephen wrote all day Wednesday, taking time in the afternoon to clean his shopping cart with the rust remover he had bought. He put on the walking cast as soon as he woke up. Although his ankle felt weak, there was no pain and no limping gait to conceal. His joints seemed to be holding up under the intense scrutiny of middle age, and despite the wilted spirit that lurked among them, they were happy limbs, tinged only slightly with restlessness. But why not take advantage of the mood, indulge in a bit of hair of the dog, get the creative juices flowing through the veins of a recently inebriated system of manic nerves and aging muscles.

Showering before breakfast, he hung his bath towel over the curtain pole and suddenly saw it in a new light. The early morning sunshine behind the plastic curtain shone through the worn cotton of his Disney bath towel. Tinkerbell's eyes were starting to look a little faded, and he thought of this iconic fairy's sage musings from Peter Pan about the place that exists between sleeping and waking. It was a place where the memories of dreams still exist, and how that can be a place where love can always reside. Somehow, Tinkerbell was reminding him of his love for Dan.

Stephen wrote and wrote and wrote:

Goodbye

When I go away for the weekend, I say goodbye to all of my possessions. This past weekend, the first thing I remember saying goodbye to was my Tinkerbell beach towel in the bathroom. I bought it at the Disney Store in the Eaton's Centre in Toronto last summer. I have an apartment close to the Centre, and sometimes, when I am feeling weary and disillusioned, I wander over to the Disney Store and gaze at all the animated characters. They comfort me. A friend once said, "One of the nicest things about being a gay man is that you can buy things for yourself that were meant for teenage girls."

Filled with so much uncomplicated life and colour, my favourite Disney characters are Tinkerbell and Pluto. I had a Tinkerbell china figurine for a few years, but it was broken in a move. Her wings were shattered. Years ago, that would have bothered me a great deal. My grandmother once sat and wept as she glued a broken lamp back together. I have inherited my strange love of objects from her.

I still have my apartment near the Disney Store, but I sublet, and live in the interior of B.C. now. I have moved so many times over the years that I am used to material and emotional loss. It can be cathartic. Like a good laxative.

Someone asked me recently, at a dinner party, what I had been traumatized by as a child, why I insisted upon reiterating that trauma in darkly comic form, and why I wasn't over it, even in middle age. I looked at them, calmly sipping from a large glass of imported ice wine I had bought at the airport, duty free. I said, quite dryly, "I think it's fair to say that people who embark—as teenagers—upon a thirteen-year affair with their mother's brother-in-law do not always come out of it refreshed and ready to party." Then I lifted my glass and pledged a toast. "Here's to trauma. A constant friend."

When my mother and I went to Disney World in Orlando in 1977, just a few months after my father was killed in a car accident, I bought two china figurines of Minnie Mouse and Mickey Mouse snow skiing. The tip of one of their ski poles broke during a move, but I glued it back on. I still have them.

I gave Mickey and Minnie to my niece when she was a baby, but took them back when she was transferred, at age five, from her family home in Calgary to a nearby group home for mentally and physically challenged children. She lived into her early thirties. I would see her once a year when I visited Calgary. I brought her fancy discount T-shirts, and I chatted away to her in the only way I know—incessantly.

Her name was Amy. I hope that I haven't failed her. I replaced the Disney figurines with a teddy bear dressed in a little white lace frock, powder-blue ribbon trimming the hem. I sewed it myself, and felt such love when I visited Amy and saw that little bear at her bedside. I wonder where it ended up.

I have just had a dark epiphany about Minnie and Mickey skiing. The car accident that took my father's life occurred on an icy road on the way home from skiing at a small resort named Devil's Elbow near Peterborough, Ontario—my birthplace and home for the first twenty-four years of my life. There was some concern that my father may have been drinking before he left to pick me up at the resort. The car accident was decades ago. Only now does it occur to me that subconsciously I must have been searching all over Disney World for a comforting memory of skiing in order to cushion the blow of having lost my father after a pleasant day participating in a much loved environmentally unfriendly winter sport.

I have had people say, in no uncertain terms, that they feel it was wrong for me to take back the gift I had given my niece. Some of them have even called me an 'Indian Giver.' I was called an 'Indian Giver' when I asked a close relative if I could have back some of the LPs that I had given him a few years before. One of them included a recording by Canadian sixties heartthrob Bobby Curtola, singing a song entitled "Indian Giver." Perhaps that was what prompted his remark.

When I confronted him on his racist reply, he responded by saying that it was just an old saying from his childhood, and that he didn't mean anything by it. I tried to explain to him that childhood is where we learn some of the greatest historical lies, and, as adults, we need to dismantle those lies and take responsibility for telling the truth about the land and the people

282

who inhabit it. He called me a snowflake asshole and walked away. I liked being called a snowflake.

I have only been in Tk'emlups a month, and have already fallen in love with the landscape and the desert light. I find myself writing emails to friends saying that living here is like being trapped in a picture postcard, only awaiting airmail stamps that will set me free from this earthly paradise. Yes, there are moments when I feel that it is time to get the hell out of paradise. But for the time being, I am happy with the few possessions I have brought along on yet another move to another province and another adventure. I could stay here forever, admiring the low-lying mountains sparsely covered with evergreens and tumbleweeds.

Tumbleweeds are my favourite part of Tk'emlups. They remind me of faintly despairing scenes in films set in the American Southwest, where whole families are ripped apart by poverty and domestic strife, forced to flee from one another in used cars or Greyhounds bound for some unappealing destination. These scenarios remind me of all I should have done in my life but never got around to. I come from a working-class background, and I thank working class gods and goddesses for my white-trash heritage every day when I am reminded of how unfeeling and filled with rage some wealthy people can be. Wealth is a relative term—my immediate family was poor, but some of our relatives were rich.

I love to dine with rich people, but find their conversations alienating. I don't mean to privilege my associations with the poor, I only want to give them their fair share of credit. If I have to say goodbye to Tk'emlups, I think that I will visit the spots I love best and perform small farewell ceremonies in the nude, tumbleweeds attached to my limbs in an artistic fashion. I will walk to the top of small mountains in high heeled shoes (they make my legs look wonderful), followed by a diligent and admiring videographer—past the Superstore and the gasoline depot named after a sled dog—and all of the restaurants

*advertising lunch specials complete with a panoramic view
of this part of the world. And when I get to the top of the
mountain, I will remember that I am only one person saying
goodbye—a single glamour-mongering entity who has failed the
people and the land in many small ways in a single lifetime.*

*Tears will stain my cheeks, and I will yodel badly and
gesticulate wildly and make impossible promises to the passing
wind. I will pay ambivalent homage to a dead uncle who
performed inappropriate acts in a distorted form of love at a
time when I should have been allowed to find love elsewhere but
needed desperately to find it somewhere. I will pledge allegiance
to a materialism that never takes itself too seriously, but always
pays respect to ritualistic objects that comprise the strained
ceremonial traditions of late capitalism. And then I will think
of Tinkerbell emblazoned across a bath towel, gazing mindlessly
into the stained glass, and I will call the airport shuttle, and I
will fly away.*

4 p.m.—Tkaronto—GARDEN

"I was with him in the garden. That's all. We made out. I met him in the lobby when I was bringing the kids back to their mom yesterday. We cruised each other. Then I went up to the roof garden for a smoke. He was there. He was really aggressive. As soon as I said hello, he pulled up the tube thing he was wearing and pulled out his cock, and I wasn't interested. I said thanks, but no thanks. He had a nice cock, but I couldn't stop thinking about you. I really like you, being here, with you, and I didn't want to fuck it up. So I left, went home, had a shower, and came back here to see you. I swear. I left him up there. He was fine. I wouldn't lie to you. As I was leaving, I noticed another guy. I couldn't see him very well, he was behind the trellis, by the basil garden, smoking, at the other end of the roof garden. They both laughed. They seemed to be together. I looked back as I left, and they were by the raspberry bushes, being like, really friendly. They were probably drunk."

"I lied for you."

"I know, and I appreciate it, but the fucking strawberry juice. They couldn't have held me for long with that evidence, and they roughed me up a lot when they found me. So I know they were nervous I would scream harassment and homophobia if they tried to push their evidence any further."

"Why did you run?"

"I was scared."

"Wow. That poor kid. The costume was so cute."

"He was cute, too. I wonder what happened. Did the other guy fucking attack him? Fuck. I could have told them all that, but I thought it would implicate me more. I was fucking terrified."

285

"They might never find out. I don't know why, but I have this weird feeling that there is nothing to find out. I think it was an accident."

"An accident?"

"Yeah. I went up there with my opera glasses. I knew the door to the garden might be locked by then, so I held my gorgeous little binoculars up against the glass door and saw the crime scene close-up. There was tape around it. About ten years ago, for Halloween, I made a dress out of strips of that yellow caution tape and went as a crime scene in drag. People thought it was really tasteless. I used duct tape as a gaff to hold my dick back, and I wasn't wearing underwear. I was very surprised how little it hurt when I ripped the tape off my crotch. The pubic hair stung a little."

"Yeah, you like it a bit rough. We are compatible that way. And?"

"And what?"

"And what the fuck did you *discern* through your gorgeous little binoculars?"

"I think he slipped and hit his head on the patio stones. I have this feeling."

"You should be a detective."

"In the first few years I lived here, a woman jumped from one floor above me and landed in the garden in front of the entrance. The trees were smaller then and there was nothing to break her fall. I had a friend who was working at the co-op beside us, in the office. She called me right after hearing about it, to see if I had jumped. I said yes, I'm still falling and I'm on my cell phone. She warned me not to look over the edge of my balcony, but of course I did. I edged slowly toward the railing, I have mild vertigo, and I put my hands on the edge of the cold metal barrier, just above waist level, and there she was. Poor thing. I noticed her T-shirt looked kind of soiled, even from that far up I could see her sad little t-shirt and her crumpled body. I felt bad, but I mostly felt numb, not different from what I normally feel. Later that night I called the suicide hotline to ask how I should be responding. They were very nice and told me to have a glass of wine, and to think kind and gentle thoughts about the poor soul who did jump. They said they didn't think I sounded suicidal, and that it was wise of me to call them, for support, for someone to talk to. And I swear to God, the next fucking morning, I was leaving the co-op, very hungover because I took the hotline's advice, but too much of it and had two bottles of wine—as I was leaving the co-op, I said hello to people working in the garden. They were fixing the flowers and bushes that her body had crushed. I think there should be a plant there remembering her. Apparently, all morning she had been knocking on people's doors trying to talk, I guess to get help. But no one answered. She didn't knock on my door. I never answer my door if I don't know who's there. I ask, but if I don't know them, I won't open the door. But I think if I had tried to talk to her, through the door, if she had knocked, maybe that would have helped. But she didn't knock. Or I didn't hear her. It's just so sad."

"Fuck, you wouldn't ever jump, would you?"

"Hell, no. I'm afraid of heights."

Day 31—Tk'emlups—Thursday, November 1

Stephen couldn't get Peter Pan out of his fucking head. The most irritating line in the whole narrative was about dying being a really big adventure. He felt he had experienced more than enough adventure in his lifetime, and dying was not something he was looking forward to.
There was a knock on the door.

Jeffrey, early for the party, alone. Stephen had expected no one to show up. An unexpected blizzard had blanketed the downtown, and by late afternoon the roads were impossible to navigate.

"You made it!"

"I took the trail."

"You walked on that treacherous trail, in this weather, dressed like that?"

"It was exhilarating. I have a winter walking pick with me. See? My boots are solid, and my coat is heavy, keeps me warm. I'm wearing long underwear."

Sitting in the kitchen, sipping po-co-mojtios from paper cups filled from a second-hand punchbowl, cocktails for twenty shared by two, minty white rum chilling frosty insides, they chatted for hours, about poetry, the unwanted pregnancy, the abortion, and then, once hope of anyone else coming to the party seemed unlikely, Jeffrey asked if he could spend the night, due to the weather, on the couch by the fire.

"Of course, that's fine. I'll turn up the heat. This cold snap really just flew in, out of the blue, the wild blue yonder, eh?"

"That's really poetic, silly, and funny, sir . . . sorry, Stephen."

"That's okay. You can call me *sir* if you like."

"Yeah, right."

"To Sir, with love."

"Huh?"

"It's the name of an old movie, and a song, about a teacher."

They both laughed, chatted, drank more, nibbled on pretzels, sushi, chocolate balls, bacon imbedded croissant puffs, and by midnight grew tired. No trick-or-treaters came to the door. The lights were off, only a single candle on the table between them, beside an almost empty punch bowl that had been filled with po-co-mojitos. Postcolonial cocktails.

At one point they moved to the living room and sat on opposite ends of the sofa. All of the bric-a-brac from Value Village watched them from the mantle. Carved ducks, ceramic angels, plush monkeys, stone carved turtles, and one singing trout. Jeffrey laughed and asked why Stephen had so many cheesy ornaments. He explained that he loved them for their unique ability to defy good taste, and that they were for the party, to give out as gifts. Jeffrey apologized for laughing and said, "Can I take one?" As Stephen nodded, Jeffery added, "you choose one for me." Stephen got up from the sofa and walked toward the fireplace. Without having to think for even a moment he went directly to the wicker rabbit and took two blue silk roses from the opening in the rabbit's mouth. He walked back to the sofa and handed them to Jeffrey. Jeffrey stood up quickly, wobbled a little from the effects of the booze, took the roses from Stephen's hand, put one over his left ear and the other over Stephen's, and then said, "I still haven't seen your bed all covered in kitsch throws." And then he leaned forward and kissed Stephen. Had Stephen been a little drunker, the kiss might have landed in a dangerous place. But he had the wherewithal to move his head in time for Jeffrey's lips to make their mark on his cheek. Jeffrey took the hint, smiled, and sat back down on the sofa. Stephen noticed the familiar tear in Jeffrey's eye, allergies no doubt. Stephen felt tears in his own eyes, thought of Dan and Craig and so many others, and had another stiff drink.

He left Jeffrey sound asleep, and not just a little drunk, lying on the sofa alongside diminishing fireplace flames, dressed in a Cinderella costume Jeffrey had found at Value Village. Stephen placed the red mohair blanket over him, leaving the Hudson's Bay blanket slung lovingly over the end of a patient, friendly cart that didn't mind sharing. Then Stephen toddled off to bed in his Bride of Frankenstein costume, wondering what another day of lighthearted fantasy-laden fear would bring. Cinderella and Frankenstein's half-crazed spouse were present, but Prince Charming was conspicuously absent, on a mad flight to Japan in pursuit of his son's own wild ways. And who was he, but a character from a fairy tale, looking for a fictional foot to fit into a fictional slipper that might mince merrily into a fictional horizon, happily ever after. Although maybe he would come back, someday, maybe he would come, that fairy-tale prince. Maybe not. In the meantime, in between time, Stephen would find a way to be happy.

5 p.m.—Tkaronto—HAPPYBACK

When Stephen got the call from Irene, he and Graham rushed out of the apartment to her apparent rescue. When they arrived by taxi, at Irene's condo, they found her sitting on her balcony wrapped in the American flag and drinking wine. When she saw them, she frowned and spit out a mouthful.

"What is this shit? Lacryma Christi? I stole it from your place. It's dreadful."

Graham sat to her left and Stephen to her right. They held hands, smiling, and fighting back tears. Irene would let go of one hand every few minutes to sip her wine.

"Weird fucking wine Stephen. Where the hell did you get it?"

"An old friend recommended it, ages ago. I was being sentimental when I saw it at the liquor store."

Graham and Stephen used their free hands to drink from the empty Dixie cups littering the balcony floor. Graham kept nodding.

"I wasn't going to jump, for Christ's sake. I actually used it as a fucking costume. And besides, I have a lot of that Amalfi-loving jilting bastard's money to spend before I die."

"What are you going to spend it on?"

"Happiness. I'm going to spend every last cent on happiness, making the people I love happy."

"Happiness. It's overrated. Tennessee Williams was right. Happiness is just a mutant form of insensitivity. In this world. Fuck. Sadness is so much more fulfilling, don't you think?"

"I try not to."

"Happyback?"

"It's not a question."

"But it always sounded like one whenever you said it to me."

"That was just the way you interpreted it."

"Goodnight, Irene."

They sat there until evening and beyond. Stephen kissed Irene. Irene kissed Stephen. Graham kissed Stephen. Kisses galore. Romantic kisses, friendly kisses, sad kisses, happy kisses, overwritten kisses. And then the silly moon kissed the silly stars. The dish kissed the spoon. The fork had left with the road. Running away in a wide and wonderful world. Laughing, crying, happy, sad. In the distance they could see the giant letters of the Trump Tower glistening menacingly on the skyline, the CN Tower one massive dick thrusting heavenward from a bitter earth. Stephen missed the huge threatened evergreens of the Rockies, but he loved the CN Tower.

The telephone rang silently in Stephen's coat pocket. Long distance from Tokyo. Perhaps there was still hope for another city in some not-so-distant narrative. Who knew.

Tkaronto—December 25—Midnight

Another holiday event had come and gone. Snow beginning
sometime in late October or early November and heaving its
merry mounds throughout Halloween, teasing yuletide lovers
with the unpredictable promise of a whitened Noel. He said
goodnight to the two dads and their son. As he walked the
few blocks to his co-op apartment Stephen felt a mixture of
seasonal joy and global dread. Merry fucking Christmas.

PROLOGUE

My Vancouver

While living in Tk'emlups, Stephen drove to Vancouver with
his roommate a couple of times, and became acquainted
with all of the Shakespearean place names along the way. The
Coquihalla was littered with sites that honoured the work of
an iconic bard. Romeo and Shylock appeared along the route
from Summit to Hope. Stephen found the Portia interchange
and Othello Road oddly intriguing. At one point, CP rail
sported the Othello tunnels. Poor absent Desdemona. Each
station along the train route was named by avid Shakespeare
readers in charge of the stolen land. Lear, Portia, Iago, Romeo,
and Juliet all clung to an earth ravaged by transport and
technology.

Alas, the history of language, what a fucking colonizing
mess. Just don't plan a leisurely picnic in Macbeth Valley,
a peaceful stroll along the trails of Coriolanus Canyon, or
a joyful family reunion at Hamlet Hideaway or Pericles
Parkette. Somewhere, history, the annals of recorded doom,
floats in an etherizing glow of time and space, between sea
and shining sea, coast to coast, rimmed by the Pacific, in
Lotus Blossom land, across oceans and time zones, through
the lives of intersecting humans.

Stephen, a few summers after leaving Tk'emlups and
returning to Tkaronto, found himself on a working holiday
painting a three-and-half-storey condo overlooking False Creek.

False Creek was one of his favourite place names in all of
Canada, because it didn't pretend to be anything other than
what it was. False. And Granville wasn't an island, not since
the 1950's, but attached to land by an obtrusive, non-idyllic
passageway encumbered by overhead slabs of concrete for
traffic to scuttle across. Stephen thought of Vancouver as a

precarious city. Beautiful and precarious, welcoming and forbidding, with weather that sent Stephen into s.a.d. mode for a prolonged period. He had taught there, at the school named after a Canadian painter who appropriated totems in their natural habitat. It happened before his Kamloops sojourn; he thought it might be a nice place to live, as a permanently impermanent tourist, with a job enabling him to leave for sunny environs whenever the lack of light and the constant drizzle became too much to bear. Las Vegas, Mexico, Hawaii just a stone's throw away, a flat polished stone skipping across puddles and continents like nobody's business but its own.

But Vancouver, yes, such a beautiful city. It suited Stephen's sadness to a T, a form of sadness he had cultivated into melancholy over a lifetime. But that's another story. This story is about a diagnosis and the intersecting relationships at its heart.

One day, during his painting job, Stephen went rollerblading on the path known as the seawall, and he noticed a face flash by in the crowd of people strolling along the edges of Stanley Park. He'd almost collided with several innocent visitors, never a full-on collision, just a near miss here and there, and the disgruntled expressions of strangers— apparitions, petals, scattered crowds. The familiar face he noticed was that of a woman, part of a same-sex couple from the way they held hands and clutched each other when a reckless cyclist flew by—a lesbian couple perhaps—a yoga instructor and a doctor. When Stephen got back to the condo, he remembered her clearly, the doctor from the campus clinic. She hadn't seen him, luckily, or she might have remembered him too, and shared that solemn sad smile he had first encountered when she embarked on her clumsy way of telling him he had a life-threatening pathology. Maybe she was right about the prognosis. Time would tell, and time was of the essence. The moron! He just couldn't let it go. In his heart he wished her well, yet held a melancholic grudge about the way she had managed to introduce him to the rest of his life.

Yes, ultimately, time was telling, and Stephen lived every minute as though it were his last. Late that night, ankles sore and throbbing, he sat on the wooden bench surrounding the small rooftop patio of the condo, sipping a martini, looking toward the Gotham-like forest of condo towers, a tiny Manhattan precariously clinging to the earth, bits of green to the west, lushly sprouting from the fragile edge of Stanley Park, and the mammoth mountains above. It was a clear August evening. The thoughts Stephen encountered made him remember a night, years before, pre-Kamloops, pre-Jeffrey, Dan, Craig, Lily, Amy, Kurt, Ben, Value Village, bric-a-brac, shopping carts, kitsch throws, telephones and postcolonial text and theory—the whole crowd who inhabited that special yet cluttered time in his life. And he wondered, the seeds of poetic form percolating in his vodka-soaked brain, if that might have been the moment when he seroconverted, just before Kamloops, when the virus made its terrible magic, and entered his body, leaving him changed in complicated ways— ways that should not all be considered negative. He was hell bent upon accentuating the positive.

He would drive back to Calgary after the painting job was done, and then fly to Toronto. Unable to find much teaching work in the years after Kamloops, and leaving his co-op for short periods to visit friends and do odd jobs for extra money, he was making the best of the situation. He thought of himself as being a member of the privileged poor. Lots of perks, but no substantial security or ongoing bourgeois illusions. He was happy. He was back home, in Toronto, a messy metropolis where he knew how to be poor. Other Canadian cities seemed unmanageable to him. He was used to the chaotic purse strings he had cultivated in the East. Cheap films, the frantic pace, the flirtations, the food banks, the waning rent subsidies.

But on that sunny sunny day late in summer, he looked forward to the drive through the mountains, along the Coquihalla, in a rented car. It always made him smile when he noticed the places named after Shakespearean characters. On this trek he did something he had always dreamed of doing. He stopped at Coquihalla Canyon Provincial Park and made his way to the Othello tunnels. But Ophelia was Stephen's favourite. Her watery death appealed to Stephen's overwrought sense of aquatic narrative device. Borrowed—artistically tailored and appropriated from earlier European stories—Italian, Spanish—these Shakespearean creatures were a group of romantic misfits finding love in, yes, all the wrong places. Hamlet. Ophelia. Romeo, Juliet, Othello, Desdemona.

Stephen stood there, overlooking rushing water. He began to jot notes for a long poem. And when he got to Banff, where he was meeting an old friend/lover just back from an unexpectedly prolonged stay in Tokyo—the saga always continues—he put Buffy Sainte Marie's drumbeat recording of "Indian Cowboy" on his laptop, went online, and appropriated, paraphrased, parodied some Shakespearean verse to scatter, like literary ashes, throughout the corpus of his newest creation—filled with fact and fiction, flight and fancy, truth and lies. He could never tell the whole truth, because he knew that he would get it all wrong.

My Vancouver

(*performed with an eclectic array of musical citations ranging from Indigenous drumbeats to classical arias mixed with pretentious Shakespearean allusions, not to mention grand elusive overdone overtures toward the urban journey of T.S. Eliot's Prufrock and the memorable mouth and buttocks of a very sweet stranger perched on this mountain rooftop*)

swilling thousand-dollar antiretroviral pills
with touches of Grey Goose
a throat full of freshly squeezed lemon
slim coiled rinds drowning gaily
at the bottom of hand-blown glass
I gaze across False Creek
toward that wobbly Gotham dipping slowly
through Pacific Rims—those lips! his ass!
once touched by glory
in the kindest stranger's oral reign
falling tickling dangling heavy dampness
hovers softly plunges lightly flailing
into anal fissures deftly cleansed in darkened showers
penile power glazed by flavoured lubricant
shadows all the godly sigmoid colons
intrarectal gaps imbricating nature's
layered trek through incredible journeys
alongside fleshy cliffs
trellises crass moraines heaving defining
ranges of my smirking carcass as we cross
those sullied sheets that wild and weary
thaw the secret of man's unweeded gardens
everlasting edicts against self-slaughter
so rank widening into vistas that absolve
all guilt abdominal plains, a pubic forest

—these thighs!
when the depths of all resolve can find
in nature an increase in appetite
for satyrs broken hearts galled eyes
the dexterity of tongues lapping
against plunging avenues windswept
by heaven's broken promise to earth
grown to seed on roads sloping
toward an English bight
to think of watery panoramic avenues, ambling streets
Jervis, Pendrell, Bute—thoroughfares gift shops
sundry owners dwarfed by glass facades and skylines
that will never tell the story of a city
once out of love with cluttered spoils of sites
colonizing bays burger joints and rainbow signs
and then the sudden memory of his lips
eclipsing an urban overview the way he slyly slid
then perched knees bent on the shifty edges
of a thinning mattress
over there on Davie Street with lush tall bouquets
by the sauna leather couches graced by patrons
draped in pure white towels entrapped
by plasma screens and lust
his tongue encircling my anus with faint white powder
from a little satin purse he bought in Chinatown
and hard as I try I can't regret the path from here to there

the immortal view of all these places sliding into
the indulgent mortality of me
these pills this vodka that view
guests ramble through as shards of dinner's
shaved pickled ginger
shift with the disarming downstairs whirr
of dishwashing cycles
this cutlery these tectonic plates that stemware
pristine apocalypse in the wake of endlessness
in love with death's glory hole
these sensations—my anus, his lips the dripping sauce
for all this pleasure may have chafed a lifespan
begging for more time and yet
well versed in this fast ride
to heaven's basement, the crackling shells
of barefoot reef walks along the sea walls
hugging wind-ravaged parks
his effervescent godforsaken chocolate balls
dangling between valleys fit for northern kings
who masquerade as southern queens
once told the limo driver that this park was named after
Stanley Kowalski and he believed me
as I blanched with glee in the back seat
sipping Prosecco and craving a screen glazed
with porn to make this flirtatious ride with luxury
complete bodies so moderately fulfilled

by substance misidentified as grave addiction
lower case abuse self-inflicted by some desire
to thrive and smile precariously beneath
those chiselled lips that tongue my horizontal haven
my gently heaving honey combing hips
I have perched here looking down on memory
sipping cocktails painting clear cedar decks
by late afternoon light
preparing a friend's multistoried town home for sale
on these multimillion-dollar fair view slopes
this gaze these rooms the fumes
his fingertips inserting digits
into pulsing patient zero laden holes
day labour insinuates memories of past hedonistic hurls
as stellar canisters of comet-like abrasive pads
scrub the stairs hands baked in acrylic white-faced palms
this toxic coat is all that's left of me
and these thoughts
this rambled muddled ode, those crows flying
back to Trout Lake from Kitsilano
marking the light onset of darkness
as it envelopes daylight hovering
along puce vistas streaks of orange and blue and him
those lips white powder anal wonder
they can't take that away from me
when Rockies tumble

among sad servings of faux creek mountain berry crumble
at a cushy bistro by those yachts
that flank ceramic serving dishes
fit for real estate hippy happy kings
my blemished love is here to stay, oh no,
this memory this thought this view
overwhelms and thrills
majesty distorting vistas shaping horizons
shaking earthen plots these quakes of mind and body
heart and soul
the tinkling ivory stealing theft
tusked claws of the only song I ever played
long enough to feed the thirst for fleeting romance
with one self-made happy whore
in love with thrill and transient tryst and turn
the cavernous beauty of chaos
—this anus that powder his lips—
as hard as missionary minions try to sacralize
obey forbid they can't take these things
away from me
these choices have been heaven sent
as lives descend along faulted coastal dreams
that slide unsteady cities into periscopic tongues
this bawdy astral glide flopping drenched and writhing
into through behind the sweeping
loss of all the resurrected pining lolling beetling into love

for measured dew along pacific rims
—this anus that powder his shattering lips
his bevelled ribs—trembling quietude of silky sweats
beaded at the edge of kitsch camp consciousness
this deeply chilling martini
the bits of flesh remaining
wholesome handsome olive pits those rinds
my heart those dead regrets this mind
half-happy—back and forth in time
drowning in some useful sunset
sinking out of measured time . . .

DR SAD

FINI

Acknowledgements

What began as an attempt to write a piece of fiction quickly became, in the opening sections, and later versions of this manuscript, a semi-autobiographical journey loosely based on the two amazing years I spent in Tk'emlups (Kamloops, British Columbia) as writer-in-residence and as term instructor in the English department at Thompson Rivers University. I have always found it difficult to create fiction without implicating myself.

The final pages of the first draft were completed in the Eastern Townships in Quebec, in a lovely second-storey room with sloping ceiling, in a country home called Lilac Cottage. After a gaily familial dinner with a family blended by postmodernity and a decidedly queer distractive gaze that gloriously upends notions of achingly heteronormative behaviour, I was inspired to take the broken remnants of a weary wicker placemat and fashion them into a strange fist-like creation of prehistoric implications, thus the accompanying photo for the opening poem *hand splint for limp wrist*. A very special thank you to Serafin, David, and their son Nicky for providing me with the time and the comfort to complete this semi-fictional journey in such a joyful setting.

Thanks also to Laurie Ditchburn, Sullivan Dyment, Shannon Maguire, and Kathleen Whelan for early readings of the manuscript, as well as Michael Mirolla (Guernica Editions, Toronto) and Malcolm Sutton (Book*hug, Toronto) for valuable advice and encouragement along the way.

Some of the poems were written specifically for this novel, while others can be found in the following collections; *Invisible Foreground*, *Impersonating Flowers*, *'tis pity*, and *Designation Youth*, all published by Frontenac House Press (Calgary). As part of a welcoming and generous community of poets in Calgary—a city I love and return to often—Rose Scollard, David Scollard, Micheline Maylor, and Neil Petrunia all contributed to the publication of these collections. I am forever grateful for the time I have spent there.

A very special thank you to Aritha van Herk and Naomi Lewis for their constant encouragement, and their very detailed and valuable editing. And thank you to the staff at the University of Calgary Press—Alison Cobra, Kirsten Cordingley, Melina Cusano, Helen Hajnoczky, Brian Scrivener—for their patience, encouragement, and guidance throughout the entire process.

I am also very grateful for the generous support of the Ontario Arts Council and the Chalmers Arts Fellowship program, funding bodies that enabled the first draft of *DR SAD* to become a daily task that I looked forward to and felt rewarded by every day for over a year, and beyond. The artist has been paid!

BIBLIOGRAPHY

Forster, E.M. *The Celestial Omnibus and other stories*. London, Sidgwick & Jackson, 1912.

———. *A Passage To India*. New York, Harcourt, Brace and Company, 1924.

Whitman, Walt. *Walt Whitman's Leaves of Grass*. New York, Penguin Books, 1855.

Austen, Jane. *Pride and Prejudice; a Novel in Three Volumes*. London, Printed for T. Egerton, Military Library, Whitehall, 1813.

David Bateman has a PhD in English literature with a specialization in creative writing from the University of Calgary. He is currently a freelance arts journalist, painter, and performance poet who lives in Toronto. He has edited collections including Patricia Wilson's *Musing From the Bunker/ Slouching Towards Womanhood* and a series of essays on the work of Sky Gilbert entitled *Compulsive Acts* (Guernica Editions, Toronto). He has taught literature and creative writing at post-secondary institutions across Canada, including Trent University (Peterborough and Oshawa), University of Calgary, OCAD University (Toronto), ECIAD University (Emily Carr, Vancouver) and Thompson Rivers University (Kamloops). His poetry collections, all from Frontenac House Press (Calgary), include *Invisible Foreground, Impersonating Flowers, 'tis pity,* and *Designation Youth*. His collaborative long poems include "Wait Until Late Afternoon" with Hiromi Goto (Frontenac House Press) and "Pause" with Naomi Beth Wakan (Bevalia Press). His collection of short stories and creative non-fiction entitled *A Mad Bent Diva: A Collection of Life Affirming Death Threats, Vignettes, and Epithets* was published by Hidden Brook Press in 2017. And he is, by degree, a mad bent diva, proven by the serendipitous fact that his name is an anagram for A Mad Bent Diva. He discovered this term of endearment in his forties at a magnificent poetry festival on Gabriola Island, and is forever grateful to Hilary Peach and Jacob Chaos for bringing this to his attention.

BRAVE & BRILLIANT SERIES

SERIES EDITOR:
Aritha van Herk, Professor, English, University of Calgary
ISSN 2371-7238 (PRINT) ISSN 2371-7246 (ONLINE)

Brave & Brilliant encompasses fiction, poetry, and everything in between and beyond. Bold and lively, each with its own strong and unique voice, Brave & Brilliant books entertain and engage readers with fresh and energetic approaches to storytelling and verse, in print or through innovative digital publication.

No. 1 · *The Book of Sensations* | Sheri-D Wilson

No. 2 · *Throwing the Diamond Hitch* | Emily Ursuliak

No. 3 · *Fail Safe* | Nikki Sheppy

No. 4 · *Quarry* | Tanis Franco

No. 5 · *Visible Cities* | Kathleen Wall and Veronica Geminder

No. 6 · *The Comedian* | Clem Martini

No. 7 · *The High Line Scavenger Hunt* | Lucas Crawford

No. 8 · *Exhibit* | Paul Zits

No. 9 · *Pugg's Portmanteau* | D. M. Bryan

No. 10 · *Dendrite Balconies* | Sean Braune

No. 11 · *The Red Chesterfield* | Wayne Arthurson

No. 12 · *Air Salt* | Ian Kinney

No. 13 · *Legislating Love* | Play by Natalie Meisner, with Director's Notes by Jason Mehmel, and Essays by Kevin Allen and Tereasa Maillie

No. 14 · *The Manhattan Project* | Ken Hunt

No. 15 · *Long Division* | Gil McElroy

No. 16 · *Disappearing in Reverse* | Allie McFarland

No. 17 · *Phillis* | Alison Clarke

No. 18 · *DR SAD* | David Bateman